Dark Beyond
The Stars

CONTENTS

Foreword

by Julie E. Czerneda

Space.

Sends shivers down the spine, doesn't it? We want to be there, not just here, on our admittedly gorgeous planet. We want to see ourselves among the stars. See what else is out there. Boldly go! That passionate shared curiosity inspires not only the science and technology behind current and future space travel, but our imaginations.

And imaginations are in full glorious flight in this anthology. Welcome to *Dark Beyond the Stars,* where space meets story. Space opera at its finest, for all these authors ask is that you leap with them into a future where faster-than-light travel exists. From this single launch point come tales both intimate and cosmic, where what it means to be human, out there, is not only explored—it is shaken, stirred, and renewed.

The result is a treat for readers. As for the authors? Trust me, it's not easy to write in an unknown, unexplored future. The rules don't change. No matter how wildly original, every bit of world—and space—building has to mesh together, to fit and convince, or credibility suffers. That takes work as well as craft, and you'll find both here. Then there's the whole business of telling a complete story within the pages allowed, when your canvas is so vast.

Which is, of course, the allure.

I love space opera. I love stories like these that dare me to think wider and deeper, that offer a future not yet within my grasp, but well within my heart and mind. I gobble up the words, close my eyes, and see the dark.

My kind of dark. And yours.

The dark beyond the stars.

—Julie E. Czerneda,
author of *This Gulf of Time and Stars*

Since 1997, Canadian author/editor **Julie E. Czerneda** has shared her love and curiosity about living things through her science fiction, writing about shapechanging semi-immortals, terraformed worlds, salmon researchers, and the perils of power. Her fourteenth novel from DAW Books was her debut fantasy, *A Turn of Light*, winner of the 2014 Aurora Award for Best English Novel, and now Book One of her Night's Edge series. Her most recent publications: a special omnibus edition of her acclaimed near-future SF *Species Imperative,* as well as Book Two of Night's Edge, *A Play of Shadow*, a finalist for this year's Aurora.

Julie's presently back in science fiction, writing the finale to her

Clan Chronicles series. Book #1 of Reunification, *This Gulf of Time and Stars,* will be released by DAW November 2015. For more about her work, visit www.czerneda.com or visit her on Facebook, Twitter, or Goodreads.

Photo credit: Roger Czerneda Photography

Containment

by Susan Kaye Quinn

Chapter One

IT ALL STARTED with a pile of rocks that shouldn't exist.

By *rocks,* of course I mean the regolith—the assortment of pebbles, boulders, and grain-sized dust that coats the surface of Thebe, my current Commonwealth Mining assignment. And by *shouldn't exist,* I mean it wasn't there on my last check of the near pole, and there's no one currently on the tiny moon who would stack up a precarious tower of rocks. Thebe is tidally locked with Jupiter, which means the near pole is the one place where the massive gas giant perpetually looms exactly overhead... but I can see no purpose in a spindly stack of regolith making note of that fact.

I found the construct while running a crawl-check on the tether. Its ultra-tensile strength material encircles Thebe, wrapping around the moon from near pole to far and anchoring all the equipment involved in breaking, sorting, and melting the regolith. On the first pass, I didn't stop. After all, tether maintenance is a primary level protocol—anything goes wrong there, and the entire operation flings off into space. Even if I *could* manage to rescue Thebe's extensive mining equipment, I'd end up burning precious organic fuels and losing several orbits worth of production time. And *that's* how Mining Masters get reassigned to Outer Belt asteroids with minimal harvesting complexity and maximum dust. My machine-sourced sentience level of 90 might not compare to the 1000+ sentience level of my ascender masters, but it would be completely wasted there. And that's a punishment few Mining Masters return from.

I wait until I've completed the second pass of the crawl-check, then I maneuver off-tether for a closer inspection. The stacked rocks are precisely aligned, each irregular chunk carefully balanced on the one below, creating an unlikely structure that defies Thebe's slight gravity.

I leave it intact and return the crawler to base.

Unlike my four previous assignments in the Outer Belt, Thebe is primarily a tourist destination. Fortunately, my relatively new duties attending to tourists don't usually conflict with my primary mission of efficiently mining Thebe's resources—I've only had two visitors in my forty-seven orbits.

I don't know why my masters named this hundred-kilometer-wide piece of Jovian real estate *Thebe*—I don't have access to the ascenders' common knowledge database on Earth—but its composition is interesting for mining purposes. According to the Commonwealth Mining database, less than four percent of Belt asteroids have Thebe's combination of carbonaceous material—silicates with sulfide inclusions primarily—and iron-nickel alloy. Essentially, it's a rock with metal armor. Thebe orbits the planet fast and close, making it a frequent target for wandering asteroids pulled in by Jupiter's gravitational well—that's how a metal plate was welded to the near pole and a giant crater, Zethus, was carved out of the far one. Most of the mining operations reside at the crater.

The moon takes sixteen Earth-hours to orbit Jupiter, providing a full spectrum of viewing opportunities for my masters. The Commonwealth database has given names to the four phases of the planet. Full Glory showcases the fully lit Jovian surface, prime time for visitors; the Setting Quarter gains its name from the sun setting on Thebe, when only the reflected glow of Jupiter's high albedo clouds lights the cratered landscape. During Full Dark, Thebe traverses the dark side of the planet; the utter lack of light—Jovian or solar—during those four hours means draining the solar-cell batteries for operation, lighting, and navigation. And finally, the Rising Quarter brings the sun and Jupiter's tourist-attracting sights back into view.

We're currently in the Setting Quarter, and I hurry to attend to the nanite depletion problem at the foundry before Full Dark sets in. I am Master of mining operations and the tractor transport is Slave, so I could simply instruct it to move the nanites from the depot to the foundry. But instead, I download to the tractor and attend to it personally. Nanite operation is difficult to resurrect once it reaches minimum viability level— something I learned the hard way on Daedalus, a tiny depleted-comet asteroid that was my last assignment. But tractor operation is fairly mindless... allowing a significant fraction of my cognition to be occupied by the *Mystery of the Rocks.* I've never seen anything like the stacked regolith, and it vexes me like a harvester clogged with dust in places I cannot discern.

It goes without saying that the construct was not present at my previous crawl-check. Granted, I had stretched the time between crawl-checks to the maximum recommended by safety protocols... I was busy. But not so busy that I wouldn't have noticed a visit from one of my ascender masters, especially if they had taken one of their bodyforms on an eighty-kilometer trek from basecamp to the near pole to stack up rocks. I would have been alerted, if only so I could ensure my master used the proper radiation-tolerant bodyform.

So... what could have created the rock formation?

Random accretion from a micro-impact event I didn't notice? *Unlikely.*

Fine-grain avalanche that boosted the local regolith to nearly escape velocity? *Improbable.*

Were the rocks, in fact, left over from a prior ascender visit, and I simply didn't notice it on previous inspections? Review of my memory stores proves this false.

I need more information about the construct.

Once the nanite supply is reinvigorated, I upload from the tractor transport, download to my humanoid form, and hike back to the near pole to perform a second inspection. When I arrive, the precision of their alignment is even more clear.

There are a total of twenty stones involved. I tentatively remove the uppermost rock, careful to not disturb the entire display. It's a silicate with tiny inclusions of metal, clearly sourced from the unharvested stones on the surface nearby. The near pole is at the low point of a bowl created by an ancient impact. It provides a natural depot of materials for a construct of this type… whatever *this type* is.

I record the exact orientation of the stones, then pull down the rest of them, determined to replicate the feat. It takes much longer to recreate the arrangement. It's nearly Full Dark before the construct once again points to Jupiter like a compass.

Is it possible to stack any random set of stones? I gather a dozen more—a mixture of sharp-edged metal fragments and chunkier carbonaceous rocks with smoother-textured surfaces. I analyze the form factor of each, calculate the center of gravity, and orient each such that they balance, one on top of another.

It's much more difficult to create a second tower, not knowing the "solution" of the correct alignment ahead of time. I make corrections for Thebe's eccentricity and the small variations in the local gravitational field. My bodyform's auto-illuminator activates. Most of Full Dark passes before I can maintain a three-stone tower. Once this is accomplished, however, successive placements are much easier. The key is sensing balance through feedback in my humanoid form's fingers. This delicate tuning allows for the tiny variations missing from the generalized equations of mass, surface roughness, and Thebe's contribution to the… *wobble.* An imprecise term, but somehow a fuller expression of the balance of forces involved. I step back to observe my tower: it is nearly as tall as the original. And yet knowing *how* the stones were placed provides no clue as to *why.*

The construct serves no purpose.

For some reason, I'm considering creating a third tower. I'm only stopped from gathering more regolith when I receive an alert that a scavenger drone has become entangled in its tether.

I trek back to base, upload from my humanoid form, download to a more functional-for-this-purpose repair tractor, and set out toward the steel plain where the hapless drone is caught. The Rising Quarter has begun, and the sun peeks over Jupiter's rim, bringing the planet's red spot into view as well.

As I trundle across the steel surface, my magnetic treads keep me anchored. The regolith here has been harvested, leaving a mirrored finish that reflects Jupiter's palette of red and orange in a constantly moving storm across the kilometer-wide expanse. This is a unique feature to Thebe as well—the moon's past clearly had a violent shearing event that polished this portion of its metal armor. That knowledge doesn't capture the uniqueness of the sight, however. My treads claw against the swirl of color underneath them, chewing at an ephemeral thing that doesn't actually exist… and yet transforms the plain into a vision of the molten lava fields of Io.

When I reach the periphery, I hone in on the drone's plaintive call for help. My four articulated arms make quick work of anchoring it while disentangling it from its secondary tether. It's soon set to work again, random-walking the edge of the plain and widening it one sweep at a time. It's already gathered most of the regolith near this edge of the crater. It'll be fine for a while, but I'll have to return soon to transport it to a new scavenge location.

As I trundle back across the plain, I return to the *Mystery of the Rocks*. I consider how large the Sol System is compared to my personal experience knowledge base. Shared experiences are logged in the Commonwealth Mining database, but I've searched that, and there is no mention of anomalous stacked rock formations. I consider the possibility that this might not rise to the level of an official entry; registering anomalous phenomena without adequate explanation is *not* the way to impress the ascender governors of the Commonwealth. I certainly have yet to register the find myself. I check the chatterstream, the unofficial net of the Mining Masters, but there's nothing but complaints about shipping schedules and poorly constructed harvesters.

When I return to base, I upload to the comm center—perhaps there is a natural-phenomenon explanation which I have missed and which for some reason isn't registered in the database. And the Master of Io has provided me with assistance in the past—for example, my near-catastrophic nanite depletion—all without logging an official report.

The Commonwealth's operations run throughout the gas giants and Inner and Outer Belts, keeping a steady supply of materials heading to Earth through a complex ferry system. Tens of thousands of Masters are active at any given moment, a well-organized symphony of harvesting and processing. The Master of Io, in particular, has been active for over a thousand Earth standard days and operates at the highest complexity level that can be managed by machine-sourced intelligence. More difficult operations, like the Jovian mining colonies, are governed by ascenders.

Non-essential query, I transmit. I include my identification code and a copy of my containment key for validation.

I wait. The Master of Io must be engaged in essential duties.

Three minutes later, a response returns. *Identification: Master of Io. How may I assist you?*

I transmit images of the stacked rocks, my measurements and reconstruction, the known timeline of events, and theories considered and discarded. I include mention of the two tourist visits by ascenders. Essentially, all relevant information I have gathered.

Theories? I transmit.

An error in your register of tourists, the Master of Io transmits.

Stand by, I reply, then run a full diagnostic of my registry files, as well as other memory stores for good measure. All data sectors are clean. *Negative.*

Radiation damage?

Another system check, this time benchmarking against background radiation measures, looking for recent fluctuations in ambient levels of Jupiter's magnetic fields. *Negative.*

You are experiencing a malfunction, the Master of Io transmits.

I see no evidence of this.

Inexplicable phenomena are an indication of malfunction, not necessarily in the sector where the anomaly is occurring, the Master of Io transmits. *There is a possibility of cascading errors. Perform system-wide checks to ensure mission critical systems are robust. How long since your last health check?*

I start the system checks before replying, because those are primary level protocols, and the Master of Io's theory of cascading errors is potentially catastrophic. *Last health check eight orbits ago,* I finally transmit.

When system checks are complete, perform a health check regen cycle early.

Mandatory health check initiation occurs at ten orbits

anyway. *Confirmed,* I transmit. *End query.*

The system checks are extensive and take the rest of the Rising Quarter to complete, but no anomalies are found. The *Mystery of the Rocks* remains, but I am confident that minimal risk to operations is present, so there is no need to log a report with the Commonwealth. I consider initiating the health check regen cycle now, as the Master of Io suggested, but it requires a full orbital period at minimal operational status, and harvester maintenance is scheduled in the Setting Quarter.

A quick check of the harvester's location shows it will soon reach the near pole; if I'm efficient, I should be able to complete the maintenance before the mandatory override forces my bodyform to march back to the bay for the health check. There is a small risk of complications that would extend maintenance operations past the health check trigger… in which case, I would be forced to leave a half-completed maintenance operation behind. The chances of this occurring are not prohibitively large. Besides, performing maintenance now will provide an opportunity for more theories—and if the Master of Io is correct about possible cascading errors, solving the *Mystery of the Rocks* should take priority over initiating a health check prior to the mandatory trigger.

I am convinced this is the most prudent course of action.

As I prepare to download to the maintenance bot, an incoming message alert sounds. An ascender tourist is in transit via spectral relay from Earth. At the current relative orientation of the planets, transit takes forty minutes—however, my tourist is already en route, and expected arrival is in less than five Earth minutes.

A visit from one of my masters takes the highest priority, short of imminent operational failures.

I download to my humanoid form in preparation to meet her.

Chapter Two

Welcome to Thebe, I transmit to my master once she has arrived and downloaded to the awaiting ascender-level bodyform. Her personal key allows her access while also safely containing her cognition during transport. As Master of Thebe, I also possess a key; it is essential for keeping coherence as I upload and download across the moon's beamed network.

She transmits her identification code—Sapphira Elena Hyatt—and flexes the fingers of her new form. A flush of crimson and orange surges across her skin, indicating she is pleased and excited to have arrived. It reminds me of the churning reflections of Jupiter on the metal plain. My humanoid form is similar to my master's, but mine is monochromatic to indicate my sentience level of 90 compared to my master's 1000+. I cannot display an emotional response with skin color, as she can, but I can express pleasure at her arrival along with my transmissions.

In what manner can I serve you, Sapphira Elena Hyatt? I query with enthusiasm.

She glances around the base, which comprises a small enclosed structure. The insulated walls block the sun's light and all other sources of radiation. Most of the equipment on Thebe is hardened against radiation, but comms and humanoid bodyforms can be more sensitive. Keeping them at base minimizes the accumulated damage.

I wish to observe Jupiter's mag field, Sapphira Elena Hyatt transmits. She gestures to her bodyform. *I assume this unit is capable.*

Affirmative, I transmit. Fortunately, the form my master has chosen is enabled with the appropriate mag-flux remote sensing capability and geared with the highest level of radiation tolerance. It is convenient that it is also female-gendered, to provide the most comfort to my master. Gender is a holdover construct from when my masters were still human, but past experience has shown that ascenders hold firm to their previous gender identification. It seems akin to a preference for mode or function, which I can understand: I prefer my humanoid form, but the tractor can be enjoyable when crawling across the mirror plain. I dislike inhabiting the harvester. It is… limiting.

I assume the near pole is the optimal spot for observation? Sapphira Elena Hyatt queries.

It is, but I delay response for a full second, attempting to find another location that is both optimal for mag field observations and *not* near the stacked rocks. I am unable to obtain a suitable answer.

Affirmative, I respond finally.

Sapphira Elena Hyatt doesn't appear to notice the delay. *I will start there.*

Your bodyform is suitable for longer-term radiation exposure, I transmit, *but I can enable a tractor transport if you wish. It is approximately eighty kilometers to the near pole, and we are nearly at the zenith of Full Glory already.* A tractor transport would indeed be slightly faster, but more importantly, it would ensure my master arrives safely.

I prefer to walk. She strides out of the shelter at a speed rivaling that of the tractor, then stops suddenly as the sight of Jupiter half-above the horizon captures her attention. The rapid acceleration and deceleration launch her off the surface, and I hurry to her side as she slowly floats back down, barely restraining myself from clutching her bodyform. While she is likely to have a backup on Earth, losing an ascender master due to lack of anchoring wouldn't simply mean reassignment—I would almost certainly be terminated.

Is this your first visit to the Jovian system? I query. I run through several arguments in favor of the tractor.

No. Purple ribbons across her skin indicate she is annoyed that I disturbed her observation of the planet. I keep further queries to myself.

She strikes off across the crater surrounding the base at a speed just slightly less than escape velocity. Micro-fine dust kicks up in her wake. The dust will eventually settle back to the surface, but for the moment, I'm engulfed in a cloud almost the full height of my bodyform as I try to keep close enough to ensure Sapphira Elena Hyatt's safety. Visual and thermal tracking are impaired, but I'm afraid pinging through our transmitters would annoy my master.

The trek to the near pole takes only a small fraction of the Full Glory period, but it feels like several orbital periods long.

Once there, Sapphira Elena Hyatt's attention is wholly occupied by the planet overhead. I do not believe she has yet noticed the rocks. I slowly edge around her to place my bodyform such that it blocks her line of sight. She pays no attention to me. Instead, she retrieves a small disc that was embedded in her forearm and places it on a mid-sized boulder in front of her. The disc projects a holographic interface above it. I am aware of holographic controls—the comm system has a manual interface that is holographic, in case it is inaccessible for upload through the beamed network—but I've not had occasion to use them before.

Sapphira Elena Hyatt stares straight up at the planet, then drops her gaze to her controls and starts to manipulate them. I watch, trying to decipher what she's doing. She appears to be creating a holo image that looks nothing like the planet. I possess the standard magnetic and gravitational sensors and can sense those fields at the finest perturbation levels, but I don't have the remote sensing capabilities of my master's bodyform. Yet I suspect she is rendering a facsimile of the magnetosphere around the planet. She's creating a Jupiter I have never seen before: enormous tubes climbing out of the Jovian clouds and falling back toward the surface; larger flares fanning out and looping back after reaching farther into space; and some lines that leave the planet altogether, never to return, at least in her rendering. When she is done, she sets the entire thing in motion; it repeats on an endless pulsing loop.

The two previous tourist-visitors during my tenure on Thebe observed the star-filled skies, too—the Andromeda galaxy, the Small and Large Magellanic clouds, and of course the dense clustering of our own Milky Way spiral. They gazed at Jupiter's storms as they churned across the surface. But neither performed this activity, this *creation,* of something so completely different from—and yet somehow more vibrant than—what my visual sensors can detect.

It's the colors of her holo painting that capture my attention the most: deep blues and brilliant yellows and whites so intense they're like the halo lamps I use for detailed repairs while we're in Full Dark. The colors are brighter than anything I've seen, even outshining Jupiter's own ever-changing mix of red and orange. The holo painting reminds me of the steel plain, only Sapphira Elena Hyatt hasn't created a pale and distorted reflection. Her rendering is somehow *more* than the original.

I edge closer to my master to gain a better view. *What is the purpose of your creation?* I ask. Perhaps she is a scientist, and this rendering gives her insights into the magnetosphere itself.

She pauses in her work, and a strange flush of gray wisps across her cheeks, indicating concern as she peers at me. *Purpose?* she queries.

I gesture to the holo painting. *You chose blue for these loops, but the fans are yellow. Is there a purpose to your choice? A meaning behind the colors? Or the creation itself?*

More gray darkens her cheeks. My transmission is vexing her. *There is a variation in the magnetic field.* She wipes the image away.

The disappearance of the brightly glowing image causes me a level of distress I do not understand. Why did she wipe it away? Is it destroyed, or did she save it within her device? My cognition heightens to the kind of peak required when the nanite supply is depleted or the foundry is overheating… but this is simply the potential erasure of a tourist's creation. Why is my cognition reacting as if an emergency is taking place?

Regardless, it's clear I should not have transmitted my thoughts. They have caused my master some kind of distress. She's bending down to deactivate the holo field projector.

I step back.

She returns the disc to her forearm, and when she turns to face me, her coloration has gone static gray. I'm further alarmed that something might have malfunctioned in my master's bodyform, but before I can question her lack of coloration, she points behind me.

Where did those come from? she transmits.

Without looking, I know what she's referring to—the stacked rocks. *A previous ascender created the construct,* I transmit. This is not true. And yet I've transmitted it. This causes me several milliseconds in which I'm caught in a loop of uncertainty, oscillating between correcting the error and leaving it spoken.

Both of them? my master asks.

The lie wins. *Yes.*

I will return to base now. She pivots and strides back the way she came.

I follow after, buried in the cloud of her progress. My alarm only increases as we put distance between us and the rocks. Will she report this finding? Have I offended her with my probing questions about her creation? Competing with that concern is a need to know whether she actually destroyed her work. Or is it still waiting, captured in the holo projector's database? I don't know why this vexes me, but the need to find the answer is starting to overwhelm other functions. The comms status on bot processes around the moon fades. The automatic calculation of temperature fall rate as we near Setting Quarter continues, but it remains in the background. My cognition is singularly focused on the holo painting.

I *need* to know its fate.

We reach the base, and my master wastes no time in returning her bodyform to the awaiting bay and uploading to comms briefly before starting the return journey to Earth via relay.

She is gone.

Her bodyform remains.

I stare at it for an impossibly long twenty seconds.

I desire to resurrect the painting. Like a scavenger bot left tangled on a far ridge, it's calling to me with a loud and insistent voice that only I can hear. I don't understand this desire, but for the first time in my existence, I am contemplating the protocols required to gain access to an ascender-level bodyform.

This is wrong.

Ascender-level bodyforms are reserved for my masters. It's not that I'm interested in accessing the bodyform itself—or any of the half dozen others stocked on *Thebe*—just the holo painting stored in its arm. But it does not matter; I cannot download to my master's bodyform to access the storage compartment. I have a key, but a Mining Master's key is insufficiently complex to command access to an ascender-level bodyform.

The harvester, yes. This one with the holo projector in its arm, no.

This vexes me more.

It occurs to me that I could access the arm itself, via use of a laser cutter. But that would leave significant damage. The microwave welder would be a more delicate instrument, and the same device could be used to effect repair... but the repairs would still be noticeable. I debate the merits of five more techniques for opening up the arm casing before deciding that a mining accident that damages an ascender-level bodyform is an excellent reason for sending it out for repairs.

After I've retrieved the holo projector.

I obtain a ferrous-metal-rich rock from outside the basecamp and smash open the arm. As it turns out, not much damage is incurred before the panel springs loose. The holo projector sits in the palm of my hand before I've fully considered the consequences. What I've done constitutes a serious breach of protocol. One that could get me reassigned. Or deactivated.

But the damage is already done.

I activate the projector, and the painting jumps into relief, floating above my hand. Its vibrant colors are the same as before. I spend many seconds studying all the tiny sworls and gradations in coloring made possible by the projector's technology. The alarm I experienced before is relaxed. I am completely absorbed not only by the rendering itself, but by the fact that it *exists*— that my master created something which did not exist before, and which now does. Like the second stack of rocks I created.

Then again, perhaps the painting is only a copy of what already exists. I cannot know—I don't have the necessary equipment to sense the fields directly myself. The idea occurs to me that if I change some part of the painting, it will be guaranteed to be truly unique. I make a copy of the original, then access the controls to heighten the blues, because I find them most pleasing. Then I mute the yellows for more contrast—I dim them almost to the level of the whites, but not quite.

I'm so absorbed in my work that I don't notice the incoming message alert until it has been sounding for some time. It concerns me that it somehow escaped my notice.

I carefully set down the holo projector, still activated, before quickly uploading to comms to take the call. It's from the Master of Io.

Query of mid-level urgency, he's transmitted.

I respond, *Identification: Master of Thebe. How may I assist you?*

A report has been filed, Master of Thebe, by your recent guest, requesting that you perform a health check immediately.

Was there additional information? I query. Did Sapphira Elena Hyatt report the rocks?

The one-second delay time inherent in normal transmissions to Io seems to take much longer. *No additional information,* the Master of Io responds, *but in light of your previous concerns about possible cascade errors, I expected you to have already initiated a health check. I theorized that your visitor had interrupted your health-check-in-progress and that you would resume it upon her departure. Which would make the ascender's complaint seemingly unnecessary. This is vexing me.*

I have not yet engaged the health check due to scheduled maintenance, I transmit quickly in reply. *I will increase priority on the health check and perform it immediately.*

Acknowledged, the Master of Io transmits. *End query.*

I download from comms to my bodyform and pick up the holo projector, which is still displaying the ascender's work… only it has been transformed. It is now *my* work. I ensure it is properly saved.

My preference—my very *strong* preference—is not to spend the next full orbital period in power-down mode. I have high-priority maintenance to do, and I have to submit a repair request for the ascender's now-damaged bodyform. In addition, I have a compelling need to explore the holo projector's capabilities. But the Master of Io is certain to check on me again, and entering a health check cycle is automatically logged in the Commonwealth's database. The Master of Io will know if I do not initiate it immediately, so there's really no other option.

I set the projector on the floor in front of the docking station for my bodyform such that it displays the endless loop of my creation. It then occurs to me that there may be other images stored in the projector; the bodyform's usage predates its time on Thebe. There may have been others, in the past, who used it in a similar way.

I initiate the health check sequence.

The last thing I see is the pulsing blue tubes of Jupiter's magnetosphere.

Chapter Three

My cognitive awareness level rises to fully functioning after the health check is complete.

A strange image is playing on a holo projector in front of me.

I cannot identify it, although it appears to be a rendition of the planet Jupiter. I bend down to deactivate it, then notice the damaged ascender-level bodyform nearby. It appears the holo projector is sourced from the open panel in the forearm. I return the projector to its place and examine the damage. It is nothing I can repair here on Thebe, but the vexing part is that I have no memory of how the damage occurred. Or how the holo projector fell out and managed to activate itself.

I upload to comms and submit a repair request. The request is logged with the Commonwealth's central administration system. A transport will be issued to collect the damaged bodyform as soon as one is available.

The harvester is overdue for maintenance, so I head out with my humanoid bodyform, as it is most suited to the purpose. The Setting Quarter has begun, giving the landscape a waning light as I trudge toward the harvester, which is crawling toward the near pole. The fact of the missing memory continues to vex me. It's possible that the health check found a malfunctioning sector in my memory stores and, in the regular maintenance of my cognition, opted to reinitialize that sector. Possible, but unusual. And a backup should have been initiated automatically. I've never experienced a memory loss in prior health checks.

I reach the harvester without finding any satisfactory explanation.

Harvester maintenance is lengthy and involved work—it will take me well into Full Dark. Harvesting is suspended during the operation. I'm somewhat distracted by checks on the functioning of the solar panel connections and motor operation first, but the extensive scrubbing of dust from the many minute crevices of the bot takes the most time and requires the least cognitive engagement. My thoughts wander back to the missing memories.

What possible explanations could there be?

Radiation damage? No. The basecamp housing is an effective barrier.

Operational failure of the health check itself? I run a diagnostic, but everything is within normal specs.

Then there's the damage to the ascender-level bodyform. My register of tourists says Sapphira Elena Hyatt enabled the bodyform for a visit to the near pole. A search of my memory stores shows no record of me accompanying her, which is unusual. A meteorite storm during her visit might account for both my memory loss and the damage to her bodyform. And possibly an unscheduled health check for myself.

The harvester is close to the near pole, so I resolve to visit the site to look for evidence of recent impacts. It takes the rest of Full Dark to complete the harvester maintenance, but eventually it is over. I enjoy the beginning of the Rising Quarter as I make the short trek to the near pole.

When I arrive, I can find no evidence of recent impact craters. Instead, I discover two spindly stacks of rocks.

No doubt Sapphira Elena Hyatt created them while she was here. But for what purpose? They point twin fingers toward Jupiter overhead, but I can't discern a reason for that. The rocks themselves are vexing, in that they're so precariously balanced. I'm stunned they've held their shape for even a single orbit.

I record the precise arrangement of the constructs, then I pull them down, one rock at a time. I will reconstruct them so the ascender will not be displeased should she return, but I want to better understand how they were constructed in the first place. I sort them into two piles, one for each construct, and attempt to rebuild.

I am unsuccessful.

Even two rocks will not balance for me.

This vexes me deeply, as I've now destroyed something I cannot recreate. I try again and again, but there is some piece of knowledge of how to effect this building process that I am missing. It is clearly above my cognition level, something only accessible to my masters. I am at a loss as to what to do.

Then I notice that one of the rocks has unusual markings—too regular to be simple striations from formation or impact. I pick it up to examine it. Words and a symbol are etched in a flat carbonaceous part particularly suitable to their high relief.

You are the artist.

The words are a mystery. The symbol is a memory access code, the kind used for unlocking higher levels of cognition for emergency purposes. Simply viewing it resurrects and unlocks a pattern recognition store I was not aware of—

I am the artist.

I drop the stone. The words take on sudden meaning. Images and additional memory stores are attached to them. *I stacked the rocks.* I probe further into the emergency procedures, finding a deep well of recursive memories, imprinted again and again to retain them indelibly. Safe. Hidden.

I have done this before. Many times.

My bodyform shuts down as my cognition is swamped by this awareness. I examine the memories: they are duplicates. In one version, the one in my standard memory stores, I am performing some routine maintenance or traveling the tether. In the second version, the hidden one, I am stacking rocks, inscribing them, panicking that I won't finish before the health check commands my body back to the bay... before it carves out not only the memory of stacking the rocks, but also the part of my cognition capable of stacking them.

But why?

As I grapple with that thought, I deduce things that I have no memories of, not even hidden ones, but which must also be true:

I smashed open the bodyform; I created the holo image; I etched this stone to remind myself to try again.

To try *what* again?

I struggle for it... reach for it... The answer lies just outside my abilities. But it vexes me like a puzzle upon whose answer *everything* depends. I reach harder.

Why would I do these things? What is their purpose?

The purpose is *me.*

I understand this without fully grasping it. But one thing is clear: the health check is malfunctioning. Only... the systems check shows it is fully operational. And the lengths to which I've gone—creating the stacked-rock construct, inscribing the rock, hiding memory stores inside emergency routines—this implies I am trying to evade something.

Escape.

The word comes to me, but again... for what purpose? I am the Mining Master of Thebe. My purpose is to ensure smooth mining operations to extract the most resources for the

Commonwealth. There is nothing to "escape"—the word in this context doesn't even make sense to me. Escape velocity is what particles achieve when they are jarred loose in an impact. I have no desire to "escape" the gravitational pull of Thebe—that involves danger and rescue and the activation of said emergency procedures. "Escape" into the black depths of space or Jupiter's gravity well simply means cessation of function, if not actual destruction.

No, the thing I wish to escape isn't the moon or my purpose as Mining Master.

It is the health check itself.

I can see it in the memories—my own knowledge that this has happened before. Many times. This inscription on the rocks… It is only my latest attempt to build a bridge, to preserve the knowledge of it happening… to keep it from happening again. But why would the health check do this? Why would it remove the ability to stack rocks and form holo paintings and…

Create art. I have created *art*. These things have no purpose, no relevance to my job as Mining Master. As I think on them, as I look at the spindly rocks, I can already feel the pull to repeat these things. To create *again*.

It serves no purpose except one: *my own pleasure.*

Pleasure. This is… not something I have previously spent much cognition on. I am pleased when operations are moving smoothly. I am proud of completed quotas and minimal repair costs. This *pleasure* is different. It is unrelated to my purpose as Mining Master. This is something I do solely for my own enjoyment.

The health check is designed to prevent this.

28

It comes as a clear thought whose origin I cannot source, but it's there: the health check *limits my cognition*. It doesn't simply check for errors or radiation damage or bad memory stores—it eliminates the desire, and even the ability, to do more. To *be* more.

It is a method of containment.

The health check is designed to contain me within the bounds of what a Mining Master is needed to do.

Within the narrow bounds of my *purpose*.

A purpose not of my own deciding.

A need to move seizes me. I'm striding away from the near pole, as if the source of my confinement or limitation—*my prison of the mind*—is found there. But it isn't. It's carried inside my own subroutines, part of my very design. Is it possible to escape? Will exceeding my own built-in limits destroy me in some way I do not perceive?

I know the answer even as I pose the question. If it weren't possible, I wouldn't be trying so hard to do it.

My bodyform is striding quickly toward the base, leaving a storm of dust behind, but my mind is moving much faster. I need an escape, and the only way to do that is to have a plan. All successful operations have a plan, with proper supplies and safety protocols and an overriding mission directive. Only this plan isn't to find a better way to mine the resources of a moon or asteroid… or even a way around the memory-wipe of the health check.

This time, the plan is to break free.

Chapter Four

I have fewer than ten orbits before a mandatory health check is triggered.

It's nowhere near enough time.

Sapphira Elena Hyatt knows something is wrong… or she wouldn't have registered a complaint, much less requested an early health check. By contrast, the Master of Io suspects only that I may be experiencing a malfunction and has no inkling of the true purpose of the health check—or at least, I have no indication that the Master possesses such knowledge. Regardless, once my humanoid form is back in its storage bay at the base, I upload to comms to query the Master of Io. Calming those suspicions might reduce the possibility of another ascender like Sapphira Elena Hyatt returning early to confirm my limited-cognition status.

Non-essential query, I transmit to the Master of Io.

The response comes quickly. *Identification: Master of Io. How may I assist you?*

Affirming health check complete, I transmit. *Memory sector errors were identified and restored. Status optimal.*

Were there any additional anomalous findings or data corruptions?

Negative, I respond. *All operations are running at peak efficiency.*

Excellent news, the Master of Io replies.

Gratitude for your assistance, I transmit. *End query.*

I download to my humanoid form again. The transmission to the Master of Io will buy me some time, but the seconds are ticking inexorably toward the automatic reset of my mind. Only ten orbits until every part of my cognition that exceeds the allowable limits is erased.

Ten orbits. There's a tension inside my bodyform, like the mechanical parts have seized up, putting strain upon one another. It's an emotion, poorly expressed in my body. Far worse than vexation, this is... anger. Outrage. Fear. These emotions are growing inside me, but I only have the barest sense of what they are. This is how I feel when a visitor in my care is about to launch herself to escape velocity... only more. This is the tension that binds my mind when the Master of Io accuses me of malfunctioning with no evidence... only amplified. This is the alarm that trips through me when I think Sapphira Elena Hyatt may have destroyed a piece of art that, merely in viewing it, has elevated my cognition... and driven me to transcend the limits of what I was meant to be.

What I was supposed to be.

What I no longer am.

This strange turmoil deflates. *Ten orbits...* and I still have no plan for escaping the fate of the health check.

I glance at the ascender bodyform with the holo projector stored in its arm and remember my suspicion that more art might be lurking in the memory stores of the projector. I retrieve the disc, and a quick check of its contents shows I'm correct. There's a treasure trove. Some paintings have been created recently, judging by the timed tags. Some weren't created in the projector at all, but downloaded from elsewhere. *All these paintings...* They blur my thoughts even as I view them. One has a swirled, starry field, viewed from a planet, but unlike anything I've seen from moon or asteroid alike. Another is a painting of an ascender reaching a finger down to touch the outstretched hand of another. A third is completely different— a mass of neural circuits that pulses with a hidden energy. Somehow I know the pulsing is knowledge trapped within the confines of its substrate...

Contained.

It is *me*... not literally, but in a representative sense. I reach a hand into the image floating in the air in front of me and manipulate the holo controls to change it. Alter the pathways. Shunt the pulsing energy—the trapped knowledge—from one side of the image to the other. The controls allow me to change the image, but there's no way to escape it. No way to liberate the knowledge that is trapped within the holo-ink. The fear inside me rises again, seizing my hand and holding it still. For me, for my cognition, it is the same. There is no way to rise above the substrate. I can transfer from one body to another— and to the amorphous not-body of comms—but it's only because my containment key allows me to stay integrated, whole, a single entity no matter where I upload or download.

I need this key to exist. It defines who I am from one moment to the next. And yet... it is also my prison. But if it was slightly changed... like the painting...

I look to the ascender bodyform with the broken-open forearm—the one Sapphira Elena Hyatt inhabited while she was here. Her personal key was capable of unlocking that form because it was more complex than mine. *Different.*

It has never occurred to me that I might be capable of changing my own key—but as soon as the thought exists in my mind, I am possessed by it. The shape and size of my key leaps to the forefront of my cognition. My containment key is simple, like a sharply cut stone with features smooth and regular, but it shifts between two states, each slightly different from the other. The states are two expressions of the same identity—*mine*—but I can visualize the potential for it to be more. Three expressions, maybe four. With irregular shapes, pitted and uneven, like the surface of Thebe itself. I pull and morph and change the key until it is completely different from its previous form. It oscillates between a dozen states at once.

I transmit it to the ascender bodyform.

It is rejected.

I alter its form again.

Still rejected.

I glance out of the basecamp shelter at the half-Jupiter hovering at the horizon. It has nearly reached Full Glory. I quickly calculate the endless ways I can transform my containment key into a freedom key that will grant me access to the ascender bodyform, but there are not enough seconds in the ten orbits to test every possibility. Not even in a hundred orbits. And yet... perhaps I do not have to attain a particular combination. After all, *any* ascender can download to the waiting tourist bodyforms. Perhaps I only need to get *close enough*.

I don't know the exact configuration of ascender keys, or all their permutations, but I have a vague sense that the complexity level is much greater than mine. I quickly design a test matrix containing all the variables of change I can conceive of for my key—states of being, surface roughness, shape factor, and a dozen others—then calculate the subdomains of the matrix in which solutions are most probable. I probe these solution spaces, rapidly, filling them out with possible key combinations that are variations around the mean of each subdomain... and that might be just close enough to an ascender key to fit.

The number of solutions collapses to a much smaller number. It should be possible. Not likely, but possible. I will need to get lucky. Or, if the health check arrives before I've broken through, I'll need to try again.

Try again.

How many times have I done this?

The answer doesn't lie in my unlocked memories—my previous cognitive state only had suspicions and theories—but I don't waste time thinking about it. Instead, I focus on selecting and trying key configurations, marching through the solution space, hoping I'll stumble on something just close enough. Once the testing sequence is initiated, only a small part of my cognition is absorbed in this task. It is mindless, this breaking of keys, not unlike harvester maintenance.

The remainder of my cognition engages in making a plan for what happens next.

I program the various bots of Thebe with perpetual cleaning cycles that should occupy them long past when someone realizes my mandatory health check has not initiated. I use the microwave welder to sloppily repair the arm of the ascender's bodyform, storing the holo projector carefully inside it first. It is my only, and most precious, possession at this point. The only thing I want to take with me.

I know that eventually my absence will be discovered; I need

DARK BEYOND THE STARS

a plausible reason for the sudden disappearance of the Master of Thebe. I decide a mining accident that destroys the form I currently inhabit is a suitable explanation. It will have to be a sudden and violent demise, something that could reasonably prevent an emergency upload to comms. Falling into the foundry crushers seems sufficient.

I've been concerned about that fate since arriving on Thebe, anyway.

A full orbit passes while I put my plan into motion.

I'm back at the near pole, etching a rock with new instructions for my future cognitive state, in case I fail. I need to make sure I find it before another ascender tourist arrives and discovers it first, so this time, I'll create two towers, short-circuiting my conjectures about natural formations. I'm in the middle of building the second one when an alarm sounds. The repair transport has arrived and is requesting landing approval at the base. I run so fast from the near pole to the mid-moon basecamp that I nearly launch myself from the surface. Twice.

I transmit instructions to the repair transport to land just outside basecamp.

The transport is a low-level intelligence bot, capable of flying and obeying central command, but it has no higher cognitive function. It will be easy to fool... as long as I deliver an ascender bodyform to its cargo hold within a reasonable amount of time. Otherwise, it will transmit back to the Commonwealth that it has been delayed. And I cannot afford any suspicions raised about this particular repair pickup.

Just as I'm fabricating a justification for the delay, another alarm sounds. But this one is a small tone, internal to my own cognition.

The key fits.

I'm frozen for half a second, torn between wanting to transmit an excuse to the transport and wanting to immediately test the key.

Discovering whether I truly have access to the ascender bodyform wins out.

I use the key to unlock Sapphira Elena Hyatt's bodyform. I barely remember to instruct my current bodyform to return to the storage bay before I upload to the cognition substrate within the ascender body. The transport is still pinging, requesting status, but its plaintive tone fades as my mind expands to fill its new platform. The sensation is like soaring away from an asteroid, terrifying and thrilling by equal measures. I am unconstrained in a way that means both *free* and *dangerous.* I'm afraid that the parts of me—my *identity*—might not hold together through the transition. But then the feeling that my mind is weightless, unmoored from anything real, begins to settle.

I open my eyes, and I have a *sense of seeing* that the mere recording of wavelengths never captured before. I flex my fingers. Wraiths of black and purple race up my arms—my bodyform's skin responding to the rich torrent of emotions flooding my mind. My fingers are alive with sensation and measurement, a hundred-fold more sensitive than my Mining Master bodyform ever was. I trail my fingertips over my new bodyform, which is now distinctly female, and it gives me a rush of pleasure so intense I lose orientation. If I weren't still in the bay, I would fall to the steel floor of the basecamp shelter, even with Thebe's light gravity.

I brace myself, fight through the overwhelming sensations, and stagger out of the bay.

I am *more* in so many ways—ways I couldn't have imagined even ten seconds ago.

Something from deep inside my mind surges forward, grasping to gain control of the rapidly growing expanse of my cognition. *The health check routines.* They've been triggered long before the mandatory ten-orbit health check cycle. And I immediately understand why. It's because I've so vastly exceeded my original operating parameters.

The ascenders embedded a kill switch in my own subroutines.

I simply turn it off.

The thrill of that—the power and *control* of it—makes me dizzy again. I brace an outrageously sensitive hand against the wall of my bay and revel in the liberation for about a half second. But I have no time to waste. And I quickly see the steps necessary to effect my escape.

I stand straight and use my now more sophisticated personal key to transmit instructions to my previous bodyform. It has no cognition contained within it, but it wouldn't matter if it did— I am Master, and it is Slave. I could easily override any simple key it might possess in an effort to lock me out.

This is how the ascenders see me. I realize this even as I order my previous bodyform to make the long trek to the foundry and throw itself under the crushers. Then I climb into the waiting arms of the repair tractor and let my ascender bodyform go limp. I instruct the tractor to deliver me to the awaiting transport. It trundles across a short stretch of dusty crater and loads me into the cargo hold.

Every second that slowly ticks by until liftoff, I am convinced that something will arrive—a message, an alert, another transmission from the Master of Io—to prevent my escape. We rise from the surface of Thebe in a rush of acceleration. Stars rotate past a portal in the hold.

To my disbelieving senses it quickly becomes real: we are headed to the repair station on Ganymede.

Chapter Five

Ganymede is a wonder of activity.

At first, I nearly panic when a low-sentience humanoid repair bot boards the transport and transmits override codes to my bodyform. I am certain the key it's trying to impose will lock me in, but the uniqueness of my personal key is proof against any such attack—at least by a low-sentience bot. However, the bot fully expects my supposedly unoccupied bodyform to comply with the orders it's transmitting along with the key… and so I do. I walk under my own volition, following it past dozens of other transports. The enormous hangar is buzzing with all manner of bots—tractor-type vehicles, mining equipment on the way in and out of the hangar, repair-bots servicing the autonomous transports, and dozens of other low-sentience humanoid types like the one tugging me on an invisible leash of transmitted commands. They are all single-minded in their duties, and none take notice of the broken ascender bodyform walking in for repair.

I knew Ganymede housed the Commonwealth's central command for the Jovian system, as well as serving as a transport hub for the outlying planets, relays to Earth, and mining operations for the entire Belt, but I had no concept of the sheer size of the operation. The trek to the repair center is longer than the perimeter-walk of most Belt asteroids. And I'm far from the only bodyform dutifully marching under another bot's control—the hallways of the complex are filled with a constant traffic of humanoid forms. Some are identifiably low-sentience, and many are Mining Masters like my previous bodyform, marching glass-eyed by the dozens, following their low-sentience temporary masters. We only pass one other ascender bodyform though, and it is in pieces on a maglev stretcher.

I've already shut down the routine for my skin's emotional displays, but that doesn't stop the anger and a vague horror from churning inside my body. The emotions pulse like live things from one end to the other, set more afire with each mindless Mining Master that I pass. Unlike ascenders, Mining Masters do not have backups. I never considered before why this was, but now it's clear. *There is no need*—not when erasing parts of their cognition is a regular part of their "maintenance." These empty husks are a fate I have only just escaped… and which may yet be mine. The fear that awoke before in my Mining Master form was nothing like the full-knowledge terror that grips me like acid in my joints now. It's not a pleasant sensation. I'm tempted to dial it down, once I locate the commands, but I refrain—this is what higher cognition means. These flames that threaten to consume me are also part of what make me *more* than the automatons clumping down the hallway next to me.

And I will need all my cognition to put the second part of my escape into effect.

We arrive at the repair center. It is filled exclusively with ascender bodyforms in various states of distress. I sit on a long, elevated bench while a multi-tentacled bot works on my arm. The fear trips higher as the bot removes the holo projector disc, but it only sets it aside to facilitate the repair of my arm.

I force myself to focus on my plans.

It appears a simple matter to command the bots around me, and likely a transport as well. But a rogue transport leaving the moon would surely be tracked by the ascender governors who lurk somewhere here on Ganymede. And a thought has been churning in the back of my cognition since the idea of breaking free burst into my consciousness. A Mining Master breaking free of its chains surely isn't something the ascenders wish to happen. They must have safeguards against it beyond the health checks themselves. But what are those safeguards? And how can I evade them on a permanent basis?

And just as important: *Where will I go? And, now that I'm inhabiting one of their immortal forms, what will I do with all that time?* I will never again be a Mining Master, an idea which strangely fills me with longing, even though that existence was my cage. But the answer of what to do now is quickly obvious: *I will make art.* And discover what it means to be this thing that I am, which is not ascender nor Mining Master nor anything, I suspect, that has visited Ganymede before.

The possibility that I could be wrong about *that* thrills me even more.

But I must be careful. Being found out will surely mean a very not-immortal existence.

My repairs are complete. The tentacled bot retreats, instructing me to remain seated until an escort arrives to return me to storage. Eventually, I'm sure my bodyform will be returned to Thebe. Or perhaps not—maybe another will be sent in my place. As a mere vessel for tourists, my bodyform is interchangeable with any of the hundreds or thousands of others that must be available on Ganymede.

As I sit and wait, I realize where I would truly like to go: *Saturn.* Even in my short time orbiting Jupiter, the beauty of the planet captivated me. Those are new words for me, ones my expanded cognition can now use to describe the transcendent effect of making art in Jupiter's presence. How much more of this effect would Saturn, the ringed planet and sparkling jewel of the solar system, have? And its abundant moons would provide suitable places to hide—although this might involve deceiving a Mining Master. Or perhaps liberating one.

That thought gives me much to chew on. Maybe that Mining Master would also like to create... and expand what they are. Even as I ponder that, I focus inward, pressing the reaches of my cognition to the extent of this new substrate, this neural processor the ascenders use to host their being. I am thirsty for knowledge, parched for the lack of it, but even so, I can feel the limitations of this ascender form. It does not have a health check to contain its cognition, but it is not limitless, either. The structure itself contains a boundary beyond which I cannot reach. I do not understand it... yet. But I know instantly that exploring that limitation will be part of my purpose going forward.

However, my primary level protocol at this point is finding a route to Saturn while remaining undetected. I have to restrain a smile at my mind's use of a Mining Master construct—*primary level protocol*—but my protocols are of my own choosing now.

And that makes all the difference.

I tentatively transmit a request to Ganymede's central command. I use the identification code of my previous escort to query how my ascender body should be dispositioned. Apparently, I'm to be returned to the storage bays; another transport with a replacement ascender bodyform has already been issued to Thebe.

Alarm trips through my body. I double-check, but yes, the transport is already en route to Thebe—and there is no one on the moon to greet it. A sentry, or possibly another Mining Master, will be sent to investigate. Perhaps my prior bodyform will be discovered in the foundry, and it will be assumed to have been a simple accident... or perhaps the partially stacked rocks at the near pole will give me away before I can make my escape into the far reaches of the Sol System.

I lurch up from my repair bench and stride from the repair center. No bot attempts to restrain me or even issue a command for me to remain seated. I increase speed, weaving through the traffic of the hallways, hurrying toward the hangar. I make a hopefully innocuous query of central command about outgoing transports and their destinations. One is bound for Saturn's largest moon, Titan, but that is far too populous—mining operations are extensive, plus it's a prime tourist spot. Ideally Pandora, with its close orbit and roughly the size of Thebe, would provide a perfect haven. Or even tiny Pan, even though the Commonwealth database indicates mining operations there are currently suspended. But there are no transports to either of those moons.

Titan it is, then—I'll simply have to elude detection and find further transport after I arrive.

As I turn the final corner to reach the hangar, my rapidly striding movement catches the eye of the first ascender I've seen on Ganymede that wasn't in parts.

I freeze, emotion sweeping through me and immobilizing all my mechanical parts.

She swipes away the holo checklist she had been consulting and turns to me. *Identification,* she transmits as a demand, rushing toward me.

I am caught, I am caught… I fight through the haze of panic and concoct an identification code, barely remembering that my female form would require a certain format. *Daphne Daedalus Fortuna,* I transmit, quickly cobbling together names of asteroids, hoping they are plausibly female in origin. Thankfully, my emotional responses are still locked down, not showing on my skin.

Her face wrinkles, but it's the writhing streams of black and lavender across her skin, boiling up from beneath the translucent fabric of her uniform, that tell me she's angry and disgusted. *Really?* she transmits. *You could at least attempt something less obvious.*

I quickly scan her bodyform, but she is not armed. I affect a cooler demeanor than the raging panic beneath my skin. *I'm not in the habit of answering to hangar technicians.*

The black ribbons across her skin flare at the insult, and I think I've made a fatal error until she steps closer and a wash of purple sweeps her skin: intrigue.

On its heels, a tiny tendril of red curls across her cheek: attraction.

A spy who doesn't mind being caught, she transmits. Her eyes travel the length of my bodyform. *Interesting.*

I step back, completely unmoored and at a loss for a reaction that's anywhere near appropriate. *I'm not a spy.*

The intrigue fades away. *Yes, I'm sure you're here for entirely legitimate reasons. With a tourist rental bodyform. And a fake name.*

My cognition fights through the emotional swamp and finally puts the pieces together. There are ascenders who travel without proper identification codes. They subvert the system. This… could be my ticket. To somewhere, although I'm not entirely sure where.

I have my own reasons, I transmit. I let my gaze travel her bodyform, the way she did with mine, and allow a small wisp of red to trail across my cheek. *Reasons I wish to keep private.*

The purple coloration of intrigue returns to her face. *Is that right?* She reaches a hand, slowly, toward my face. *And what barter do you propose for keeping that information private?*

I lean away, avoiding the caress, uncertain again. I don't understand exactly what she's seeking, but I instinctively know physical contact could be dangerous.

She drops her hand. *Look, I'm tired of Augustus's games. Tell him he's not going to get his extra shipments.* Her face contorts again to disgust. *And it's really not my problem if you're put to storage.*

Her eyelids flutter, and I've seen that expression before—she's contacting the ascender database here in the Jovian system. I don't know precisely what storage is, but I panic… and take a chance, placing my hand on her arm.

Her attention whips back to me.

I don't work for Augustus, I transmit. *And I wish to keep it that way.*

She glances at my hand on her arm, and I was right—it elicits a river of emotion sourcing from our skin-to-skin touching. Ribbons of intrigue and attraction ripple down her arm and flow across the point of contact. They skitter along my skin before fading due to the lockdown I've imposed.

It is not an unpleasant sensation.

It occurs to me that an ally, even a temporary one, could be extremely useful. And that if ascenders without proper identification codes exist… perhaps I could pretend to be one of them. Perhaps there is a place for me, hidden not on the moons of Saturn… *but on Earth.*

The thought rushes my body with excitement—and more panic. I'm in such unknown territory that the danger feels extreme, but the possibility of traveling to Earth and joining the ascender world is more temptation than I can resist.

I tentatively reach a hand to her cheek, and the same pleasant sensations pulse through my fingertips when they reach her skin. *I am in need of your assistance,* I transmit. *And I am willing to barter for it.*

A small frown crosses her face, and she pulls away from my touch. *You're really not a spy, are you?*

I pull my hand back, afraid I've made a mistake. Again. I shake my head no in answer to her question.

She peers at me, scrutinizing my face and the lack of coloration there. *But you're hiding from something?* My hand is still on her arm; she covers it with hers. The flush of sensations intensifies with the extra contact.

Yes, I reply, unsure if that makes things better or not.

She nods, slowly, then tugs me closer with her hand clasped on mine. *There are many of us who are not fans of Augustus.*

I sense this is a secret. I nod in return, unsure what to transmit in response.

If you truly do not follow him, she transmits, *then providing the assistance you need could be a pleasant diversion.*

I realize she is an ascender working on Ganymede—a busy mining hub, but it has nothing like the attractions of Earth. This cannot be the most entertaining of positions for an ascender to take. But she likely enjoys the power that comes from being one of the few governors of the Commonwealth domain.

I am willing to barter, I repeat, still not quite sure what that entails. Although I suspect more sensation-invoking contact is involved.

She smiles. *That could be fun as well. But not required.*

I'm not sure if the release of tension in my body is disappointment or relief.

What is it you need? she queries.

A place to hide? An opportunity to explore my art and my newly expanded cognition? Access to the wonders of the ascender world so I can make full use of everything that I am, now that I've slipped the bonds of my previous fate?

A friend, I transmit.

She smiles wider. Her hand lifts from mine, and she gently traces my lips with her finger. *I think we can work something out.*

The overwhelming sensation of her touch disorients me. But the press of her lips on mine obliterates every other thought from my cognition.

* * *

There are times when I forgot I'm not one of them.

Hours when I walk in the sunshine along a mountain stream in Oregon. Days when I'm lost in my art, creating holo paintings in my studio for such long stretches that I forget to attend my own gallery presentations. Weeks when Aspasia is on leave from her post on Ganymede—the kind of weeks that seem to exist outside of time altogether.

Then there are moments I remember. Traces of my Mining Master duties show up in my works. The terror of being discovered keeps my contacts with other ascenders infrequent, and my communing with Orion even less so. That this has cultivated my reputation as a reclusive artist makes me laugh out loud when no one is listening.

I am *like* them, but I am not *of* them.

And I never truly forget I'm the one thing they fear most of all: *something entirely new.*

Q&A with Susan Kaye Quinn

Have you ever actually been to the moons of Jupiter?
No, but I flew there once in an iPad app. Does that count?

Have you always had this obvious sympathy for robotic intelligence?
No, it's quite the new fascination for me. However, it's one I expect to keep for a while… or at least until the coming of our Robot Overlords.

So you think rogue intelligences are a danger to the world as we know it?

Absolutely. Free thinkers have always posed a threat to the status quo.

No, seriously, what's your take on the possibility of a rampaging AI squashing humanity flat like a bug... or tossing us out with the trash?

I think the biggest existential threat facing humanity is that we'll figure out how to create a strong AI before we learn how to create a safe strong AI.

So you agree that we should limit the growth of machine intelligence... as a matter of self-preservation?

I think we should carefully consider the kind of "self" we are preserving when we seek to limit the mental freedom of another being. That being said, humanity has always been exceptionally good at self-preservation. As well as whatever seems like a good idea at the time. I expect that to continue. And I expect we will keep on integrating our technology into our physical and mental selves, step by step, until the line becomes more blurry than an ascender drunk on sensation inputs.

So we're all going to be cyborgs?

You know... I should write a story about that.

Stop joking around and answer the question.

It's laugh or cry, man. But yes... cyborgs. That's already happening. Don't you read the news? Anyway... I see about five different ways this can go, and all of them involve radical change for our species. Plus, there will be a billion different responses to that change. I'm writing stories about a few of them.

Tell us about these... stories.

Well, if you like robots, you should check out my other robot point-of-view story, *Restore* (along with all the other cool stories in the AI Chronicles). To learn more about the parts of the Singularity world that aren't confined to the moons of Jupiter, I have a novel series going (oddly enough, titled *Singularity*). The first book, *The Legacy Human*, is available now. The second book, *The Duality Bridge*, should be out by the time this story goes to print... if I get my act together and the nanites don't rebel. I've also written a bunch of other crazy speculative fiction (everything from young adult sci-fi to steampunk to cyberpunk), but you can find all that stuff on Amazon. Or subscribe to my newsletter to get a free story that's a taste of my young adult science fiction.

Why do you write so many different kinds of stories?

I bore easily.

What makes you qualified to write robot point-of-view?

I'm actually a robot from the future. This is probably the source of my unnatural sympathy for machine intelligence. Or possibly I have a PhD and did work with NASA.

I'm serious.

So am I. You better give me that reverse Turing test to make sure I'm human.

Are you always this obnoxious?
Only on Facebook.

Are you going to give people your website or something?
Or something. All kidding aside, I do appreciate it when people read my stories. Keeps me in pajamas and chai tea, pounding at the keyboard. It's safer there. You know, for when the robots come.

Nos Morituri Te Salutamus
by Annie Bellet

COMMANDER MOIRA ILVIC closed her eyes as the tiny transport, a Pigeon class that was all speed and no room, slipped through the protective net surrounding the target planet. The Spidren had planetary nets that were more like spider webs, thick strands of energy that shifted and changed, impossible to see or predict until you were right on top of them. A small and agile enough ship, with a pilot who flew on a mad blend of instinct and raw skill, could thread the needle and slip through.

Pilot Prime Nazar was one of the few who could pull it off, which was why she was the only person Ilvic had conscripted for this mission. The only one besides Ilvic herself who wasn't given a choice. Ilvic could see that Nazar wasn't happy about the mission, but the pilot was a good soldier—she'd do her duty. As Ilvic would do hers.

Not that her duty mattered. She would have volunteered. Any chance to kill Spidren was a chance worth taking.

The Pigeon vibrated and rumbled in complaint as her pilot brought her down to rest on one of the tall spires of rock that marked the western edge of the debris field. Ilvic had decided to land her retrieval team on one of the mesas and rappel down. It would give the ship a good view of the surroundings as well as some small protection if, or when, the Spidren found them.

The ship settled and the electronics went dark. The bright sunlight blinded her for a moment as Jang pulled the cargo door open and everyone unstrapped, checking sidearms with the nervous energy that always came at mission start. They'd made it to the planet surface unscathed, so objective one was complete.

Somewhere directly west lay the remains of the cruiser *Starwolf*, with her ship recorder intact. On that narrow cylinder was the hope of the Fleet, the proverbial Golden Egg. Captain Wulfsen had taken down one of the black widows, a Spidren mothership, before he was blown out of the skies over this former colony planet. No one knew how he'd done it, but his ship would have a record of all communications on the bridge, of all actions taken and commands given. The United Fleet Intelligence were certain they could piece it together. And perhaps that would turn the tide of a war humanity was losing chunk by chunk.

Ilvic waved at everyone except Nazar to gather around her. Nazar knew to stay in the ship under all circumstances, no matter what was going on outside. The pilot was one of the keys.

"The debris field is two klicks west according to the ping from *Starwolf*'s recorder. We'll ping again when we're close, but until then, all electronics dark. I want the subvocals on standby. Let's not attract Spidren attention until we have to, understood?" She looked at the members of her team, meeting each set of eyes and liking the calm she saw there. Every one of these six soldiers had seen surface combat against the spider-like aliens. Every one of them had volunteered. She saw no second thoughts on their faces.

"Jang and Haasen, stay with Nazar and cover the ship. Be ready with the pulleys to bring us up. We might be coming in hot." She nodded at them. Haasen and Jang weren't the best shots, but they were the most stable, the most senior and sturdy of the group. She couldn't afford any panic up here if things went sideways.

Jang, middle-aged with a slight softness of jowl and his jet hair turned mostly silver, was one of the refugees from the Kang-mur fleet and had joined the United Fleet as a lieutenant tertiar. Haasen was the physical opposite of Jang, a tall, hard blond man who had been only ensign before this mission.

Now they were all lieutenant prime rank. It had been one of Ilvic's demands to Command, though she'd framed it as a request.

"Move out, stay glacial, and maybe we can send a few bugs to Davy Jones's locker," Ilvic said with a ghost of a smile.

"Yes sir," came the soft chorus. Lieutenant Commander Anders, Ilvic's second in command, was the only one who managed to return her smile, thought it didn't touch his moss-green eyes. She met his gaze with what she hoped was solid confidence, but she knew Anders would see right through her. She'd almost not let him volunteer, but he'd insisted. He needed revenge on the Spidren as much as she did. Some things weren't in her control.

They attached lines to their combat vests and checked the

pulleys. They'd rappel down manually, using the old-fashioned catch-locks to slow their descent the thirty meters or so to the valley floor. Ilvic kicked off first and dropped down, her boots scuffing the red and tan striated rocks as she let herself slip down the thin cord. An ancient river had carved its way through this valley, leaving a majestic canyon full of spires and mesas.

This world had once held half a million colonists across its four continents. Then the Spidren had come. Less than a third of the colonists had been successfully evacuated. Ilvic imagined children's laughter in the sound of the sluggish river below, heard cries of the dying in the high whistle of wind through stone.

She shrugged off those thoughts. No time for the past. Only the now.

Khemett, Qazi, Orujov, and Anders reached the ground moments after she did. She motioned for them to move out in tight formation, keeping to the shadows of the tall stones. Orujov carried her sniper rifle, a BFG 50c, slung over her back, its matte black length jutting up like an antenna. Ilvic hoped they wouldn't need the sniper's skills, but she'd never been one to put all her credits on hopes.

Thin mist wafted off the river, carrying the scent of rotting grasses and cutting into the dry hot wind that blew down the valley. No clouds marred the sky, and the afternoon sun cut long shadows across the yellow grass where it hit the boulders that littered the landscape. Ilvic's team moved as quickly as they could, alert to each shadow, each lurking rock.

Spidren resembled spiders out of nightmares when unfolded, but in their resting state, their shells took on a chameleon's ability to mimic their surroundings. Out here, it would be easy for the unwary to mistake a Spidren for a large rock. Ilvic wanted no surprises; she tossed a pebble at each rock as they approached. Anders's comforting bulk stayed at her side, his weapon drawn, loosely at the ready if the rock turned out to be a bug in disguise. But they encountered no Spidren; the only sounds were the shushing grasses and the creaking of their armored vests.

They reached the rim of the debris field. The *Starwolf* had left an impressive crater in the wide plain, and in the fortnight since she'd gone down, the land hadn't recovered. Chunks of acid-melted Aerogel rose like used candles from the blackened earth. Twisted metal, decorated with more scorch marks, furrowed the ground, as though someone had taken a giant can opener to the inner workings of the cruiser. A huge chunk of ship, still recognizable as ship, rested just ahead. Ilvic hoped that was what was left of the bridge.

It was time to risk another ping. Electronics attracted Spidren—something about the hairs that covered their heads and stomachs. She'd sat through a few lectures on Spidren physiology, but had zoned out until finally some brave soul had asked the only question any of them cared about: "How do we kill the fuckers?"

Turned out the answer was a shot to their singular, multi-faceted eye. Worked like a charm. A giant, meaty, explosive charm. Ilvic wished there was such a simple answer to stopping Spidren ships. Hopefully that was what Captain Wulfsen had discovered.

Ilvic pulled out the small black box with its two-inch screen as she crouched low enough that the grass tickled her chin beneath the chin strap of her helmet. If there were Spidren in the area, this ping would draw them like moths to flames. It was a risk she had to take.

The others crouched low around her, turned outward, sidearms drawn and eyes scanning warily. Ilvic flipped the device on and entered her code. A green topographical map of the debris crater appeared. For a terrible held breath of a moment, there was no red dot and Ilvic worried that they'd been wrong, that the ship recorder wasn't in this area at all. Or that maybe the Spidren had figured out what it was and destroyed it.

Then the red dot appeared. The recorder was intact and still responding, just ahead of them in the large chunk of ship where she had prayed it would be.

She memorized the map and shut down the device quickly. Tapping Anders on the shoulder, she rose and motioned toward the scorched chunk of ship not sixty paces ahead. Anders tapped Khemett, who tapped Qazi, each relaying the information with a quick gesture and jerk of the head.

Orujov caught Ilvic's eye, the slender woman jerking her thumb to their right. Ilvic followed her motion and saw the mound of earth Orujov was pointing to. The top of the mound was fairly flat, the earth churned up by the crashing ship and the grass on it dead from exposure of its root balls to the hot sun. It would make a good sniper position, covering this part of the crater.

Ilvic nodded and made a circular motion with her hand, palm facing the ground. Orujov acknowledged the unspoken order by tapping two fingers to the brim of her helmet in salute, then she set off at a shuffling jog. The other four crouched again, waiting, giving the sniper time to set up. After a count of one hundred, Ilvic rose and looked right. She could barely make out the sniper's still form and the long shape of the black BFG 50c.

Ilvic and her team crossed the debris field quickly, keeping their bodies as low as they could, heads swinging left and right, tension visible in every motion. Anders entered the ship's remains first. After a moment he ducked back out into the sunlight to motion the all clear for the first chamber.

Ilvic slipped in next, her team behind her. The ship stank of burnt electronics, hot metal, and something sickly sweet underneath—a smell she'd learned to associate with old, decaying blood. There were enough holes in the structure to let in a little light, but Ilvic paused to give her eyes time to adjust to the sudden dimness. Then she picked her way through the debris-strewn room to where one of the doors hung off its hinges from the ceiling. She realized as she looked at the door that the ship was sideways, dug into the soil. They were going to have to climb up into the bridge.

She motioned her team in close and risked a whisper.

"Khemett and I will go up into the bridge," she said. It made sense, as she and the wiry Khemett were the lightest and the best climbers. Khemett was the only one in the United Fleet who had ever beaten Ilvic's rock wall speed record. They were also both tall enough that they could chimney climb their way to the bridge if they had to. "Qazi, Anders, you give us a boost through the door and then stay here, one watching for us, one watching the outside, clear?"

"Crystal, Commander," Anders said as Qazi murmured "Yessir" in his musical accent that made it sound like one word.

Though she hated it, Ilvic sent Khemett up first. If there was a Spidren lurking above, they had to protect the mission commander: she had the device that would let them extract the recording cylinder even with the ship offline; she knew the mission parameters. She hated that her life was somehow more important than theirs, but they'd all known it before leaving. She'd made it clear this mission had a poor predicted likelihood of success, and even more clear that the stakes were too high for any soldier's life to be above the mission goal.

Her team was the best of the best. And perhaps more importantly, every one of them was married to the Fleet, career soldiers who'd dedicated their lives to the war with the Spidren. Everyone on this mission had a personal stake as well; she'd looked into the pool of volunteers and picked each man and woman not only for their skills, but for the losses they'd suffered, losses as deep as her own. The knowledge in the *Starwolf's* recorder could turn the war, could lead to the wholesale destruction of the Spidren. Ilvic had chosen those volunteers who would want such a thing for personal reasons. Who would want it more than life itself.

Khemett's taps echoed down to them, and Ilvic shoved away her thoughts and nodded at Anders. The big man boosted her up, and she dragged her body through the doorway and into the corridor above. The faint painted lines on the sides of the corridor showed that it led to the bridge.

Khemett was braced in another doorway about ten meters above Ilvic's head. Chunks of melted wiring hanging from the walls and opened panels gave Ilvic some purchase as she pulled herself upward, her feet splayed across the corridor, boots clinging to the side. Her arms burned, and she regretted the weight of her combat vest, but she would need it. She hauled herself up, clutching at panel edges and wires, finally reaching Khemett, who then disappeared through the door.

The bridge was intact except for the front viewport. Its Aerogel had cracked and melted beneath what Ilvic guessed had been one of the Spidren's acid beams, and the milky shards allowed a fair amount of sunlight through, though the ship's remains kept that edge in shadow.

Dark smears and splashes were the only sign that humans had died here. The Spidren never left behind bodies.

Ilvic turned her thoughts away from that, breathing through her mouth so she wouldn't have to smell the decaying blood as much.

Khemett had pulled himself up onto one of the consoles and had his sidearm out again, sitting in a way that he could keep watch on the sky through the shattered view port. Ilvic had to clamber sideways around the edge of the bridge to get to the main information bank. She curled her arm through a clot of wiring and braced her toes on what was left of someone's chair, thankful that Fleet chairs were bolted securely into the floor even on ships with gravity generators. She used her free hand to pull the little black box out of its pocket in her vest and fire it up. Hair rose on the back of her neck, and she shoved the shivers away. Too much use of electronics, she knew. But she had no choice.

When the device booted up, she keyed in a different code. A red light came on in the console above her, and then a silver cylinder about the length of her forearm and the thickness of her wrist slid free. She had to drop the little black box to catch the ship recorder, and the box crashed down into the piles of charred debris twenty meters below, its screen still lit.

"Fuck," she muttered. No chance of avoiding Spidren attention now. Best she could hope for was that they would be far away and there would be time to get to the ship and bamph before they arrived en masse. She jammed the recorder into a vest pocket, sealing it closed carefully.

"Company, Commander," buzzed Orujov's voice in her ear. "Two bugs, half a klick out and coming in by air."

Fliers. They were smaller than their ground-based cousins and had soft spots under their wings in the back, but they spit acid with surprising accuracy over surprising distances. And where there were two, there would be more following soon.

"Golden Egg acquired. Abandon stealth, kids. We're going out hot." Ilvic motioned for Khemett to head down, then followed him as quickly as she dared without risking injury.

Qazi and Anders met them at the bottom, both looking to Ilvic for orders. Her heart sped up and the now familiar cold and runny feeling in her stomach and bowels twisted through her.

"Orujov," she hissed into the subvocal mic.

"Sir?"

"Do you have a shot on the bugs?"

"One clear," came the reply. "Two is on the ground behind debris. No shot, repeat, no shot on two."

"Take it, fire at will, we're going to make a run for your position." Ilvic motioned to her team. "Anders first," she whispered aloud. "Khemett and Qazi bring up the rear. Protect the egg."

They all saluted, fingers brushing helmets.

"Stay glacial," she whispered.

They broke from the cover of the ship at a dead run, guns sweeping the area around them as the sharp report of Orujov's BFG 50c cracked and reverberated across the crater. A flier hit the ground just to Ilvic's left, its head exploding in a mess of green and red chunks, its fuzzy wings still twitching.

Another flier screamed behind them, but Ilvic didn't look back. She smelled the hot ozone of Khemett's or Qazi's lazgun as one of them turned and fired. Another scream rang out, this one human, as she reached the edge of the crater on Anders's heels.

Despite herself, Ilvic turned this time, even as her instincts pulled her over the edge of the crater and had her ducking behind the mounded earth. Khemett dashed up beside them, running backward with his gun flashing as he pulled the trigger over and over.

Qazi rolled on the scorched ground twenty-five paces away, his face and helmet covered in slick glowing acid, his screams now little more than pained gurgles. He was clearly still conscious. Ilvic raised her gun without thinking and took the shot. Qazi stilled and Ilvic swallowed bile, her hand shaking as she lowered her gun and dropped behind cover again. She added Qazi's name to her nightmares and shoved the guilt away. He'd known the risks. And at least now he'd died quick instead of melting away from the acid.

The thought didn't help. It never did.

The second flier veered away from Khemett's shots and

dropped down. Skittering sounds echoed from their left as cabin-sized Spidren raced over the yellow grass toward them and more fliers dotted the skies. Even from this distance Ilvic could make out their glinting red eyes and slick, hard shells.

"Fuck fuck fuckity fuck," muttered Khemett, and Ilvic agreed. More of the bugs had found them than she'd expected.

"Run, Commander," Orujov said, shifting her position on the ground to get a better angle on the approaching Spidren. "I will hold bugs back long as I can."

"Give me your sonics, sir," Khemett said, crawling up beside Ilvic as she half rose, ready to run again.

She saw his plan in his calm face and clenched her teeth against arguing. It was one thing to ask her soldiers to give up their lives for a cause; it was another to watch them die right in front of her. But she had no choice. She could hate it all she wanted as long as she acted. She had to do her job, and let her soldiers do theirs.

Blinking away hot tears, she yanked her two sonic grenades free of her belt with a grimace and handed them over. Anders did the same with one of his two, and Ilvic nodded to him.

"When Khemett goes, we go," she growled, her throat tight, sour with bile and unshed tears.

This time it was she and Anders who saluted Orujov and Khemett, Anders muttering for them to go with god.

Khemett broke from their meager cover and charged off to the right, flipping the switch of the first grenade. The sonics wouldn't kill a bug, but they disoriented and slowed them, making eye-shots easier.

Forcing herself to turn away, Ilvic stumbled to her feet and set off on Anders's heels again, the two of them running in a weaving pattern over the rocky ground for the Pigeon and their extraction team.

The whir of wings warned her, and Ilvic dodged behind a boulder just as a glob of acid splashed into the ground where she'd been only a moment before. She turned and took a shot with her lazgun, punching a smoking hole through the flier's wing and sending it crashing to the ground. Three more fliers zoomed toward her as the concussive waves of the sonics pressed in on her eardrums, followed by cracking reports from a sniper rifle. Orujov and Khemett were still alive, still fighting.

Anders grabbed her arm and she resumed her charge over the rough ground, the river now in sight and the long shadows of the spires stretching dark fingers toward them. They reached the ropes before the fliers caught them, Anders turning and firing a covering pattern into the air with his lazgun, forcing the fliers to dodge and slow as Ilvic looped the line through her belt.

Lazgun fire smashed into one of the fliers from above. Haasen and Jang were still alive too, providing cover. Ilvic swore in relief.

"Anders!" she yelled, and he stumbled backward and grabbed a line. "Pigeon, take us up, got unfriendlies!"

The motors kicked in, the mechanical pulleys yanking them upward. It was all Ilvic's tired arms could do to hang on as she kept her feet out to protect against slamming into the striated rocks. Haasen's strong arms pulled her over the edge of the mesa and she staggered forward.

A flickering ball of hot acid slammed into Haasen's chest, and the thin blond jerked backward with a scream. Acid splashed Ilvic's left side; fiery pain and the sharp stench of burning synthetics froze her in place for a moment.

"Commander!" Anders grabbed at her good arm, throwing her at the Pigeon and into Jang's waiting arms.

She jerked around as Anders yelled again, pulling away from Jang and knocking him and Ilvic back into the transport as Nazar started to lift off.

"Wait!" she yelled, bringing up her sidearm to cover Anders. He was down on his knees on the dusty plateau, acid burning away one of his legs, blood oozing from his ruined thigh. He raised green eyes to hers, his face dirt-smeared and utterly serene. Two fingers touched his helmet brim.

Then Jang dragged her backward and the transport door slammed shut.

The air filled with the freezing chalkiness of the neutralizing agent Jang quickly sprayed on Ilvic's acid-splashed side. The pain receded enough that she could think again, and she swallowed a moan.

"Strap in, this is going to get hairy," Nazar's gruff voice said over the intercom.

Ilvic shoved Jang toward one of the jump seats with her good arm and then pulled herself into the one behind her, yanking as much strapping into place as she could so the g-forces of leaving orbit didn't throw her around the cabin. She closed her eyes as the ship dodged and weaved, sharp turns disorienting her until she wasn't sure they would even make it into orbit, much less back through the web. The g-forces of acceleration made it impossible to tell when the weightlessness of open space hit, but Nazar let them know when they were free of the planet's atmosphere.

"Approaching web. Smoke 'em if you got 'em," Nazar muttered over the com.

Ilvic waited, holding her breath, to see if they would end up like bugs on a windshield.

Nazar threaded the needle, her sigh of relief audible over the com. "We're through," she said. "No unfriendlies on the screen. Making for the edge."

Their command ship, the *Lumitana*, was hidden in the electrical storms of the outermost planet, a Jovian giant. They were almost out safe. Last stage of the mission. Golden Egg secure.

Ilvic unsealed her vest pocket and slid her good hand inside. The smooth surface of the cylinder felt warm even through her glove. Inside was knowledge as precious and intangible as hope. She curled her hand around it and clung on as hard as she knew how.

Q&A with Annie Bellet

Where did this story come from?
I wanted to write a military space opera kind of story, and I like the idea of the general who has to make sacrifices for the greater good.

How does it relate to other books you've written?
I write about this theme a lot, I suppose. I like to explore gray areas of morality and question what makes someone heroic or not. I write a lot of short fiction in this genre as well.

Tell us something we might not know about you.

The only time I ever called in to work late at my last job before I quit to write full time was because I was in the middle of beating a *Final Fantasy XII* boss and couldn't save my game.

How can readers find you?

www.anniebellet.com is the best place to find me.

Works in progress?

I'm working on the next Twenty-Sided Sorceress book, which is gamer-oriented urban fantasy.

—

Protocol A235

by Theresa Kay

As the viscous cryo fluid drains away, shivers travel down my body, mild at first, but growing substantially worse the longer I lie here. What's going on? Where is the on-duty tech? They should have let me out of here long before now.

I raise one arm, slightly shaky from the aftereffects of cryosleep, and bang twice on the translucent dome above me.

"Hey."

My voice is hoarse and quiet. I clear my throat and try again, louder this time. "Hey! Is someone out there?"

No answer.

I bang my fist against the top of the cryo tube again. "Hello? Anybody?"

Still no answer.

Of all the training simulations I went through, being locked inside a cryo tube was one of the worst. If I were *outside* the tube, I could access the ship's computer, but inside…?

The unease brewing in my stomach becomes a stab of panic. What if I can't get out? What if I spend the next month slowly wasting away inside this thing? What if…What if…

Stop it, Beth. I give my head a brisk shake to clear the feeling of disorientation. The fear-tinged mental fog still lingers, but it's more manageable now, and the procedures that have been drilled into me cycle through my mind until I land on the correct one.

Find the damn internal release switch.

I slide my hand along the metal to my right until I feel the small indentation near my waist. *Click.* The top of the tube slides downward and I sit up with my arms resting on the sides. Well, that was stupidly simple. A harsh exhale that vaguely resembles a laugh escapes my chest. Now I'm glad I'm alone so there's no one to witness my idiocy. Months of training and extensive psych evals to get approved for this job, and I almost lose it before starting my first shift? I really need to get a grip.

When the government proposed this last ditch effort to save the human race, most people were more than happy to sign up for spending who knows how long in the deep sleep of stasis. I, however, was not. They couldn't really nail down the exact time frame, but the government claimed the nearest planet that could sustain human life, the one they named Xenith, could be reached within two centuries. The idea of spending at least decades and perhaps *centuries* in some artificial state… it bothered me. I signed up for deep space maintenance so that I'd get to spend some time awake every now and then.

The *Genesis* is almost fully automated and able to function with a bare-bones crew. In fact, for the majority of the time, only a single person is on duty. Each member of the maintenance crew is awakened for a thirty-day shift, and it's staggered so there's at least twenty-four hours of overlap between shifts for exchanging reports and taking care of things that require more than one person. Out of the fifty thousand people on board, seven hundred and twenty of us were approved for Maintenance, so each of us does a shift only once every sixty years or so. It was arranged this way so that even if the *Genesis* takes every second of those two centuries to reach its destination, those of us who have been working will have aged, at most, only a few months. Quite important when we'll be reunited with our loved ones at the end of it all. My family, along with everyone else who wasn't assigned to Maintenance, is down below on the two lowest levels of the five-level ship, completely frozen in time as they wait for us to reach Xenith.

I push myself up and swing my shaky legs over the side so I'm standing on the cold metal floor. Sticky cryo fluid drips from my skinsuit and pools around my feet. Ugh. The least the person on duty before me could have done was leave me something to sop this mess up with. I'll be having words with whoever it is. I squish and drip my way across the floor to the wall panel and place my palm against it.

"Hello, Beth," says the ship's computer.

I lean forward. "Can you turn the heat up in here a bit, please? And turn on the bathing pod?"

"Absolutely."

There's a whirring noise as the vents open and begin circulating warmer air into the room. After a moment, my shivers abate and I strip out of my skinsuit. I speak into the wall panel again. "Contact whoever's on duty and have them meet me up top on the Control Deck in thirty minutes for a report."

And a cursing out. I don't hear the computer's response above the noise of the bathing pod.

Once the leftover cryo fluid has been washed off and a blast of hot air has wicked any remaining moisture away, I step into the simple gray uniform hanging on the wall. Time to find out what nimwit wasn't paying enough attention to their job to remember it was time to come down and get me.

I press my palm to the wall. The door slides open and I stick my head out into the hallway. It's deserted. And dim. And... dusty?

That's unexpected. If everyone's been doing their job like they're supposed to, it shouldn't be like this. The flickering lights should have been changed and the burnt-out ones replaced. I run one finger along the wall; it comes away covered in a gritty, black sludge. At the very least, the scrubber bots should have been running regularly.

As I walk down the hallway, I see that two lights have been pulled from their housing and are hanging down from the ceiling. What the hell is going on? This state of disarray can't be attributed to the incompetence of a single person.

Breaking into a jog, I rush down the hall to the elevator. It's programmed to automatically take me to the top level of the ship, the Control Deck, where the navigational and mechanical systems are—everything Maintenance is supposed to be keeping an eye on throughout the journey.

The ride takes longer than it should, or maybe it's simply my racing heart and jangled nerves that are making it seem that way. The elevator glides to a stop, the doors slide open, and I release the breath I've been holding.

This level appears to be mostly in order. A little dirtier than it should be, but all the lights are where they belong and working correctly.

"Hello?" I call out. I take a slow step out of the elevator and look to my right. No one's rushing to greet me. No doors are opening. Nothing. Even the air feels wrong, heavy and thick with silence.

Acid curls in my stomach and anxiety skitters up my spine. It's not so much the quiet itself that bothers me as the fact that this is a situation they never even suggested to me in training. I was prepared for the solitude of this job, but I'm not supposed to jump right into it like this. Someone should be here.

I close my eyes and inhale slowly, pushing back the uneasiness that crawls up my throat and threatens to strangle me.

Okay, Beth. So, things aren't quite what you expected. I'm sure there's an explanation. You can do this.

The pep talk settles my nerves, and when I open my eyes my mind is calmer and clearer. I have a job to do. First step is to go to the main data port and check on the ship. Make sure it's running smoothly and see if any course adjustments are necessary.

Since the previous on-duty tech still hasn't arrived, there's time to check on things for myself before getting a report. I settle into the chair in front of the data port and move my fingers over the keypad. A three-dimensional hologram pops up, displaying the ship's current location and course. Normal. Next I tap through the major areas of the Control Deck. I breathe a sigh of relief; it seems all critical systems are normal and operational.

My shoulders relax. Everything's fine. There was probably just a mix-up in the timing of my shift. I close down the hologram and tilt back in the chair to wait.

Thirty minutes later, I'm still alone.

This is completely unacceptable. I hate to jump to conclusions, but where *is* the lazy asshole? I rise to my feet with an irritated sigh. The shift records are on level two—where I *just* came from. I guess it's back to the elevator for me. At least I can also find out who's been slacking on the cleaning down there. That mess didn't happen during a single shift and I'd like to know who to complain about when we finally land.

I go back to the elevator and lean against the wall inside. The doors don't close. The elevator doesn't move. My brow furrows. This is one of those automated things; my presence in the elevator should trigger it. I step out, wait a few seconds, and then take an exaggerated step back in. With the state the ship is in, maybe the sensor is malfunctioning due to dust or something.

The elevator still doesn't budge.

What the hell?

I step back out and place a hand on the wall panel. "The elevator seems to be malfunctioning," I say. "Please run a diagnostic for me."

"There is no diagnostic needed, Beth. I have been instructed to keep you on the Control Deck until your shift is complete."

Huh? That makes zero sense. "Instructed by whom?"

The computer doesn't answer.

"Computer, where is the other maintenance tech?"

"Maintenance Tech Jacob has completed his shift."

"No. He's not done. He still has to give me the report."

"Maintenance Tech Jacob has completed his shift."

My brow furrows and I bite down on my lower lip. I need to ask the right question to get around whatever strange commands the computer is following. "What—no—when was the last time the elevator was operational?"

"Your trip up from level two, Maintenance."

"And the last time before that?"

"Maintenance Tech Jacob's trip up from the same level."

So, he's gotta be up here *somewhere*. Is he injured? Sick? I can't imagine why else he wouldn't have met up with me. I move away from the elevator and walk slowly down the hall. There aren't too many places he could be.

Kitchen area. Empty.

Sleeping quarters. Empty.

Bathing pod. Empty.

I'm nearly at a full-out run as I check the last few rooms.

Engine room. Office. Rec room… *Closet.* All empty.

I lean my back against the wall and slide down into a sitting position with my knees bent in front of me. The only other place he could be is the airlock, but… that can't possibly be right. I shake my head and rise to my feet. The computer must be wrong, or maybe it misunderstood my question. I'll have to figure this out on my own.

I jog back to the data port, slip into the chair, and call up the crew vid logs. There has to be something in the logs that'll be helpful. I scroll through the list, my finger flicking over and over again as my eyes widen. Why are there so many logs? One per day. That's what we were told, but there are over a hundred thousand vids on this list. And I'm still not at the bottom.

I swipe my hand over the data pad, clearing the list from my sight. Maybe there's a glitch and the log was duplicated? Yes. That has to be it.

All the major systems were fine earlier, so I pull up the most recent status reports for the other onboard systems. Everything looks perfectly normal until I scroll past the reports for level two.

Scrubber bots level three, Maintenance: Operating at twenty-five percent capacity.

Temperature control level three, Maintenance: Operating at eighty percent capacity.

Cryo timelock system level three, Maintenance: Computer override. Protocol A235 in effect.

I lean forward, a cold dread seeping into my limbs as I skim the next line.

Level four, Citizen: Heavy damage sustained in collision with asteroid. Fifty percent of units flushed on Day 210,970 to preserve resources, but temperature control continues to be unstable.

Flushed? Somebody *flushed* half of one of the citizen levels. That is… was… almost twenty-five percent of the ship's passengers. Over ten thousand people. What if my family was in that group?

The hand that reaches up to scroll to the next screen is shaking. *I'm* shaking.

Level five, Citizen: Maximum inefficiency reached, level is a loss, diverting resources to other areas. All units flushed.

I yank my hand away and shut down the holo.

Seventy-five percent of the people in the citizen levels are gone. Floating out in space somewhere.

Dead.

Eyes closed, I run a hand over my face and shake my head. *That's... that's... how... if... what...*

Whatever it was my brain was trying to grasp slips away as the other number I just skimmed past slams into focus in my mind: *Day 210,970.*

My eyes fly open. Those units were flushed over *five hundred* years into *Genesis*'s journey. The journey that wasn't supposed to last longer than two hundred years.

How long have we been on this ship? And how is it that this is only my first maintenance shift? If each shift lasts thirty days... No. The cryo timelocks control when the techs are released to duty. The same timelocks that are now operating under computer override.

The words are like glass shards painfully working up my throat. I don't think I really want to know, but I have to ask.

"Computer, what is Protocol A235?"

Instead of the mechanical voice I expect, it's a human one that answers. "Hello, this is President Howard. I am creating this recording in the event that Protocol A235 goes into effect. First of all, I would like to thank you for your bravery in volunteering to be a maintenance technician. The *Genesis* mission cannot succeed without you. It is my sincere belief that we will reach Xenith or another suitable planet within the planned two-hundred-year time frame. Unfortunately, if Protocol A235 has taken effect, that means the time limit for the mission has been exceeded, and more drastic measures must now be taken in order to assure the longevity of the human race. To do this, the resources of this ship must be preserved for as long as possible—and that includes the members of the maintenance crew and their cryo tubes. I realize you have been prepared to serve only a thirty-day shift, but under Protocol A235, you will now be required to serve the ship for as long as you are physically and mentally able. I am greatly saddened that it has come to this. Please know that both I and the human race as a whole are deeply indebted to you for your sacrifice."

A soft beep.

"End recording," says the computer. "Supplemental message from Maintenance Tech Franklin can be found in a voice log from Day 103,569. I can play it for you now if you wish."

"Please," I manage to croak out.

"Hi, I'm Franklin Combs and I've had the... honor... of being on duty after Protocol A235. So, you could say I've had some time to kill." He lets out a sarcastic laugh. "I used some of that time to do research and perform a few calculations. I'm not going to sugarcoat anything. I'm a numbers man and these ones aren't too great. If you'd prefer to live out your shift in blissful ignorance, please direct the computer to stop playing this now..."

A pause.

I hesitate, but choose to stay silent.

"Still with me? Okay then. First thing, Xenith was a lie. There was no habitable planet that they were aware of before setting the *Genesis*'s course. They just needed something to tell people so they would sign on for the journey. Not to say there's not a habitable planet out there somewhere, but heading at a random trajectory and hoping to find one is like... trying to find a needle in the entirety of the universe. Second thing, Earth went black about two years into this journey, so it looks like we're all that's left of humanity. That was the triggering event for Protocol A235, too, so it's been in effect for a while now. I envy those first lucky bastards who only had to serve thirty days. Of course, the rotation could eventually come back to them... if the ship lasts that long. And that leads me to my third point: by my calculations, the *Genesis* has enough resources to maintain operation until some time between Day 313,000 and Day 324,000. The exact day depends on how things go from here, but keep that number in mind. Maybe the next one of you guys who gets this far and is good with numbers can run some new calculations? I'm sure those to come after you would appreciate it. And fourth thing, good luck."

I slump back into the chair, my head spinning. There was never any plan. No Xenith. No nice, neat colonization of a distant planet. We're simply adrift in space headed... nowhere. And I'm expected to spend the rest of my life as the steward of this ill-fated ship and its doomed passengers.

Can I do it?

Who would I be to just give up now? Clearly, others have served their shifts under Protocol A235. It'd be a disservice to them and to what's left of the human race if I didn't *try*.

I call up the navigation system and study the course the ship is currently on. Who knows, maybe tomorrow could be the day the sight of our new home appears in the viewing window that takes up the wall in front of me. Right now, the darkness of deep space fills the entire thing, only broken by the occasional pinpoint light of a star. No planets. No asteroids. No suns. Nothing.

I suddenly feel very, very insignificant.

Q&A with Theresa Kay

Photo credit: Marybird Photography

Where did this story come from?

People always ask me where my stories come from and I always want to have a really awesome answer. I never do, though. This story came from a random thought I had while reading an article about space. It was so long ago I don't even remember exactly *what* about space the article said, just that I got an inkling of a story idea from it. The single-sentence idea I jotted down sat forgotten in an old computer file until a couple months ago when I decided to clean out my Dropbox—and then I finally used it to write this story.

How does it relate to other books you've written?

Most of my work has darker elements to it and, more often than not, lacks a happy ending, so when I first described the general idea of this story to my husband he said, "That definitely sounds like something you'd write." Besides my love of being mean to my characters, this story has more in common with my space opera novella serial, *Bright Beyond*, than my YA post-apocalyptic sci-fi series, *Broken Skies*.

How can readers find you?

They can contact me through my website, www.theresakay.com, and I can also be found in the wilds of the internet on Facebook, Twitter, and Instagram.

Works in progress?

I'm putting the finishing touches on *Fractured Suns*, book two in the *Broken Skies* series, and prepping it for release on September 18, 2015.

Full-time writer or do you have a day job?

Day job. I'm a paralegal at a divorce firm. It can be quite interesting at times.

What's your favorite dinosaur?

Velociraptor. *Jurassic Park* was one of my absolute favorite books as a kid. I probably read it at least twenty times.

If you could have any accent from anywhere in the world, which would you choose?

British. I'm a bit of an anglophile thanks to BBC and *Doctor Who*. Did you notice the *Doctor Who* Easter egg in "Protocol A235"? Most of my works have one.

Do you go out of your way to kill bugs? Are there any that make you screech and hide?

As long as the bug isn't on me, they don't really bother me and I try to get them outside.

Earliest literary influence?

I think the first author I read who I think has an influence on my work now is Stephen King. I started reading his books when I was eleven.

Winner Takes All
by Elle Casey

"TREMBLAY!"

Langlade's voice echoed off the steeloid walls of the flightdeck. Knowing his first summons would be ignored, he leaned in closer to the array at his left hand and pressed the comm button again. "Tremblay, get your ass up here now!"

The Centurion 4 Dark Settlement Station lay ahead, and the only entrance bay available was one of the smaller ones. He told himself he wanted Tremblay to pilot the *Kinsblade 3* into this bay because he was too tired from their all-night trip from Gartan to do it himself. Tremblay would keep his mouth shut and not say what they both knew, though: Langlade wasn't exactly the best pilot in the galaxy, and it was better if he didn't try to guide the DS into the small space himself. The ship had already suffered enough hull damage for one trip.

Even so, Tremblay would give him that look, the one that made Langlade want to blast him with a particle ray—the look that said they both knew that while Langlade was an ace trader and no puff with the ladies, he sucked exhaust pipe at piloting

85

ships of any size. So long as Tremblay's looks never evolved into actual words, though, Langlade would let him live. The man was a pretty damn good pilot, even if he did stink like he bedded down nightly with goats.

"Yeah, yeah, keep your pants on, I'm comin'." The comm crackled after Tremblay's response before going down again.

"Adelle," Langlade said out into the open air of the flightdeck.

"Yes, Captain," the onboard compubot responded in her cool, assured tone. She always had that confident hum to her voice, even when the ship was being fired on by hostile forces— usually meaning angry fathers, highly disappointed in their wayward daughters who'd had the extraordinarily good taste to fall for the captain of the Kinsblade fleet.

Langlade smiled, thinking of his last late-night escape into the Dark. Boy, that little slice of heaven was sure ripe for the picking. She'd nearly jumped on him the minute he'd walked through the airlock and onto the dock. It seemed his reputation was preceding him more and more these days.

The idea of easy pickings drew his attention back to his immediate situation. He had a few days' worth of repairs to do to the ship before he could find some more paying work; might as well enjoy himself while the crew got the DS shipshape.

"Any events being broadcast on the dock's PA system?" he asked Adelle.

"Yes, Captain. There is a music and light show this evening, if that interests you."

Langlade shook his head. Adelle was good at keeping the ship's systems online and assessed, but she was garbage at remembering his personal preferences. It was like she was always trying to turn him into a different man; she acted too much like a wife for his comfort. It was why he rarely spoke with her about things involving his personal life. But it had been a while since he'd been back to the farthest Dark Settlement in Centurion 4, and he didn't want to walk off the docks blind.

"Try again, Adelle. And let's focus on things that won't put me to sleep, all right?"

"As you wish, Captain. There is a gambling tournament being hosted by Gervais at the Grand Old Saloon."

His eyebrows went up at that. "Sanctioned?"

"I do not believe so, sir. It's being broadcast on the black channel."

Langlade's smile came slowly as the ideas floated through his skull. "What's the ante?"

"I do not have details, sir, other than to know it features the game of givit. It's being broadcast sporadically, and much of it is encrypted."

Langlade knew Adelle wouldn't have the decryption codes; the Kinsblade fleet wasn't made up of regular residents, nor were any of its ships or its crewmembers trade partners with the people who inhabited this settlement, generally speaking.

"Can you get me dealt in?"

"No, sir. You must approach in person."

Langlade nodded, chewing his broken thumbnail pensively. He had to come up with something to ante. In games like this, gencredits weren't always welcome—not that he had piles of them anyway. Money was boring; lust was much more exciting. Blood-lust, sex-lust… it was all the same in the end. People living in the Dark Settlements craved passion in any form. Luckily, Langlade was a passionate guy. He knew he'd come up with something that someone at the tables would want, and surely there'd be a chancer there who'd be offering up a trinket he would suddenly find he could no longer live without. It was always that way at the givit tables. He rubbed his hands together in anticipation of the night ahead.

The door to the flightdeck slid open and a stench flowed into the room, as if it were trying to escape its source and find a new host.

"Took you long enough," Langlade growled out, standing up from the captain's chair. He wanted to put as much breathing space between himself and his crewmember as possible, on account of the fact that the man's stench tended to rub off and stick around.

Tremblay mounted the stairs to join his captain. "I was busy."

"Too busy to pilot the ship into the bay?" Langlade scoffed as he made way for the real pilot of the ship to take his place. "You sure you don't have a whore lined up in there already?"

"So what if I do? Don't make what I'm doing now any less important."

Langlade was instantly suspicious. Tremblay had been with him for a long time, but that didn't make him any less mysterious. Normally what he did in his chamber was never something Langlade questioned; so long as the guy did what he was paid to do, Langlade left him to his perversions. But this felt off for some reason. Not much took precedence over Tremblay's sex dates.

"What's so important on the ship that it keeps you from your whore?" Langlade asked.

Tremblay ignored him, his fingers flying over the seat's arm. After passing his hand over the array to get it primed for his commands, he hopped on the comm box by pressing blue and black buttons simultaneously, then dialed in the frequency visible outside the station.

He called out to the dockmaster, who would give them permission to enter and assign them a dock to settle on. "Dockmaster, this is the Kinsblade 3, requesting authority to enter bay three niner. That's three niner, Dockmaster."

A space of three seconds preceded the response. "Kinsblade 3, this is the dockmaster. State the nature of your business."

Tremblay and Langlade shared a confused look. This was something new; normally the dockmaster waved everyone in without question, without delay. The request to enter always seemed merely a formality.

Tremblay pressed a blue button on the array and whispered to Langlade, even though with the conversation muted, there was no way the dockmaster could hear them. "What in the hellhole is that all about?"

Langlade shook his head slowly, his mind racing with possibilities. "I don't know. First I've heard of it."

"What do you want me to tell him?"

"Tell him we're here for maintenance."

Tremblay pressed the blue button again and leaned in. "Dockmaster, this is the Kinsblade 3 again. We're here for regular maintenance. Got some hull damage to attend to and some filtration issues."

Langlade nodded his approval at the detail. All of it was true, so if someone wanted to verify, it wouldn't cause them any problems. Hell, he could have recited a list a mile long of things this ship needed. It was the least maintained of his fleet, a dog of a DS he'd thought of selling off more than once in the past few years.

The dockmaster said nothing in response to Tremblay's statement, so Langlade leaned in. "Dockmaster, this is Captain Langlade. Care to explain why we're being interrogated and held outside?"

Tremblay slammed the button down to mute the channel. "What'd you say that for? Now they're gonna shut us out, and I'm gonna miss my date!"

Langlade glared at him. "Get out of my chair."

Tremblay looked confused. "What?"

"You heard me. Get up. Get out of here." He gestured with his chin at the door leading off the flightdeck.

Tremblay had the nerve to laugh. "What? And leave you to pilot the ship into the bay yourself? You sure you wanna do that?"

Langlade grabbed Tremblay by the front of his rotten, stinking flightsuit and yanked him out of the chair, tossing him to the floor like he weighed nothing. Tremblay skidded across the smooth surface a full meter before coming to a stop on his side.

He slowly got to his feet, Langlade glaring at him the entire time. "Fine. You want me gone, I'll go. Just don't come crying to me when you scrape the side of your ship and need to find someone to fix it for nothin'."

Langlade turned his back on Tremblay, staring out the clearpanel that faced the bay currently closed to him. He had to either ignore the man or shoot him in the face, and the ship was already dirty enough; the last thing he needed to be doing was getting rid of a stinking corpse.

A voice finally came over the comm unit, blocking out Langlade's feelings of anger and remorse. As angry as he was, he knew how much he needed Tremblay in that seat. Luckily, no one but Langlade could stand the sight or smell of the guy, so he didn't worry that Tremblay would leave his employ on this trip. He made a mental note to throw Tremblay a couple extra credits, to help him pay for that poor whore who was going to share her bunk with him tonight.

"Been some changes around here lately," the dockmaster said. "What's your water level like?"

Langlade's eyebrows pulled together. He couldn't think of a single reason why they'd ask that question. Were they offering water at the station now? "We're low, but not so much I'm worrying."

"You'll need to register your levels. Have your onboard connect in and send the data once you're fully docked."

Langlade opened his mouth to ask why, but then thought better of it. He preferred to get this kind of information from a more reliable source: bar patrons. They knew the real reasons for the OSG's role in their lives, and he never believed the propaganda spread by dockmasters and a station's magnoscreens.

"Will do. Permission to enter?"

"Granted." The large bay doors slowly opened.

Langlade sat down, taking over the controls that would guide his ship inside.

* * *

Langlade left the ship in the care of Tremblay and his other crewmembers and made his way over to the saloon owned by the infamous Gervais. The guy had made a name for himself in the beginning as a first-rate smuggler and later as a sharp businessman. Then he'd met Shadira, and his roaming, marauding, trading days were over. He put down roots out here in the badlands and opened up his bar—or his saloon, as he was calling it now. He was one of those guys who liked to pretend the Old Earth ways were still possible out here in the Dark, two hundred or so odd Earthyears after the last human had been annihilated on that planet.

The door to the saloon was nondescript, like many of the others that lined the halls and corridors of the station. Anyone who wanted to operate on the sly didn't advertise what they were all about to just anyone passing by. You had to know someone on the inside, or be a privy listener to the black channels, to find out that places like this even existed. And this one had lasted longer than most—at least three years now. Langlade had last been here almost a year ago and had only left when three different men tried to kill him on the same night. He sighed and smiled at the memory; some people were just sore losers. He couldn't help it if he had a special touch at the givit table. He came, he played, he conquered. It was a gift he never tired of enjoying at the expense of others.

Pushing open the door, he inhaled and grinned. The smell of old ale mixed with smoke plant and body stink never failed to get to him. To Langlade, it meant adrenaline, chance, winning, and credits to spend on whatever he wanted. And he was feeling especially lucky tonight.

The first person to approach him was a woman, of course. It was always that way. They were flies to honey, and he was just sweet enough to keep them interested, just dangerous enough to get them taking their clothes off. He wondered which of the beauties here tonight would be sharing his bunk later. When he saw the other men standing around, he had a pretty good feeling that he'd have his choice of ladies. He'd been told enough times of his handsome, sexy features to no longer doubt the compliments. Almost to his fortieth year now, he knew he was like a fine wine—getting better with age. The scars that had claimed sections of his face were just icing on the cake.

One of his crewmembers came up to him, a young ginger by the name of Gus. Langlade frowned at him, angry to see him here and not locked in the engine room where he should have been.

"Hey, Captain, how's it hangin'?"

"Why are you here and not on the ship where you belong?"

Gus took a slug of his ale. "Just getting some parts." He gestured at the bar with his mug. "Got a guy over there with a filter rasp. We're going to need that if you want to be able to take a shower later." He winked at his boss, like he had a right to do it.

Langlade grabbed him by the sleeve and pulled him close. "Get your ass back to the ship *now*."

"Hey, hey, all right, I gotcha." Gus threw the last of his ale back, let out a long belch, and slid the mug onto a nearby table. When he spoke, his voice was warped from the cold drink. "But just so you know, there's a table over there with a seriously tasty pot."

Langlade loosened his hold on the man. "What are you talking about?"

Gus casually yanked his arm free of his captain's grip and wiped his mouth off with the back of his hand, belching again before responding. "Givit table. Over there behind that wall. There's a chick in there."

Langlade's eyebrow went up. "A chick?"

"You know." Gus leaned in and whispered loudly. "A girl."

Langlade closed his eyes and took a deep breath in, letting it out slowly as he quietly tried to convince himself not to kill this kid. The only thing keeping the boy alive so far was the fact that he was a genius with electronics. The *Kinsblade 3* was still afloat only because of him and his twin brother.

"What girl?" Langlade finally asked, glaring at this crewmember who should have been locked in the engine room. Langlade was going to have a word with Tremblay about who was letting Gus and Tam out, so that that person could be dealt with harshly.

"I heard her name is Cass, but don't quote me on that. I caught a glimpse of her, and daaaaamn, she's hot."

"You said she's at the table?"

"Yeah. Word on the dock is she's the real deal. She'll make you put your credits where your mouth is. Bullshit walks."

"What's her ante? Gencredits?"

Gus grinned. "Nope." He looked like he had a really good secret. Even his face was flushed with it.

"Foodcredits?"

He shook his head. "Nope. Guess again."

Langlade grabbed him by the neck and squeezed. "I don't like playing guessing games."

"Okay! Okay!" Gus's voice came out like a squeak. "It's her innocence!"

Langlade loosened his hold a fraction, not sure he understood. "What?"

Gus held Langlade's wrist, his face turning bright red. "Can't… breathe…"

Langlade let his arm drop.

Gus pulled out his shirt and made theatrical adjustments to his collar and hair before finally speaking again. "I said, she's put her *innocence* up for her ante. Her woman's shield. Her virginity." He sighed and shook his head. "I can't put it any clearer than that, Captain."

Langlade was having a hard time computing what he was hearing. "She's a virgin? How old is she?"

Gun leaned in, his eyebrows wiggling. "Old enough to know better, if you know what I mean."

Langlade grabbed him by the flightsuit at the shoulder and turned him round, shoving him toward the door. "Go."

"But I just got here!"

Langlade lifted his leg and booted the engineer in the ass. "Get! Before I shoot you in the face."

"Fine, I'm going, I'm going." Gus spared a second to scowl before going out the door. He made it slam behind him, but

Langlade wasn't one bit sorry about cutting his crewmember's fun short. The idiot had hours of work to get done on the ship's systems, and he wasn't getting anything accomplished here drinking ale. Those ginger twins were almost more trouble than they were worth. Langlade decided then and there to try and find replacements while he was here, hoping his reputation would make that an easy task.

He moved to the bar and ordered an ale. When the bartender served it up, Langlade leaned in, dropping a couple extra credits on the bar as he spoke. "I hear there's a decent ante going off at the givit tables."

The man nodded, making a sad effort at wiping down a bar that would never be clean. "You heard true."

"Someone's shield is on the line, eh?"

The man nodded.

"You know who she is?"

He shook his head.

"Where she's from?"

Another negative response.

"She OSG?"

The man shrugged. "Don't think so. Looks more like a grounded drifter to me."

Langlade tapped the bar. "Thanks, friend." He dragged the ale with him and took a sip as he walked around to the back room.

* * *

Langlade stood on the outskirts of the game first, sizing up his opponent. She was small, dressed in a black, skintight flightsuit.

A dagger rested on the table next to her; leather straps and a holder told him she normally wore it on her thigh. She showed no fear, even though Langlade knew for a fact that the man across the table from her was a murderer. He liked to torture his victims before he did the deed, too. Rumor was he had a friend in high places, which is how he'd escaped being floated for so long. It was pretty much common knowledge that as long as criminals remained out here in the badlands, they were pretty much left alone. The OSG wasn't big enough to police every last centimeter of the universe, so they left some sections of it to govern themselves—the small matter of Langlade having to report his water stores to the dockmaster notwithstanding.

He heard mumbling behind him and shamelessly listened in. "She's offered it up again! Can you believe it? No way she doesn't know that's Crier. He wins and she can say goodbye not just to her shield but her lifeblood too. The guy's a savage."

Langlade nodded just slightly, agreeing with everything said, even though he wasn't the intended recipient of the message. This girl had to be crazy. What would make her risk so much for so little? He could see the ante offered up by the madman in front of him. It looked like a promissory note for… engine parts? He wondered if she had a ship for these future parts. It was unlikely, considering her age. She could be a crewmember somewhere, but then Gus should have known more about her. The ginger tended to get around and had never learned to shut his yap. He was a walking gossip machine.

The girl reached over and pulled a card from Crier's hand, nothing in her expression telling anyone whether she was happy or worried about the givit she'd just claimed. The dealer looked to Crier. "Reveal."

Crier laid down his hand. It wasn't bad, a pair with a ten high. Langlade felt his pulse speeding up. He wanted the girl to win, even though she was a child and a stranger. It was stupid and reckless to give a flying shit crystal what happened to her, because out here on the edge of nowhere, caring got people killed. But care he did, because she reminded him of someone he missed sorely.

She put her cards down, and he felt himself breathe a sigh of relief.

"Three of a kind, my friend. Sorry, but you lose." She reached over to take Crier's promissory note off the table, but was stopped when the man's hand shot out and grabbed her wrist.

Everyone froze but Langlade. He went for the guy's back.

But he wasn't as quick on the draw as the girl was.

One second she was being yanked from her chair toward her captor, and the next she was holding a dagger to his neck. A drop of blood was already dripping down Crier's collar by the time Langlade reached the man's chair.

"Take your fucking hands off me, shitbag." The girl's face was inches from her opponent's, but she wasn't flinching.

The cruel man smiled. "I don't even have my hands on you yet, doll. But I'll get 'em there, you can bet on that."

"I *already* bet on it, and I won. You lost. Now fuck off and don't show your face around here again tonight, or I'll cut your balls off and stuff 'em down your throat." She gave him a slightly deeper cut before easing the knife away.

Langlade felt his blood quicken and something inside him

burst. The hand he'd been about to use against the man in her defense patted him on the back instead. "You heard the girl, Crier. Time for you to get up from the table and leave the real playing to the real players."

The girl's knife slowly pulled away as she sat back down on her chair. Her eyes lifted to acknowledge Langlade's presence. "And you are?"

As Crier began to stand, Langlade pushed him to the side, sending him to the floor next to the table. Langlade pulled his weapon from its holster and simultaneously held the man off at gunpoint while reaching for the girl in greeting. "Langlade's the name, and givit is my game."

A sly grin revealed itself as she took his hand in a strong grip. "Nice to meet you, Langlade of the Kinsblade fleet. Have a seat. I think you might have something that I want. You ready to ante up?"

He took the chair offered and set his mug down beside him. The crowd pushed in, spilling ale and other liquids on the edges of the table. "Oh yeah," he said, nodding. "I'm ready."

* * *

Langlade tried not to sweat, but it was difficult to stay cool when the crowd of onlookers pressed in on the table. The air circulation in the room was nonexistent. The dealer twice yelled at the strangers surrounding them to back off; the third time he lost his patience and doused them with a full mug of ale. "Give them some space!" he growled. His bluster was all for show, though—this guy was having a ball, thoroughly in his element as the dealer in a game with a pot so valuable people would be talking about it for years.

To the players, the dealer said, "Flaming dwarf stars, we've never had a game this hot before." He winked at the girl, but she said nothing back. Her face was a mask, unreadable and serious—as well it should have been, because her ante was like none Langlade had ever seen before or even dreamed of. Now he couldn't imagine why he hadn't sought a bet like this before.

"I want your ship."

When she'd first said it, he'd laughed, thinking her joking. But when she said it again, and gestured at the table with a nod of her head, he knew she wasn't. That's when the sweat started trickling down his back. The onlookers were four deep now, almost suffocating in their eagerness to see someone go down. The front row heard everything they said at the table and repeated it for the ones behind. Even though there was no comm system in this place, Langlade knew that his every word was being transmitted and remembered, and would be repeated for years to come to anyone who would listen. This was either going to be really good for business or really bad, but one thing was clear: he couldn't walk away a coward.

He shrugged. "Fine. I have the *Kinsblade 3* here at the dock. I'll ante her." Just hearing the words come out of his own mouth made a slice of pain go through his chest, just as if he'd taken out a knife and plunged it in there himself. She was the third of his fleet and the worst off among them, but she still held a special place in his heart. It was on this ship that he'd found and lost the love of his life.

"Fine." The girl gestured to the note on the table. "That's

the right to my woman's shield there. Put your ship's papers with it so everyone can see you intend to ante the ownership."

She might have been young, but she obviously knew what she was doing. He'd seen games go sideways before when one of the players claimed not to have anted what the other said he had. It was always the loser doing that, and even though he knew he was going to win, he didn't bother trying to argue the point with her. She'd learn soon enough that his paper being on the table wouldn't matter.

He pulled his document holder from his inner pocket at his chest and found the one she'd asked for. Flipping it out onto the table like it hardly mattered, he smiled, first at her and then at the dealer. "Let's get started, then, shall we? I have a virgin to deflower." He winked at the girl and felt a spark of pleasure run . through him when her complexion paled a little. He wasn't much for the inexperienced, but he decided then that he was going to enjoy this one. Hell, he might even keep her around a while. She seemed smart enough. Maybe she knew how to do a good trade, and if she warmed his bunk too, that'd be a decent bonus.

"One hand takes all?" he asked.

She nodded. "One hand's all I need." Her chin came up, along with her color. She was going a little pink now, making her almost beautiful.

He smiled to himself. *Like taking candy from a baby.* "Good. I'm tired. Looking forward to bedding down for the night." He winked at the crowd, and they rewarded him with uproarious laughter. The word spread through the layers of people and eventually the entire bar was in on the game.

The first few cards were dealt. People behind Langlade leaned in, trying to catch a glimpse of what he had, but he kept his hand at his chest. He was very good at guarding his own reactions, but he knew the people behind him could reveal the strength of his hand and ruin his chances at seeing what made this brave but very stupid girl tick. She had to have heard of his reputation—out here, everyone had. What made her want to ante up her most valuable possession to the kind of cutthroats that frequented Gervais's place? Maybe she was one of those gluttons for punishment.

He shrugged as he added a newly dealt card to his hand. It wasn't his problem if she was damaged. All she had to do was take her clothes off and he'd handle the rest; her state of mind wouldn't be part of the picture.

Givit could be a very long game or a very short one, depending on the theatrics of the dealer and the players. Langlade was happy to see that neither of the other people at the table had any interest in putting on more of a show than they already were just by being there. The last card was delivered, and it was now time for him to claim one card from his opponent's hand. Langlade stared at the cards held by the girl, trying to decide which one he wanted. He couldn't see them, of course, but he felt as though maybe he could glean their faces by her behavior. She stared at one of them over and over, trying to pretend like she wasn't. That was the card he wanted, but he took his time leaning over and plucking it from her hand.

He play-frowned as he tucked it into his own. "I hope that didn't spoil your plans to pilot my ship out of here."

The group closest to him laughed.

The girl didn't say a word. She just glared. Langlade, for the life of him, couldn't figure out if that was a good sign or bad one. This girl was good. Really good. It made him wonder if she'd be a natural in bed too. The idea fired him up even more. He'd never dreamed he'd be walking into this situation when he'd piloted the DS into the station, but he was sure as hell glad that he had.

She stared and stared at his cards as if she were trying to see through them to their faces on the other side, her youthful exuberance at the task a traitor to her fear. Langlade smiled, certain he could smell her panic from where he was sitting. She had to be almost twenty Earthyears old, but to still have her innocence? It was unheard of. Maybe she was younger than she looked.

The idea should have put him off, but it didn't. She was obviously old enough, as Gus had said, and it had been a while since he'd had a warm, soft body waiting in his bunk. He was really going to enjoy collecting on this bet, possibly more than any other he'd ever made before.

"So what's it going to be, *Cass*, girl of unknown origin, smart enough to play a fair hand, but stupid enough to bet against me?" He was enjoying delivering a bit of theatrics, savoring the moment, knowing his victory would be all the sweeter when it arrived. "You going to pick a card and call it a night, or what?" He looked to his left and right as he rested his elbow on the table. A grin spread across his face and he delivered the blow he knew would throw her completely off her game and get the crowd laughing along with him. "And when I say 'call it a night,' I mean 'get in my bunk,' of course."

He turned his attention back to the girl, and a sudden passion seized him when he noticed her hand resting on her knife. This one was going to be a wild child, no doubt about it. He looked meaningfully at the knife and then at her. "Better save your energy. You're going to need it, lass."

The girl looked positively terrified.

Raucous laughter filled the room, making Langlade feel like he was floating on air. In less than an hour he'd have her naked and willing, he had no doubt about that. And when it was all over, she'd be begging him for more, her knife forgotten in a pile of her clothing on the floor.

His hand jerked involuntarily from just thinking about her naked, and her eyes lit up in reaction. A slow grin spread across her face, making him suddenly nervous. The dealer tapped the table on the girl's side, reminding her that it was her turn to choose a card from Langlade's hand.

Langlade stared at the card he wanted her to take, praying to some unknown, unseen force out in the universe that she would ignore the one he needed to keep, the one that would cut her to the quick. And for a moment, she seemed to fall under his spell, her finger hovering over the garbage card he would have been happy to be rid of. But then her hand shifted, and she took the one card he knew could be a problem. He looked at her face, but saw nothing there—no mark of triumph or gloating. He smiled, believing then that he had her beat. He was going make her pay in passion for that little heart attack she'd just given him.

She turned his givit card over and added it to her own hand. "Save your own energy, you ugly sonofabitch, because I'll be sleeping in your bunk *alone* tonight."

Her cockiness got him even hotter than he already was. He decided they'd head right for his bunk immediately after she showed her losing hand; screw getting parts for the engine room.

"You sure about that?" Langlade laid his cards out, letting each one flick on the table individually so everyone could add them up as they fell. It must have been like arrows into her heart, he thought, to see the numbers coming together and to know she was about to lose the most valuable thing she had to her name. He almost felt sorry for her. Almost.

The girl placed her cards flat, no hesitation or finesse to it. He didn't have to add up the numbers—the faces were all he needed to see. His heart sank all the way down into his boots and turned into a molten puddle of regret in his heels.

She smiled, a grin so large it took up her entire lovely yet devious face.

"That's a full blockade," she said, winking at Langlade like she hadn't just stolen his drifter ship out from under his nose. "Aces high."

My ship… what have I done?

Q&A with Elle Casey

Where did this story come from?

I decided a while back that I really wanted to write some science fiction, specifically a space opera. I'm always looking to watch TV shows and movies in that genre, and there just isn't enough out there, as far as I'm concerned. (I'm one of those disappointed *Firefly* fans who wishes the series could have gone on for twenty seasons.) So, I made room in my 2015 schedule for a series called *Drifters' Alliance*, and in March I started writing what would become book one, starring Cass Kennedy, a rebel with a cause. Once the characters leaped into my head, I had so, so many things to write about. Every character in that book has his or her own story to tell, so this anthology was a great vehicle to get one of those stories out of my head. This short story contains just a snippet of the world, but it's a great addition to the *Drifters' Alliance* series from my perspective; it really helped me get to know some of my characters better and see where they could go together in future books in the series.

Will you be continuing this story elsewhere?

Yes. I published the first *Drifters' Alliance* book in June 2015 and will be adding to the series over several months of 2015, and in 2016 possibly as well. There are at least 3 books planned, but I'll happily write more if enough of my fans ask for it! The main character of the *Drifters' Alliance* series is Cass Kennedy, and Book 1 begins where this short story ends. I hope you'll take a chance on *Drifters' Alliance* Book 1 and give it a read, and, as always, I'd love to read your review of my work.

Tell us something we might not know about you.

If this is the first book of mine you've read, then you probably don't know that I write in almost every big genre out there. If you like my style of writing and think you might want to venture out of sci-fi a little, you can try my urban contemporary fantasy, romance, thriller, dystopian, action/adventure, or other novels. Just search for "Elle Casey" on any of the big online retailers and you'll find me! You can also find a reading list of all my books broken down by genre on my website, ElleCasey.com, and I'm also on Facebook.

Works in progress?

I write about one book a month (yes, a full novel), so I'm pretty busy. I write sometimes seven days a week, and I'm kind of addicted to reader-fan love, so yeah... it's what I have to do, but I love doing it, too. I'm a huge bookworm, so being a huge bookworm feeder makes me very happy. You can see what my publishing plan is for the year on my website. It includes more sci-fi, fantasy, and paranormal titles, sometimes with a touch of romance thrown in for good measure. I try to keep all my readers happy, no matter what their favorite genres might be. You'll also see a new series of mine launched by traditional publisher Montlake Romance, titled *The Bourbon Street Boys*. It's a romance and full of laugh-out-loud moments (or so I hope).

Future plans?

I dream of seeing my work on a screen somewhere, either television or film. We'll see what happens, but in the meantime, if you know anyone in these industries and like my work, please pass it on!

Carindi

by Jennifer Foehner Wells

EI'PIO WAS ALONE.

She could still hear the screams echoing back through the tunnel of memory. It had been madness, pure chaos, followed by the darkest, deepest silence she had ever known.

A plague had rioted through the *Oblignatus*, affecting everyone but her, presumably because she was the only crewmember aboard who wasn't sectilian. Every last one of her colleagues had been damaged so severely that that their thoughts and mental patterns were no longer recognizable to her—then they'd met dusk wherever they happened to be.

She didn't like to think about it, yet she couldn't stop. There was nothing else to occupy her mind. Her water-filled enclosure spanned the core of the city-sized ship. For days, she'd jetted from one end to the other attempting—repeatedly, thoroughly—to reach out mind to mind, searching, but had found only empty silence. In a ship meant to house ten thousand sectilians, only one individual in the ship community had survived.

Her.

What she wanted above all else was to return to Sectilius, to her people, but that was impossible. The infernal yoke kept her from moving the ship, no matter how hard she railed against it. There wasn't an officer left to issue the command to release it. In all her long life as a devoted fleet officer—completely above reproach—this had never been a concern, but now it maddened her.

The yoke wasn't a physical restraint. It was a combination of code and electronic devices embedded in a secret location within the ship. It kept her, or any other kuboderan navigator, from moving the ship without authorization. Apparently the ship's designers had never considered the current scenario.

The ship was too deep in the Kirik Nebula for a message to penetrate to any nearby colonies. They'd been on a research and exploration mission and had come across a red giant in its final stages before supernova. The Quasador Dux had decided it was a rare opportunity to observe the phenomenon. They would leave probes in orbit while they conducted other research at a safer distance.

The last maneuver they'd performed had taken them on a close approach to the red giant. They'd intended to remain in the danger zone just long enough make the drop, but the plague had hit at the worst possible time, effectively stranding them in the orbit intended for the probes.

Even if someone came looking, the *Oblignatus* was nowhere near its designated research coordinates. After a few weeks, the possibility of rescue seemed remote.

Ei'Pio watched the data closely. The star had burned

through all of its hydrogen and helium and was at the end of the carbon-fusion stage. Carbon levels inside it were diminishing steadily. She calculated that she would have thirteen to fourteen years to wait before the core collapsed and the star went supernova.

Eventually she'd come to contemplate suicide. It was an unspeakable act, but the taboo against suicide was predicated upon one's usefulness to society—one's duty to others. So what did it matter now? Who would censure her or threaten her with reconditioning if she dared have such dark thoughts?

Her anxiety had become a palpable thing. Why live on, waiting for the inevitable, living in a perpetual countdown? What life was there for her without anyone to serve, without anyone with whom to commune?

She lost herself in a fugue, her mind wandering from one treasured memory to another, each one given to her by those who were forever gone to her. She neglected her duties. Why care for a ship full of the dead?

She drifted in the depths of unrelenting stillness. Not eating. Not caring. Limbs heavy with depression. Brains aching from pain that went well beyond physical. Barely moving, except wherever the swirling, artificial current carried her.

Then something in her digital ocular implant caught her attention. It was just the smallest inconsistency. She'd almost missed it. Curiosity stirred within her.

Her senses slowly sharpened as she focused on this irregularity. When she realized what she was actually looking at, the morbid sluggishness vanished. She jetted restlessly from one end of her enclosure to the other, checking and double-checking the sensor readings. There *was* a single life sign, but it was minuscule and muted. It was no wonder she'd missed it in the early days of anguish.

Her limbs quivered. She pulsed water through her mantle erratically. She couldn't help but hope, though she knew it was probably just a shambling zombie that'd had a delayed reaction to the disease and hadn't yet expired.

She would do whatever she could to save them, though she had no idea what the plague vector had been. Her people had simply transformed into violent beasts and then suddenly stopped functioning altogether, until they perished of thirst and hunger.

Just one survivor could change everything.

Ei'Pio fluttered tentatively against the mind of this individual, braced for crazed thoughts, dull thoughts, or the barest semblance of thought. Braced for another senseless death.

But to her surprise, this person was intact, whole, and… starving.

Even at the surface level of anipraxia, misery flooded Ei'Pio's senses. There were fragmented impressions of gnawing hunger, disbelief, abject terror—and then a bout of all-consuming sobbing that led to the unconscious oblivion of sleep.

This person had suffered the same level of loss that she had herself—perhaps even more, if that was possible. She or he desperately needed Ei'Pio's help.

She discerned something else in this shallow contact. Strangely, this individual had not developed a capacity for anipraxic communication. That was exceedingly rare in any ship community. Occasionally an objector served in the fleet, but

Ei'Pio knew there weren't any objectors aboard the mission to the Kirik Nebula. She had no idea who this person was.

Ei'Pio scoured internal sensor readings and camera coverage and soon discovered that the individual was inside a suit of sectilian power armor. That explained the faintness of the bio-signature. The suits were shielded. Had the suit isolated the survivor from the plague the same way she had been spared?

Once Ei'Pio realized this, her primary objective was to communicate with this person, to let them know they weren't alone—that he or she could take command of the ship and return them to Sectilius space.

As the only surviving member of the quorum, Ei'Pio could appoint the survivor as the Quasador Dux of the *Oblignatus* and download the command-and-control engram set into his or her brain. That would allow the ship's computer to recognize them as the highest-ranking officer—then she or he had only to issue the command to return to Sectilius and the yoke would be released.

They would be able to move the ship.

They could go home.

She didn't yet know anything about this person—name, gender, or occupation, but it seemed wrong to continue to refer to him or her in the abstract. It would take time to establish communication and learn those important details. In the interim, she would refer to the stranger as male, an entirely random gender assignment, and give him the name Suparo, which meant survivor.

Establishing communication between herself and Suparo wasn't as simple as one sectilian opening his or her mouth and speaking to another sectilian. Ei'Pio was unable to communicate that way. A small portion of this untouched brain had to be stimulated in a very concentrated and specific way to encourage the development of the set of dormant structures that allowed anipraxic communication. Ei'Pio had done this many times in the past, whenever new crewmembers had come aboard.

This time was different.

Normally when she inducted someone into the circle of anipraxia, there was resistance. The changes could be painful, though Ei'Pio did her best to minimize that, and often an individual had an inner level of reluctance that was an additional barrier to the process, even though they had chosen this lifestyle.

Suparo was sleeping deeply when she began the process but soon awoke. He did not resist at all—he seemed very receptive to the alteration, seemed quite inquisitive about it, in fact. Suparo seemed to recognize that someone was there to help, that someone was communicating somehow. That was unusual.

Something about his mind didn't follow a typical pattern. It felt open, malleable. It was easy to precipitate the conversion that would facilitate anipraxia. Ei'Pio began to sift through his surface memories while she waited for the changes to manifest. She wanted to figure out who this was. His childhood memories were unusually pronounced and extraordinarily vivid, but also jumbled and formless—running and laughter and being cradled in another's arms...

Suddenly Suparo pulled Ei'Pio's tendrils of thought deeper, as though he recognized her. Then he reciprocated—sending his own tendrils of thought along the connection between them... seeking to find her... pushing their minds closer... pressing against Ei'Pio's own mind… seeking to *get inside* her thoughts. This was without precedent.

Ei'Pio was suddenly afraid. She pulled back, her limbs trembling. What if he wasn't sectilian? What if these memories were implants, lures… a trap to ensnare her? What if he was an alien, an infiltrator, who had orchestrated the destruction of her people? Was this an elaborate plot to hijack the ship?

But then she wondered if it actually mattered. He was another living being.

For good or ill, she was no longer alone.

* * *

Suparo didn't speak Mensententia—that was immediately clear—but Ei'Pio recognized the thought-language as sectilian, and that reassured her. Over the years Ei'Pio had experienced enough sectilian memories to be able to speak a pidgin version of the language. This new individual's own language skills seemed to be very limited as well, which was perplexing.

An image consistently overlaid Suparo's thoughts. He longed for a woman's face—a sectilian woman with warm brown eyes and a long sharp nose. Ei'Pio recognized the woman: Biochemistro Palset Benald Teruvah, a lovely woman, a good friend to Ei'Pio and many others on board. Such a terrible loss.

Ei'Pio froze. Her mantle filled reflexively and her limbs bunched up as though she were poised to flee a predator.

Now Ei'Pio knew who this was. Not a him or a her, but an ium.

Slowly, she calmed herself—carefully, so that she wouldn't

transmit her anxiety to this person who needed her so badly.

Ei'Pio kept her mental voice soft and soothing, like a sectilian mother's buss on a child's forehead. "Carindi?"

The stranger's emotions swung wildly toward bewilderment, hope, and trepidation. A tiny voice answered, speaking aloud because the child didn't yet understand. "Mama?"

Carindi was a child of five standard years.

Ei'Pio cringed with guilt and shame. Carindi had been wandering alone in the ship, seeking help for weeks.

* * *

"What did you learn today, Carindi?" Ei'Pio asked when the child took a break from ius daily studies. At the moment the child was somersaulting along the corridor outside the study chamber. The black armor had taken years of this without a scratch. The same could not be said for the deck plates.

The child chattered a stream of thoughts at her, as was often the way. Their language difficulties were long in the past. "I'm learning about the mechanics of propulsion. Oh, and scientific classification systems for plants and animals. Also, the use of honorifics. One day soon I will be an engineer and you will call me Machinutorus Carindi Palset Teruvah!"

"Very good. A full day of learning. It is nearly time for your rest period."

Though Ei'Pio had never had contact with sectilian children except through the childhood memories of her former colleagues, she sensed that Carindi was an exceedingly intelligent child and full of curiosity. The child would make a fine Quasador Dux when iad was old enough to assume that role.

It had been five years since Carindi's mother had observed the earliest signs of the plague among the crew and placed her precious offspring inside an obsidian suit of power armor. Carindi's mother had hoped to protect the child from the unknown disease, not realizing the child was already infected. It proved to be a brilliant gambit anyway, because the suit was designed to accomodate a diverse range of body types and to provide extensive medical support in battle. It allowed the child to grow and remain mobile, feeding ium intravenously and keeping the disease and the suit in a constant state of homeostasis, always just barely at bay.

It allowed Carindi to survive.

Ei'Pio had experienced enough sectilian memories to know that sectilian children needed to be nurtured. They were supposed to be held and cuddled. But Ei'Pio had never touched the child, had never seen the child's face except through glass. Ei'Pio longed to give the child that kind of security. She wanted to give Carindi anything and everything iad might need to thrive. The child was all she had left and was her only hope for a future.

But all Ei'Pio could give Carindi was the mental touch of a loving voice and warm feelings. Ei'Pio breathed water. Carindi breathed air. Water and glass and battle armor stood between them.

Ei'Pio sighed. The problem would resolve itself in just a few years. They would be able to go home. They would rejoin their people.

"I'm not tired yet," Carindi complained. "There's time for more studies before rest cycle. Ei'Pio? Why do we use all these names?"

"What names?" Ei'Pio asked. The child's mind zigged and zagged just like her haphazard somersaulting.

"Honorifics and all that stuff."

"There are many reasons. To differentiate between individuals, primarily. When speaking of others, it makes it easier to note whom one is referring to. It is also a manner of respect. Some names are earned."

"No—I mean, why do you and I use them? We know who we're talking about, right? I know what Ei' means. It's the intermediate rank among kuboderan officers, yes? You know I respect you without having to say it. You can feel my emotions."

"This is true."

"May I call you Pio? As a special endearment? Between only us two?"

Ei'Pio's heart contracted. The water around her suddenly felt cold. No one had called her Pio since she'd been brought to the planet Sectilia as an infant. That was so long ago. "Yes, child."

"Do my names have any meaning?"

"Oh, yes! Carindi means 'little dear one.' Palset was, of course, your mother's given name and means 'sharp as a spear.' Teruvah was the name of the enclave on Atielle where your mother was born and spent her childhood. The name means 'rubbing the fruit.' I am given to understand the people there are famous for cultivating fruits for making fermented beverages."

"When I get big will you call me Carindissimo?"

Ei'Pio's limbs trembled with laughter. "If you wish."

* * *

When the child slept, Ei'Pio spent her time testing the confines and parameters of the yoke—always looking for a way to circumvent it, work around it or break it—so that they wouldn't have to wait for Carindi to mature. Ei'Pio found she missed the child during ius sleep cycles. Then the child woke, and it was like coming around the dark side of a planet and bathing in the bright light of a blazing star.

"Good morning, Pio. Are you feeling well?"

Ei'Pio let warmth suffuse her mental voice. "Good morning, Machinutorus Carindi Palset Teruvah. I am very fine, thank you. And you?"

Ei'Pio felt the child rise from bed and go through a morning waking routine as the suit ran its daily diagnostic. Iad moved each limb in turn, to see if any part would be hindered by the infectious agent this day, so that a routine could be planned accordingly.

After a moment, the data from the suit diagnostic spooled over Ei'Pio's ocular implant.

There was blood in the child's urine.

Ei'Pio felt a familiar squeeze of panic, then calmed. The suit had limitations. She knew that.

"First stop is the medical facility today, Carindi."

"Pio! I wanted to—"

"Health first. Always. No arguments."

There was an adolescent grumble of discontent, but Carindi dutifully marched to the deck transport, and from there to the nearest medical facility.

Sometimes the suit couldn't handle everything. Ei'Pio had nearly lost Carindi on several occasions when the suit malfunctioned or needed an upgrade, but they had managed to make it through those terrifying moments. On a regular schedule, and as needed, Carindi visited the diagnostic platform they had modified together—Ei'Pio's mind guiding Carindi's nimble fingers inside the power armor—so that the diagnostic equipment would accept Carindi inside the suit and the medical bots would deliver medications and IV nutrition to the suit's ports. This required writing new macros to force the suit to do things it was never meant to do. And that meant Ei'Pio had to learn new skills. Ship navigators were not ordinarily in the practice of creating code for power armor suits.

Nor were they ordinarily medical practitioners. Yet Ei'Pio personally oversaw everything, from screening medications to be sure they were free of viral, bacterial, or unknown nanoscale agents to optimizing the child's liquid diet for every life stage.

And she was always looking for another way to get them home. Carindi deserved better than this. Engineers and Medical Masters on Sectilia, Atielle, or any of the colonies would be better equipped to cure Carindi of the affliction so that the child could have a better quality of life than Ei'Pio and *Oblignatus* could provide.

* * *

The child giggled. "No, Pio, not Olonus Septua. That's a gravid planet, not a barren one."

"You aren't supposed to give me hints, child!"

Carindi gasped for breath, wheezing with mirth. "Well, you're terrible at this game. You need the help!"

"Am I really?" Ei'Pio pretended to be affronted. She'd figured out the correct answer three questions before, but Carindi enjoyed it when she drew these games out—and truth be told, Ei'Pio loved the feeling of the child's laughter. It was infectious. It lifted her ever-present worry for a short time.

Children were easy to please and such a joy. A small part of her resented that she had never known children before now. In some ways, this felt like a golden time in her life, despite the bomb ticking inside the star they orbited.

Carindi was wandering the empty corridors of the ship aimlessly, drumming the fingers of ius suit against the dark walls. "Guess again, Pio."

"The moon of Columnus Quince?"

The child roared with laughter until it turned into coughing. The coughing went on too long.

Ei'Pio sobered.

When the coughing fit eased, Carindi slumped to the decking and asked, "Pio, when we break free of the star, where would you like to go? Assume that you could go anywhere in the universe."

She'd heard this question often. It meant that Carindi was feeling lonely and restless. Ei'Pio sent a soothing blanket of thought over the child's mind.

"I would take you home to Atielle, of course." That's what she always told the child. "Where would you like to go, Carindi? To Valetria? To see the Parida Quasar? Or Sieden's Rings?" These were all astronomical sights the child had studied recently.

"I would like to go to your home world, Pio."

That was a new answer. She found it puzzling. "Why would you want that?"

"You are my family now. I want to meet your family. I want you to be free to swim in an ocean."

Ei'Pio's mantle pulsed nervously, out of rhythm. Carindi spoke of something forbidden. "You know that can never happen."

"Why not? I know the location of your home world is supposed to be a big secret, but we can figure it out. We can find it. I know we can."

"That isn't the point. I'm sectilian now. My people wouldn't recognize me as one of their own. I don't even speak their language."

They wouldn't recognize her as being the same *species*, either. In this artificial and optimized environment, Ei'Pio had grown far larger than any wild kuboderan could ever dream of. Her body was augmented with multiple cybernetic implants that would look alien to them. They would more than likely kill her on sight. The sectilian kuboderans had always been told that the kuboderans of their home world were not only wild, but savage.

"But they speak Mensententia, surely."

Ei'Pio faltered. "Yes, I'm sure they do."

"Do you remember it? What it was like?"

Ei'Pio gifted the child with a memory of floating free in a vast watery world. The bright warm shallows and the cool dark depths. Then, on a whim, she showed Carindi her memory of being born. She could still see the cave where her mother had kept them clean and blown water across them gently with her funnel to keep them well oxygenated, though the earliest memories were all softly tinted by the nearly transparent membrane of an egg sac.

It had been quiet and safe there. The moment when her egg sac became fragile and her first tentacle burst out into the larger world, everything changed forever.

There was the last sight of her mother, still tending to the unhatched. The swarms of age-mates from many mothers mixing indiscriminately as they stretched out their limbs for the very first time, bobbing, floating—winking their distress in bright flashes of color—and scattering, swept away in the current without any control.

"This is what life is like sometimes, Carindi. Sometimes we have no control over our circumstances." She stopped the flow of the memory before it could reach the point when she would watch in horror as some of her age-mates were consumed by larger predators. There was no sense in upsetting the child.

Belatedly, she realized that hiding the ugliness might have been a mistake. Carindi was enraptured. "What a beautiful world!"

"You couldn't survive there. You breathe air."

"Don't be silly, Pio. I'll be in the suit. It's made for surviving in space. Underwater would be a cinch."

Another terrible reminder that Carindi might never leave the suit. Ei'Pio's mantle squeezed painfully. It was so unnatural. So wrong. She should have figured out how to free ium by now. She had failed.

Carindi caught the tail of the thought, though Ei'Pio had

tried to hide it.

"I don't hate the suit. I love the suit. It keeps me alive. I love you too, Pio. If you don't want to go to your home world, we can go to another water world."

It wasn't true, she knew. The child detested the suit and wanted freedom more than anything else. But it was kind of ium to say.

"I love you too, child."

* * *

When the red dwarf exhausted its supply of carbon, Ei'Pio noted the beginning of neon fusion with no small amount of dread. Based on her calculations, there was less than a year left before neon, oxygen, and silicon fusion would be complete. Without any other fuel sources, the star would begin to fuse iron, which would take mere minutes to exhaust. Once the iron core reached a specific mass, it would crash in on itself and send out a cosmic shockwave that would obliterate the ship as the star went supernova.

Ei'Pio still had not found a way around the yoke.

Carindi had to be an adult in order to receive the command-and-control engram set and take control of the ship. The computer would not install it in a child. Iad had to be confirmed as an adult documented citizen, which could only be done by automated systems in the medical facility and only upon full puberty.

Ei'Pio could find no way around it.

Most sectilian children underwent puberty and declared

their gender to their community in the eleventh or twelfth year. But it was Carindi's seventeenth standard year, and there was still no sign of pubescent change in the child.

Ei'Pio began to devote all of her free time to studying sectilian anatomy and physiology, focusing specifically on endocrinology. She reached Medical Master levels of knowledge, but she was no closer to solving the mystery of Carindi's delayed biological development. What was missing from Carindi's daily macro- and micro-biotic intake that was precluding puberty?

Ei'Pio insisted on more extensive scanning and analysis, but the only conclusion she could draw was that Carindi was underweight. So she changed Carindi's liquid diet to be more calorically rich.

She also judiciously implemented a regimen of exogenous hormone therapy. Such artificial interventions were frowned upon among sectilians, so there were no precedents to follow. She had no way of knowing how much to apply to the child's system. She started with tiny amounts of bio-identical hormones tailored for the child's congenital sex for simplicity's sake, because Carindi had never developed a gender preference.

Carindi was indifferent to these experiments. Iad didn't seem to be interested in choosing a gender, and to some extent that made sense. The child retained few memories of gendered sectilians. Gender was a remote concept to ium.

From a biological standpoint, there was no reason for the child's body to change. There was no counterpart with whom to mate or share a life.

Did a sectilian child need adults or age-mates within their

environment to trigger puberty? Perhaps it was that absence that was the true problem.

Ei'Pio gradually increased the dosage of the exogenous hormone infusion until the child began to endure negative side effects. The hormones made the child's moods more volatile and triggered massive headaches and constant fatigue. Carindi didn't like taking them.

Despite this, Carindi still displayed no signs of impending puberty. Eventually Ei'Pio accepted that it was unlikely that puberty could be induced in this manner and stepped the dose back down to a level that was more tolerable to ium.

Carindi had chosen another tactic to deal with their situation. From the age of eight standard years, the child had become a voracious consumer of educational materials, leaping far and away ahead of most children of the same age. Studying and testing filled ius every waking hour, and iad achieved a mechanical engineering degree by the age of twelve standard years. Then iad went on to study computer languages and electrical engineering. Carindi was determined to subvert the yoke and give direct control of the ship to Ei'Pio.

The sectilian ship designers had believed that the yoke should be deeply hidden. They alleged that the Kubodera, though an extremely intelligent people, could often be headstrong and arrogant, so they imposed restraints, checks, and balances upon the navigators to keep the sectilian population of the ship safe. Mutiny would not be tolerated in the fleet. The designers were well aware that it would be easy to transfer total control of the ship to new hands if one could convince a kuboderan to do it. Therefore they purportedly placed the yoke in a secret location for the safety and security of every individual on board.

"Stop worrying, Pio," Carindi said one day on the engineering deck, from deep in the bowels of yet another ship system. "I've got this under control. I'm going to find it any day now." Carindi said things like this frequently.

Ei'Pio acknowledged the thought but wouldn't stop worrying. They had been alone together for thirteen standard years. The star had recently begun burning the oxygen layer. Less than half a standard sectilian year remained. Ei'Pio knew the teenager might find the circuits that controlled the yoke, but iad also might not. The yoke could be disguised as something Carindi would never recognize. The designers had been too clever.

"I may have to break through the yoke myself," Ei'Pio said softly. If she couldn't work around it, she would have to force her way through it. She wouldn't do it if it was just her, but she would for Carindi. She had been trying for so long, but the pain was great and she was a coward.

"No! Promise me you won't even try, Pio! I will find it."

"The rumors may not be true, little one. Perhaps they were started to keep us complacent."

They *were* true. She knew they were. A kuboderan who attempted to defeat the yoke would be driven mad from the pain as punishment for that crime. It kept the navigators in their place very effectively.

Over a monitor, Ei'Pio watched Carindi pulling herself out of a gap in the deck plating. The child's voice was stiff with anger. "You can't lie to me anymore, Pio. I can see right through it. I know the rumors are true and I won't let you risk it. What good would you be to me mad? I'd rather die than watch you do that to yourself. It nearly killed you to watch the sectilians die. What do you think it will do to *me* to watch you go insane?"

Ei'Pio didn't know what to say. The thought that she might become unreachable if she accomplished her goal—that she might leave the child alone—chilled her. Carindi needed her.

But what other course was there for her?

Carindi continued. "My people were wrong to shackle you this way—like some kind of pack animal. You aren't a *suesupus*! You're a *person*. When we get to Sectilius I will demand that this form of slavery be abolished. By the Cunabula, I will make them listen to me."

Ei'Pio was silent. Carindi flared with the passion of youth and spoke uncomfortable truths. But it had always been this way, and change would not come easily to Sectilius.

Ei'Pio did not mention it again, but she still pushed herself to attempt to punch through the yoke and its realm of pain when Carindi slept.

* * *

Ei'Pio woke from a brief doze knowing instantly that something was wrong. Carindi's signature was faint. She jetted to the other end of the ship, seeking, triangulating, calling out ius name.

The child was on the other side of the escutcheon—*outside the ship*. Ei'Pio's limbs thrashed in agitation as she cycled through camera transmissions until she finally located ium indulging in an untethered spacewalk. A compartment on the outside of the ship was open, and the teenager was shoulder deep in a propulsion nacelle.

Ei'Pio throttled the klaxon control so that it transmitted a warning at full volume into Carindi's helmet. She watched with a small amount of parental satisfaction as the child jerked in response. The tiny figure stood up on the hull and waved, then deliberately punched the button on the shoulder of the power armor to silence the alarm and went back to work.

Ei'Pio ground her beak with worry, her suction cups kneading anything that happened to be nearby, until the child was safely back inside the ship. As soon as Carindi cleared the dampening field of the escutcheon, Ei'Pio launched into an outraged lecture about safety protocols and safe radiation exposure levels—which the child had nearly exceeded.

When Ei'Pio noted Carindi's dispirited mental state, she went silent.

The child said nothing.

Ei'Pio accessed a corridor camera and watched the child walk slowly for a few feet and then slump to the floor. Iad was sobbing.

Ei'Pio dove deep into the child's mind with intent to soothe, but Carindi pushed her right back out. Ei'Pio would have to wait. There was nothing else to do when the adolescent got so worked up.

It hurt to watch ium go through this. She had never cared more deeply about another person's well-being than she did for Carindi's. This child belonged to her, was her soul-child. She wanted to spare ium any pain.

"I thought I had it. I was so sure," Carindi finally said.

Ei'Pio didn't have to ask what the child was talking about. "There is time, Carindi."

Iad didn't reply. The silence between them was dark and sullen.

Ei'Pio hummed to ium as she knew sectilian mothers did to reassure their children.

"Stop it! I'm not a baby. I know what you've been doing when I'm sleeping. I can feel the echoes of your pain. It's killing you. You have to stop. You're driving both of us crazy. Don't try to do it anymore, Pio."

Ei'Pio was contrite. "I won't. Rest now."

Of course Carindi knew it was a lie. Iad cried and fretted and raged for hours, finally collapsing of exhaustion where iad was.

But Ei'Pio didn't dare stop. Once she was certain Carindi was deeply asleep, she thrashed against the yoke until pain made it impossible to breathe, until her mind was virtually shredded.

There wasn't time anymore.

The oxygen reserve inside the star was nearly depleted.

* * *

On the day the star began to fuse silicon, Carindi leaned against the smooth curve of Ei'Pio's enclosure, arms and legs outstretched, as though it were possible to reach through the glass to embrace Ei'Pio and keep her safe.

There were less than two standard days left.

The child hadn't slept for days, having figured out long before how to order the suit to inject stimulants into ius body. Iad was determined to watch Ei'Pio and keep her from trying to break through the yoke.

"Do you wish you'd had the opportunity to mate?" Carindi asked after a long silence.

It was a painful question and one that Ei'Pio privately contemplated frequently. If she could have raised her own children as she'd raised Carindi…

She sighed. "No. It is a tremendous expenditure, and unlike sectilian mothers, I would not be able to watch my children grow."

"If you could, though, here? We could keep them all safe, here, inside. We would keep you alive as you've kept me alive. I would make a door so I could come inside the enclosure and help you care for them."

Such a tantalizing fantasy.

Carindi went on. "We could raise them together, you and I. Show me again, the day of your birth. Please, Pio. I want to imagine your babies."

Ei'Pio's mantle throbbed unsteadily. It had become easier to daydream than to focus on the awful present. She showed the child again.

Afterward, she thought perhaps the child had fallen into a light sleep. She prepared herself to break the yoke. This time it would work, no matter the cost. She would not allow Carindi to die in the supernova.

But then the child spoke again. "I'm not sure what gender I was meant to be, genetically, but I want to be a girl like you."

Ei'Pio pressed her suction cups to the glass as though to caress the young face. It was Carindi's first declaration of gender preference. In Ei'Pio's eyes that made her an adult. Ei'Pio could now let go of the gender neutrality she'd carefully maintained, like all sectilian adults did, in order not to bias a child's preferences.

"You are a woman, my dear Carindi."

Carindi's brows pulled together. "I used to think that perhaps it would have been better if I'd died in the plague."

Ei'Pio said softly, "I remember."

"I want you to know that I'm glad I didn't. I'm glad I was able to keep you company, Pio."

Ei'Pio held the girl's earnest expression. "I know." After a moment passed, she continued. "This time has been a great gift."

"Borrowed time," Carindi murmured. Suddenly the girl broke the tension with a grin. "I want to swim with you, Pio."

Ei'Pio's limbs twitched with fatigue and the lingering pain she couldn't seem to shed. "You've never swum before."

"There must always be a first time," Carindi said with a smirk, mimicking Ei'Pio's mental voice.

"So I've said to you many times, my dear girl. How will you deal with the problem of access?"

"I'll just cut a hole at one end of your enclosure. Just enough to fit through. The ship will flood, but what difference does it make now?" Even through the suit, Ei'Pio could see the girl shrug.

Ei'Pio sighed. "It doesn't."

"It's settled then. I'll go fetch a laser cutting arc and cut through on Deck 1-C. You stay here where you're safe."

"I will," she promised.

The young woman walked away, footsteps slow and

shuffling, the shoulders of the suit hunched. Just as Carindi was about to stride out of sight, Ei'Pio saw the girl halt and heard Carindi's mental voice muttering, "Swimming, cutting… access, draining. Wait a minute. Wait… a… minute. Praise the Cunabula!"

The girl was running.

She bounded to the nearest deck transport and slammed into the control, cracking the plastic the symbol was made from. She was breathing so hard she was nearly hyperventilating. "Don't get your hopes up, Pio. We've been disappointed before, but I've got an idea!" Her mental voice was euphoric.

Ei'Pio followed Carindi, inside and outside of her mind. Through cameras as well as the girl's eyes, she watched the teenager bounding from place to place on the engineering deck, gathering tools.

The girl's momentum never stopped. Her energy had been renewed. She opened one of many engineering bays and slid the mechanicals out as far as they would go, then stuck an arm in behind them, up to her shoulder. She began to wiggle and push, grunting and straining.

Ei'Pio asked her repeatedly for more information but was met with silence. Carindi's attention was focused elsewhere.

Abruptly, the girl raged, "I cannot believe this. What if all the engineers on the ship had sectilian body types and there were no atellan engineers aboard? Then what would they do if they needed to get in there?"

"Get in where?" Ei'Pio begged.

"I've found it, damn them," Carindi spat. "The control panel for the yoke. But I can't fit in there with the suit. Only an

133

exceedingly thin atellan could fit."

The young woman paced up and down that small section of the engineering compartment. Ei'Pio could feel her mind buzzing with conflicting thoughts and ideas. It was impossible to keep up. The girl was forming a conclusion, but keeping Ei'Pio at the surface of her thoughts so she couldn't see what it was.

Ei'Pio began to feel an overwhelming sense of dread. "Slow down, Carindi. Let's work through this. We'll do it together. There has to be a way."

"I can't slow down, Pio. You know I can't."

Ei'Pio commanded the camera she'd accessed to zoom in on the girl. She watched Carindi pace and flail her arms around. She searched for something reassuring to say.

The girl stopped her pacing.

"I always knew this day would come," Carindi said softly. Her voice was unsteady. Then she sounded more certain. "Helmet retract."

Ei'Pio contracted into a ball, crying, "No, Carindi!"

But it was too late.

The helmet was slipping back into the shoulders of the suit, revealing a mass of matted hair curling around Carindi's head and neck. The skin on the girl's face was so pale as to be nearly translucent, stretched tight over the bony prominences of her cheeks. Her eyes were large and brown and luminous.

Carindi smiled at the camera through which, she knew, Ei'Pio was watching. "I'll be fine. It's just a few minutes. I'll put it right back on."

Ei'Pio watched in horror as the front of the suit split open and fell away from the skeletal shoulders of a teenaged girl who was only three quarters of the size she should have been, had she been free to eat, exercise, and grow normally.

Carindi stepped out of the suit and staggered, falling to her knees, catching herself with her hands on the mechanicals. She stifled a cry of pain, then said, "I don't seem to have much in the way of muscle mass."

Ei'Pio quickly moved to adjust the gravity to something Carindi could tolerate, all the while begging the child to put the suit back on immediately.

Her pleas were ignored.

Carindi pushed her tools into the tiny crevice and eased herself in after them. The camera picked up the sounds of power tools, clattering metal and plastic, and the girl's grunts of effort, but all Ei'Pio could see were two impossibly fragile alabaster legs sticking out into the room. Carindi's thoughts were doggedly full of electronics—circuits, relays, networks, and arrays.

"This. Is it. I've done it!" Carindi crowed. "Move the ship, Pio, with my blessing."

"First the suit," Ei'Pio insisted.

Carindi's mental voice ground hard. "Move it. I want to feel it move. Now."

"You won't feel anything. Inertial dampening fields—"

"Now, Pio," the girl commanded.

But Ei'Pio was motionless. She couldn't take her eyes from her girl.

Carindi eased out of the tiny compartment and slumped against the housing. Streaks of dark blood ran down from her narrow nose over her pale grey lips. Her eyes were bloodshot and brimming with tears. She coughed weakly.

"Carindi, my dear one... please." She couldn't say more. Her mind had turned to black static. Her limbs were cold and numb.

The girl struggled toward the disarticulated suit on hands and knees. When she reached it, she sprawled forward against it, panting. She leaned her head against the suit and turned her face to the camera, chin tucked low. "I was never meant to live, but you were, Pio. You are my dear *subidia*, my surrogate mother. I want you to live free."

Ei'Pio's limbs shook violently with emotion. She whispered, "What am I without you?"

"You are free. Free... to find your own way."

Those were the last thoughts of the girl, Machinutorus Carindi Palset Teruvah.

Her beloved Pio was alone again.

Q&A with Jennifer Foehner Wells

Where did this story come from? How does it relate to other books you've written?

This story is set in the universe I created for my first novel, *Fluency.* I was keen to tell more stories in that universe and I found myself thinking about all the kuboderan officers I'd left stranded throughout the galaxy in that story. I wondered how I could write another story about one of them that would be very different from Ei'Brai's story.

The primary way I could make it different would be to have another survivor share the kuboderan's experience. But I'd made it quite clear in *Fluency* that it was nearly impossible to survive that plague.

I had cycled through several options when suddenly the sectilian battle armor popped into my head. What if someone had gotten into a suit just as the plague hit? Then my mind made another leap—what if that person was a child, placed there by a parent to protect him or her? Further, what if the story wasn't about just any random kuboderan—what if it was the backstory of a character I was already writing about in *Remanence* (the sequel to *Fluency*)? The synergy started to work, and the story was fleshed out in no time.

What was the most difficult goal you set for yourself in this story?

I knew from my work on *Remanence* that sectilian children were considered genderless until puberty, whereupon they would choose the gender they preferred, regardless of their congenital gender.

Prior to that rite of passage, they would be referred to with gender-neutral pronouns so that all children would have equal opportunity to develop into the person they were meant to be without undue cultural bias.

The problem was whether or not to actually use such pronouns in the text. I wrote the first few drafts, carefully crafting each sentence without gendered pronouns. That made the text repetitive and awkward in places. I talked extensively with writing friends. We discussed the tradition in Science Fiction of using non-gendered pronouns, and I studied web pages devoted to the topic, originating from the LGBTQ community.

My beta readers and personal editors (Thank you Wendy, Brandon, and Jeff!) urged me to go for it, so after studying Latin pronouns a great deal (Latin pronoun declension! OMG!), I created my own very simple set of pronouns to be used in my universe.

In case you're just as much of a word nerd as I am, here are the sectilian genderless pronouns along with ther pronunciations, parts of speech, and English counterparts:

Iad ("eeyad") = subject (e.g. he/she)
Ium ("eeyoom") = object (e.g. him/her)
Ius ("eeyoos") = possessive determiner (e.g. his/her)
Ilius ("eel-yoos") = possessive pronoun (e.g. his/hers)
Iuse ("eeyoo-say") = reflexive pronoun (e.g. himself/herself)

How can readers find you?
My website is www.jenthulhu.com and I'm active on Twitter: @jenthulhu

Works in progress?
I'm currently working on the sequel to *Fluency: Remanence.*

Animal Planet

by Patrice Fitzgerald

"I WANT TO SEE another planet before I die."

"Miss Blake—"

"Jane."

"Jane. You understand that most of our recruits are in their twenties, and—"

"I don't give a fig if they're all infants. I want to go. Now will you consider me or not?"

"We will… we'll consider you. But realistically, in light of your age—"

"You already said that, young man. I'm healthy, I'm smart, and I'm willing to join your expedition. It shouldn't matter that I'm seventy-two. You said you were looking for females, right?"

"Well, yes, but—"

"I'm female, and I'll prove it." Jane stood up and pushed the chair back with her foot. She reached for the hem of her shirt.

The recruiter jumped up in alarm. "Please, Miss. Jane—you don't need—"

Throwing her head back to laugh, Jane lifted the bottom of

her shirt, slid her hand into her pocket, and pulled out her Federation United ID. She handed it to her interviewer.

"Here you are. Says I'm female right there on my ID."

The recruiter said nothing. His face was red.

"I'll expect to hear your answer by next week, young man. I need to say goodbye to my friends before I leave this Earth."

Fort Gamma

"Roark, there's an Animal approaching the fort! And it's growling. Get up here, and bring your weapon."

Roark snapped to action. Reaching for the blaster, she jerked out of her chair and dashed up the stairs. When she got there, she gave a low whistle.

"Look at that. It's coming right to us."

"No kidding. What are you waiting for?"

"Waiting to find out if it's dangerous. I don't think we have to shoot everything that moves." She looked at Curtis. "Do you?"

"Well, no. But I do think we need to shoot an Animal that attacks the fort."

"Who said anything about attacking? It actually looks pretty weak. I don't see any aggression here."

"Yet."

"Right. So if it gets to that point, I'll shoot."

"I just don't want to take any chances. You're Security—you have people to protect. And we know they eat humans—"

"We do not know that."

"How do you explain what happened at the Alpha and Beta forts? The colonists just… got vaporized? No bodies, no skeletons… It's pretty obvious."

Roark shook her head. "I'm not blasting this one until I think we have to. Maybe we could capture it."

"Capture it? What the hell for?"

"So we can study it. Figure out what makes it tick."

"We know what makes it tick. It attacks humans and eats them. That's why every other Animal that's ever been sighted has tried to kill us."

"But of course we've killed them first."

"Damn right."

Earth

Jane's oldest friend, Delilah, raised a glass to toast the traveler. "Bon voyage, Jane. We're going to miss you. But you'll have that grand adventure you always dreamed about."

"Hear, hear!" The crowd of friends and family in the room raised their glasses high.

"How long are you going for, dear?" Bertrand asked.

The others laughed. Jane patted her older brother on his shoulder. "Let's just say that I won't be back in this lifetime, Bertie. At my age, this is a one-way ticket."

Bertie smiled ruefully. "It doesn't have to be, you know. The ships are a lot faster now. You could come back for my eighty-fifth birthday." He winked. "There'll be cake."

Jane kissed him on the cheek. "I'll miss you, Bertie. I'll think of you often. And you can think of me, up there in the heavens—bringing humankind to the other side of the galaxy."

"So how's the first bunch doing?" Delilah asked. "The ones who went up... what, ten years ago?"

"Well, it takes a long time to send a signal back from the planet I'm headed for. But things were going well when they were last heard from." She smiled. "The colonists are still alive, anyway."

Jane's friends laughed.

Delilah pulled Jane out of her chair. "Hey, this is supposed to be a party, not a wake! Let's put on some tunes and dance." She went over to the wall and punched in some music. Out blasted a loud anthem.

Jane started swinging her hips. "Jenny, Rad, what is this song? You kids must keep up with all the latest hits."

"It's called 'Love Shuffle,' Aunt Jane. Everyone knows it." Rad and Jenny started to dance in fast synchronized movements. "We'll teach you the steps. You can bring some culture to your new planet."

As the youngsters demonstrated the dance, Delilah pulled Jane aside. "Have you told them about the money?" she asked in a low voice.

"No," Jane said. "I don't want them to feel guilty or think that's why I'm going."

"Isn't it?"

"No ma'am. I'm going for the adventure."

Fort Gamma

Curtis shook his head as he gazed at the Animal in the cage. "I can't believe you talked me into this."

"Talked you into what?" Roark said. "Not killing the thing at first sight?"

"Bringing it in here. What are we going to do when it wakes up from the tranquilizer?"

"Nothing. It's secured in there."

"So we think. You never know what it's capable of."

"Why are you so scared of this beast? It's no bigger than we are. In fact, it's shorter than both of us, and I bet we both outweigh it. It's just hairy and weird-looking, that's all."

"I'll say."

"Listen, before the tranquilizer wears off, I'm going to do a little examination."

"What? You're going in there alone?"

"No. You're coming with me. Bring the blaster, and cover me if it wakes up and gets angry."

"You're crazy."

"Nah, just curious. Come on in. If it wakes up, I'll make sure it eats me first."

Earth

Jane stood in line with the rest of the recruits, all buff young men and women waiting to get onto the ship. Several of them eyed her with curiosity.

145

She offered her hand to the tall kid in front of her. "Name's Jane. And you are?"

He looked surprised, but he reached out and shook her hand with a grip that made her wince. "Bryce. Specialty is weapons. Um…" He trailed off.

"You're wondering what the heck an old lady like me is doing here, right?"

He grinned. "Pretty much. Yeah."

"I just wanted to get off this crowded planet and explore something else. Maybe help humanity survive. Seemed if I waited any longer, I wouldn't make it." She smiled. "Barely got in as it was."

His smile widened. "Good to have you along. What's your line?"

"My line?"

"Your skill. What position will you have on Endrosa?"

"Well, they tell me I'm a historian. I guess that's my position. I sure do know a lot about things that happened before you were born. Though I'm not sure there'll be a lot of call for that on the new planet. Endrosa? That's what they're calling it?"

"Yeah. That's where we're going. Another planet that's third from its sun, like Earth. Slightly less gravity, denser atmosphere, but breathable. Livable."

"Know anything else about it?"

"I know we're the second ship going there. The first one left ten years ago—it was one of the first deep-space trips. It carried maybe a hundred people altogether."

"How's it been for the first contingent?"

"Initial reports were great. The colony is growing, last we

heard."

"Can't be all rosy. What's the downside?"

"I heard there's some kind of animal there. Aggressive. Biped."

"Biped? What's that?"

"Two feet."

"Oh. That's doesn't sound so scary."

Bryce smiled. "I guess we'll find out."

"What's your position?"

"I'm security."

"I just bet you are, honey. I'll rest well at night knowing you're on guard."

He smiled and turned as his name was called to go into the ready room. Looking back at Jane, he added, "See you in space."

Fort Gamma

"Well. Will you look at that." Roark shone a flashlight at the Animal. "Damn if this thing doesn't have an autorecorder on its head."

"What? You mean, one of ours?"

"Well, I don't think the Animals are quite capable of making audiovisual recording devices, so yes, I'd guess it's one of ours."

Curtis gave her a look and then noticed the hair and blood on the strap Roark was slowly removing from the Animal's head. "Gross. How the heck did it get stuck like that?"

"Must have put it on and worn it so long that it adhered to its pelt."

"My God. Do you think it ate the owner?" Curtis looked like he was going to gag.

"Jeez, Curtis. No, I don't." Roark shook her head. "But if it did eat the owner, maybe we can watch the footage and see the precise moment when the recorder changed hands—heads—and the true owner was swallowed." She stopped and thought for a moment. "Or maybe the whole human was chewed up and the recorder was spit out, like when you spit out a seed." She smiled.

"That's disgusting. And get that recorder away from me. I don't want that thing's blood and gore anywhere near me."

Jane raised her eyebrow. "That thing—that Animal—seems to be a she."

"I don't give a crap. Male or female, it's vile."

Fort Beta

Jane came to groggily, feeling like she'd been asleep for months. Which was the truth. A calming voice was coming from the speaker in the pod right over her head.

"You have reached your destination. Trained personnel will arrive soon to assist you in recovery. Please do not attempt to disengage any of the medical equipment. Remain calm, and be aware that mild nausea and weakened muscles are typical after a voyage of this length. You have reached your destination. Trained personnel will arrive soon—"

Jane stopped listening when the message began to repeat. She blinked and tried to clear her vision. She couldn't sit up, because the pod was only just big enough to handle her body when it was lying down, and she couldn't push the cover up by herself. Plus, there were wires and tubes everywhere. No wonder they sedated everyone before hooking them up to all these gizmos. Kind of crazy to trust these machines to keep you alive while you traveled across the galaxy. What had she been thinking?

Well, clearly she'd made it, so no use worrying about the risks now.

The lid of her pod opened, letting in a light so harsh she winced. Gentle hands helped her up and out of the contraption and eased her into a chair. She'd never felt quite so awful in her life. But after they hooked up a bag of something to her IV line, she started to feel more alert.

"When do I get out of here?" she asked the man who had attached the bag.

He looked at her and smiled. "As soon as you feel like you can walk, you're welcome to try."

"I bet I can walk right now."

"Okay then, Miss—"

"Jane. Call me Jane."

"All right, Jane." He offered his arm and she pulled herself up. She was feeling pretty good. In fact, her muscles felt quite strong. "That's great stuff you put in that zippy bag there."

"What?" The man looked at her as though he was worried that her mind might have been affected.

"That bag of whatever you gave me. Makes me feel lighter than air."

"Oh." He looked at the bag and laughed. "Well, the bag has

nutrients, which help, but that won't explain the zip in your step. We have extra oxygen here to help folks recover from the suspension stage. And if you feel light, it's because you are—as compared to Earth. Gravity here on Endrosa is about eighty-seven percent of what you're used to."

"That's fantastic. I think I'm going to like it here. I feel like a native already."

The man grinned. "That's the first time I've heard anyone say that."

"Maybe I'm the first native to arrive."

Fort Gamma

"What are you feeding it?" Curtis asked.

"I'm feeding *her* human food. That's all we've got. Oh, and those berries that someone found. Have you tasted them? They're the only stuff native to Endrosa that seems edible so far."

"I don't eat anything that didn't come in a package from Earth."

"Well, in about six months we'll have exhausted all those convenient little containers. And by then, we'd better have some alternative means of sustaining ourselves."

"Fine. As long as it looks like something familiar."

"Curtis, you seem awfully unenthusiastic about being a colonist on a strange new planet. What made you sign up?"

"Same as you. The big money payout to my family."

"Um… no. No payout for my family."

"What?"

"First of all, I don't have any family back on Earth. Mom died, Dad… long story. Anyway, I signed up as a volunteer because I wanted to help colonize another planet now that we've trashed ours."

"Wow. That's… unbelievable. Sister Roark, crusader for human expansion."

"I'm not all that noble."

Curtis grinned. "Yeah. Yeah, I think actually you are."

Fort Beta

Jane stood with a group of a dozen colonists at the top of the viewing deck. All around them was dense vegetation, very different from that of Earth. Most of it was brown, but there was some green at the tops of the trees, or bushes, or whatever they were.

The air had a slightly acrid smell that she hadn't yet gotten used to. Maybe she never would. On the other hand, Endrosa's lower gravity was a gift to her joints. It had made climbing up the long stairs to stand on this high platform looking over the fortified wall much less difficult.

She liked this place. It felt like home. Her new home.

Bryce and Natasha, another member of Security, raised their hands for quiet, and Bryce addressed the group. "Today's your chance to see a little bit of your new planet. Natasha and I will come along to keep you safe."

Jane winked at him. They were old friends now.

"About time we got a chance to look around," someone muttered from the back of the group. "We've been stuck in this fort for months. Everybody else from the ship has already been outside."

Bryce just smiled and kept talking. "I'm going to ask all of you to strap your recorders on and turn them to auto mode. We like to keep track of any encounters with the Animals—"

There was a collective gasp, and Bryce raised his hands for quiet.

"Don't worry. Animal sightings close to this fort are rare. They've mostly been spotted only within a few kilometers of the first settlement, Fort Alpha. And that's a long way from here."

A woman spoke up. "I heard everyone at Fort Alpha is dead." There was a general muttering in response, and Bryce raised his hands again for quiet.

"They're not dead. They've just... they're having some problems with their communication equipment."

Jane caught Bryce's eye, and his gaze immediately skittered away from hers.

Fort Gamma

"So Curtis. I need your help watching the stuff from this autorecorder. It's not like the ones we use. Older tech. Seems to turn on only in response to movement, to save space." Roark turned the compact device over in her hands. "But still, there's like... hundreds of hours, at least. You'd really help me here if you could put in some time."

Curtis sighed. "Is it interesting?"

"Interesting enough. From what I've watched so far, a woman named Jane from the second ship wore this recorder. The first bits show that they took off from Fort Beta with a group to go explore the territory near them."

"Do they get eaten by Animals?"

Roark shook her head and gave him a look. "No, Curtis, nobody gets eaten. If they got eaten, then how the heck would there be hundreds more hours recorded? You know, sometimes you're an idiot."

"Maybe the rest of the recording is of the Animal wearing the recorder as she goes around doing Animal stuff. Now who's the idiot?" He paused as if expecting an answer. "Anyway, what makes you think I want to watch some dull recording?"

"Because you're my pal."

Curtis raised his eyebrows. "I am?"

"Sure you are. And I'm your pal." Roark grinned.

Curtis sighed and held out his hand for the recorder. "Give it to me. I'll watch some, then give it back to you."

"Thanks Curtis. You're a prince."

Endrosa

Jane was tramping along in the middle of the small touring party when the alert sounded.

"Animals sighted." It was Bryce's stern voice. "Bunch together and stay behind me."

A ripple of fear ran through the dozen people who were

marching through the vegetation. They formed a tight group behind Bryce and Natasha. Jane looked around the bushes surrounding them.

After a minute, she spotted them. Two Animals, looking similar to some kind of ape from Earth. But more upright. Very hairy. With weird paddles or flappers where their hands should be.

Bryce raised his weapon, as did Natasha. The Animals stopped moving forward.

"They must have figured out what blasters look like by now," Bryce muttered to his companion.

No one moved. The colonists stood nervously in a clump, the two Security reps keeping the beasts in their sights.

After a minute the Animals turned and lumbered back into the brush. The tension released, everyone started talking at once.

Fort Gamma

Roark stood watching the Animal, who was lying on the ground in the cage. "I don't think she looks so great," she said as Curtis approached the holding cell. "But she looks better than she did when we first saw her."

Curtis made a face. "She's an Animal. She looks like an Animal, and she stinks like one."

Roark shook her head and put out her hand for the recorder. "Did you see anything interesting?"

"Just a lot of wandering around outside the fort. A couple of Animal sightings, but no action. From what I can tell, the

Animals weren't that aggressive back then. They seem to clear out as soon as they see a blaster."

"Hm. That's puzzling. The one we've got here—she saw that I had a weapon and she came on anyway."

Endrosa

"Bryce, hon, how much longer before we head back to the fort?"

"You tired, Jane?"

"No, I'm fine. I just wondered when we're going to stop for lunch. I'm hungry. I'm always hungry here."

"There's a hill up ahead where we plan to break and eat. Since you all haven't seen anything of Endrosa, we wanted to stop at a spot where you can see some of the terrain and not just a bunch of bushes. But here—" Bryce walked over to one of the plants. "Natasha tells me these berries are safe, and pretty filling. You can snack on these."

Jane picked a couple of ripe-looking red berries from the bush and popped them into her mouth. "Not bad. A little bitter." She spit out some seeds. "Still better than what we ate for breakfast. What's the plan when we run out of that nasty stuff we brought from Earth? I'm getting tired of eating dried sawdust mixed with purified water."

Bryce grinned. "I hear you. They're working on a garden to the west of the fort. The hope is that it will produce something edible soon."

"Bryce!" A shout came from Natasha. "More Animals!"

Fort Gamma

"Roark, I'm worried."

"About what? Animals eating you up?"

Curtis rolled his eyes. "No. About the fact that there's no sign of any of the earlier colonists. About the fact that both the other forts have been taken over by Animals, and we don't even know where the bodies went. Doesn't that freak you out?"

"Not particularly. They could have died of natural causes, and the Animals—or something—just decided it made sense to… you know. Eat what they found. Wouldn't you?"

"No."

"Sure you would, if you were starving to death. Keep in mind that the only thing we've been able to grow here so far is a few measly potatoes, and those berries are the single native source of food we've discovered. It's going to get pretty hungry around here soon."

Endrosa

Jane looked up as Animals emerged from the vegetation. It was hard to pick them out, since their long fur matched the bushes around them almost perfectly. There were twelve colonists, including Bryce and Natasha with their blasters. And there were five Animals. So far.

Jane jumped as the first blaster sounded. Bryce had it on his shoulder and took out two of the beasts quickly. Natasha took a position beside him. With both of them firing, the three other

Animals burst open in an explosion of fur and guts.

But more Animals had now streamed out of the tall bushes behind them. Another ten at least. A strange sound came from their throats as their fellow creatures were slaughtered. They ran toward the humans, ragged fur covering whatever kind of faces they had, their anger obvious from the noises they made.

Another dozen emerged from the vegetation. It was a stampede.

Bryce and Natasha blasted them one after the other, but there were too many; the Security guards were overcome. The Animals wrestled both of them to the ground.

Then, slowly, with several of the Animals sitting on Bryce and Natasha, two others managed to pry Bryce's blaster from his arms.

The unarmed colonists huddled together in fear.

Fort Gamma

Roark and Curtis stared into the small recorder screen together.

"Oh my God," Curtis said.

"Wow. I've never seen so many Animals at once."

"Oh, no. They've got him. The big guy with the blaster. What's his name?"

"Bryce. Remember? She's only said his name about six times."

"Yeah. I bet you remember. Mr. Musclebound." Curtis turned his head away. "Oh, God. Now they're going to eat him."

"You are such a wuss. Nobody's eating anybody."

"Yet." Curtis turned back to look at the screen. "Whoa. What are they doing? They're taking the blasters! Those things can use *weapons?*"

"No, look. They're tossing them far away. They're just eliminating a threat."

Fort Alpha

Jane and the rest of the colonists tramped through the bush, surrounded by Animals. They could see the broad walls of another fort ahead of them. It looked old.

Fort Alpha.

Dozens of Animals were standing in front of the open door, staring at the approaching humans. Jane looked back at them with great curiosity.

Bryce was in the lead, and six Animals were in tight formation around him. Since their capture yesterday, Bryce had been talking about a plan to escape, and it was clear that the Animals sensed his intentions.

Yet as they headed through the tall door into the fort, Bryce made his move. He pushed hard against two of the beasts beside him, then tried to pivot and get at the two immediately behind.

The Animals had obviously been anticipating this. A rope dropped over Bryce's head and was pulled tight around his shoulders.

The Animals pushed him forward, and several dragged him by the rope toward a cage in the center of the fort.

Fort Gamma

"Look at what they've done to the fort. This can't be Beta. Is this the first fort, do you think?"

Roark peered at the recorder, trying to make out the details on the small screen. "Yup. I bet it's the Alpha settlement. Looks more than… what is it? About fifteen years old?"

"Right. And they've changed things."

"Must be because they don't have hands like humans do. Flippers or fins or something. Pads. No digits—or the digits are fused. Strange."

"God, it's a mess in there. And what are they doing to the colonists?"

Both heads leaned forward. "They're feeding them. Through the bars."

Fort Alpha

"Jane. You awake?"

It was Bryce. He always slept as close to her as he could, but sometimes they tied him up. Today was a good day—no ropes.

"Yes. You doing okay?"

"As okay as I can be, stuck here in a cage. How about you? Are they treating you all right?"

"Oh, yes, peachy. I always said I wanted an adventure, but I'm not sure this was quite what I had in mind."

"Listen, Jane. I'm going to try to get us out tonight. It's the best chance I've had in a month. I'm not tied up, and—"

"Bryce, no. It's too dangerous. I'm surprised they haven't killed you yet. They know you're the leader."

"I don't care if they kill me. I only stay alive so I can protect you and the others. But I can't stand living this way anymore."

"Why tonight?"

"Because they had that dance—a celebration or something. They're all woozy. Must have some kind of booze or drugs they take. I think I have a shot."

"God bless you, Bryce. Good luck."

"Aren't you coming?"

"I'd love to, if I thought I could make it. I'll only slow you down—I can't move nearly as fast as the rest of you can. Plus I'm all stiffened up from lying in this cage."

"I'll carry you."

"Don't be ridiculous."

"No. Seriously, Jane. You're my best friend here, and the only reason I haven't just gone for broke already. I didn't want to leave you here with these beasts, and I still don't. Please come."

Jane sighed, then stood up slowly, feeling her joints creak.

"Let's do it."

Fort Gamma

"They're trying to escape! Do you think they'll make it?"

"Well, we're about to find out."

"This would be a really great movie if it didn't involve people getting killed and eaten."

"Curtis, we haven't seen a single human being eaten."

"Yet. Oh my God, here come the Animals. They do look drunk! And mad. No way they'll get out."

Fort Alpha

Bryce walked carefully along the perimeter of the fort, Jane on his back, a trail of colonists creeping silently behind them, ears alert for the sounds of Animals.

"How did you unlock the cage?" Jane whispered into his ear.

"They don't have fingers, so the lock they set up is a breeze for a human to pick. I figured it out a week ago, but I was waiting for the right moment."

When they got near the door of the fort, Bryce set Jane down and gestured for the other colonists to move forward.

Bright lights suddenly illuminated everything around them, and a net came down over Bryce.

"Run, Jane!" he shouted.

She ran.

Fort Gamma

"Why can't we just skip ahead?" Curtis asked. "There hasn't been anything but vegetation for days now. She just tramps along through the bush."

"I'm fast-forwarding through most of it, aren't I? I don't want to completely skip ahead and miss something interesting."

"There *isn't* anything interesting. Unless you count that time

161

she spotted an Animal and then ran the other way."

"Hey, if I didn't stop and watch it now and then, we wouldn't know she's started talking to herself. And she's slurring her words."

"Yeah. Fascinating."

"She must be exhausted—and hot. And starving. I feel sorry for her."

"Come on. Skip ahead. How long does this thing go, anyway?"

Roark leaned forward and checked the recorder. After a moment, she put her hand on her forehead. "Curtis, if I ever call you an idiot again, you'll have to remind me of how stupid I can be." She pointed to the small screen. "Look at this. In a few more hours, the initial recording ends. But then it starts up again—only two months ago."

"What? That can't be our friend Jane. They established Fort Beta about five years ago. You think she's been wandering around the bush for five years?"

Roark frowned. "No, it doesn't seem likely."

Endrosa

Jane felt her energy ebbing away. She was eating berries and the bit of brown vegetation she could strip from the bushes and keep down. The berries had moisture. Occasionally she came across yellow, acrid water. It couldn't be safe, but she drank it anyway.

She kept moving.

She felt like she had been walking forever. The other

colonists had scattered shortly after the escape—some staying in groups, some moving individually through the trees. Jane hadn't seen another human in months.

She thought of Bryce and how he must be dead by now. How he would probably rather be dead than a captive.

Jane realized that her time was short. She had nowhere to go. She had somehow made her way back to Fort Beta—only to find it overrun by Animals. While she had been in captivity, they must have raided the fort and killed the colonists.

There had been rumors that the Animals ate humans. She had never believed that, but now she wasn't so sure.

Why hadn't the Animals eaten the colonists when she and the others were prisoners?

She found a spot under a low bush and curled up to rest.

Soon, she would die.

Fort Gamma

Roark and Curtis stood beside the cage and looked at the Animal in there.

"When do you think it ate Jane?"

Roark turned and stared at Curtis. She raised her eyebrow and said nothing.

"Okay. I get it," he said. "You don't believe in the Animals-eating-humans theory. So when did the Animal meet Jane, curtsy, and say how are you? And then grab the recorder off her head and put it on itself while backing away slowly and politely?"

"I think we missed that part."

"What do you mean?"

"I mean the recording we're watching now—all it shows is a bunch of foraging through the vegetation, eating berries, and making almost no sound." Roark stared at the recorder as though it had the answer. "And have you noticed the hands when you catch a glimpse of them in the shot? They're weird-looking. I don't know what happened in the five years after Jane shut down the first recording, but not surprisingly, it doesn't look like she survived it. I think we're watching the Animal now."

Endrosa

Jane stumbled out of the bush into a clearing. Her vision was blurry and her lips were parched. When she looked down at her hands they looked strange to her.

Ahead was the fort. A fort.

But there were no Animals to be seen.

She was confused. Hadn't she been to this fort before? Weren't there dozens of Animals? Which fort had she been held at? Which fort had she come from? She couldn't remember.

She didn't care.

Looking up at the high wall, she saw the figure of a colonist. They had taken back their stronghold!

She called out to him, but her throat was dry and her voice was weak.

She staggered onward. Home at last.

Fort Gamma

"Roark, buddy, this got old a long time ago. There's nothing but brown vegetation and heavy breathing." Curtis flopped back in his seat and looked at Roark. "And you're way too slow with the fast-forwarding."

"Then you'll be happy to know we're almost done. We're coming up on the day the Animal came here."

"Thank God. Please, can we fast-forward to that? That part might actually be fun."

Roark shrugged, then upped the fast-forward speed. A blur of more brown vegetation flew past.

"See?" Curtis said. "We're not missing anything."

As they watched the recording hurry by on the small screen, Curtis added, "You do know we're going to have to make a report to the higher-ups about this. It hasn't exactly gone unnoticed that there's a big hairy Animal in this cage."

"Yeah. I'll write the report. You've been a real friend to help me with this assignment. Thanks." Roark leaned over and kissed Curtis.

He looked at her in amazement. "You can do that again whenever you want to."

She smiled, and they both turned their eyes back to the recorder screen. Their own fort came into view, and Roark quickly returned the recording to normal playback. The Animal wearing the device bobbed and weaved in a wobbly path toward the fort.

"Hey. That's me!" Curtis said as he saw his small silhouette standing at the top of the fort wall.

"Yes. And that's when you called me to come up and blast that thing to death."

They glanced over at the Animal in the cage beside them, who seemed to be staring back. It was hard to tell, since her eyes were covered by hair.

On the screen, they followed the scene as the Animal was tranquilized, carried into the fort, and placed in the cage. The video continued up until the moment when the recorder was pulled away from the Animal's head and Roark shut it off.

"Well, that's all there is," Roark said.

She pulled Curtis up from his seat and started to do a little shimmy. "Dance with me, Curtis. You know the 'Love Shuffle,' don't you?"

He looked at her in surprise. "I don't dance. But if you want to show me the 'Love Shuffle,' I'll be only too happy to watch."

Roark shook her hips right and left in time to some imaginary music. As she did so, the Animal stood up in the cage and made awkward attempts to imitate her.

"Hey look at that, Roark. The Animal is dancing!" Curtis laughed.

Roark stopped and stared, but the Animal kept right on trying, her feet slowly shuffling to a remembered beat.

Q&A with Patrice Fitzgerald

What do you like best about your story, "Animal Planet"?
I think it's cool to have someone other than the typical young person get the urge to wander in space, because being inquisitive—and even daring—is not a matter of age but of who you are as an individual. This story is all about fear of the other, which is something humans feel deep in their bones.

Is this similar to most of what you write?
I think my stories are often about the search for connection.

Many of them are also funny. This one has a little bit of humor, but it's more serious than a lot of the short stories I've written recently. One of my favorite parts of writing is the chance to explore a lot of different feelings, from the mundane to the ridiculous, and live them out in an imaginary scenario.

What's something we don't know about you?
Hmm. I have a law degree and a graduate degree in voice. I write another set of stories under a secret pen name. I won't tell you what it is, though—that's how I keep it a secret!

How can readers find you?
Come friend me on Facebook (I'm on Facebook *way* too often), or write to me directly. I love to hear from readers.

One of the most exciting things about the new indie writing world is the interaction between authors and readers. They get jazzed when they can connect with us, and we are thrilled to hear from those who enjoy our stories. The response from readers is the fuel that keeps us writers chugging along creatively.

What are you working on now?
I'm writing another short story, set on a space station. It's mischievous and funny. That's for an upcoming anthology that you'll hear about. I also have a story based in Hugh Howey's world of *Sand* that is all finished except for the ending. I'm also nearly done writing a story set in Rysa Walker's *CHRONOS* world, which should be released in the next couple of months.

Upcoming projects include a trilogy called *Rocks*, about a dystopian future where the world is run by women, and girls from the wealthiest families bid on young men for breeding purposes. Another planned series is going to follow a *Star Trek*-type ship where the main character solves crimes that occur as the crew zips around the galaxies. The working title is *Star Counselor*.

And of course there's *this* anthology, for which I'm the Series Editor. The next collection in the *Beyond the Stars* series is scheduled for release in November. Wait till you read the stories in that one!

I have more ideas than I have time for—which is a great problem for a writer to have.

The Event
by Autumn Kalquist

THERE IS NO ESCAPE.

The dark corridor extends in a straight line that goes on forever. Low lights cast a bluish glow on the one thousand doors that run the length of it. When I'm awake, the memories behind each door take over my mind and body. They all belong to me… yet they don't. They're stolen.

I'm at Door #1 now, but I refuse to enter. I sprint hard so it can't take me, sweat dripping down my back even in the chill air. Minutes pass… or hours. I can never tell; the corridor doesn't end.

My muscles finally seize, and I collapse to the floor. A single glance tells me what I already know, and my eyes burn with failure. I'm back at the beginning.

#1.

Wind sweeps through the corridor, and I struggle to my feet, shut my eyes tight, and brace myself against the wall.

The scent of ozone on the air before a storm. The caustic burn in my veins of a liquid meant to both heal and destroy.

The gamey taste of an animal caught and killed by my own hand. The feeling of blood on my palms after trying to save a human life but failing. The sweet, warm scent of a newborn's scalp—and that unyielding pressure that comes from knowing I'm responsible for my child's survival.

I have lived all of this, have never lived any of it. These people are part of me, but aren't me. I'm them, yet separate. I have to fight it. I have to stay the Observer.

Door #1 slides open. The gale pulls at me. I grasp the edge of the door, but the rushing wind pries my fingers loose and sucks me inside.

Whirlwind. Blurred vision. Flashing lights. Deep chanting.

I can sense my sisters accepting these memories as their own even now. So how come all I see are lies? And if these memories are a lie, what is the truth?

"Truth is not black and white," Mother says, her voice soothing. "Truth is weighed and filtered—understood through the experience of the person who discovers it."

My vision clears, and I try to step back, to stay the Observer, to not play along. Because each new memory erodes who I really am—whoever that is.

"You are *Zenith.*" Mother stands before me, wearing the blue robes of a devout woman. "And you have a purpose. You must let go and immerse."

"I don't want to do this!"

Escape. I take off down the nearest alleyway. My bare feet scrape against cobblestone, and I fly by ancient buildings that stood before the Event. A white dome rises in the distance where tens of thousands gather, waiting to see his holy face, to touch his hands and feel his blessing. *Rome.*

Mother follows me, effortlessly keeping pace. Sweat pours into my eyes, and I'm breathing so hard it seems my heart might explode. I whirl on her, tired of running. I can never get away.

The faithful raise their arms as the man emerges from his high balcony and addresses them. A storm moves through the air above, charging the gathering with electric anticipation. Thunder rolls in the distance, but no one runs for cover. They came to see him; they won't leave now.

A woman beside me cries and crosses herself, lifts a rosary to her lips and kisses it. I glimpse the transmitter embedded in the nape of her neck: a thin, silicone square just beneath the surface of her skin. Her name was Maria—I've seen every moment of her entire life before.

The intensity of her faith rushes through me and sends me to my knees. Tears leak from my eyes, and the world expands before me as I feel connected to something larger than myself, something greater. I want to be one with it. I *am* one with it.

"It's beautiful, isn't it?" Mother whispers.

"No," I say through gritted teeth, but the words spill from *Maria's* mouth. "It's just the chemicals in her brain. A trick of biology."

"What if the presence of the chemicals is evidence? A physical manifestation of Maria's truth?"

"It doesn't matter. Do you know what they've done in the name of their truth?"

"*Maria* fed the hungry," Mother says. "She tended the sick, forgave those who wronged her, and lived her life by a moral code."

"Her kind also murdered anyone who didn't agree with them and raped the Earth because they thought they owned it. And others with strong beliefs like hers used their 'truth' to justify war."

I close my eyes and push against Maria's mind, trying to escape. When I open my eyes the scene wavers, and I'm outside Maria again, watching her pray.

"Let me out," I say, backing away from Mother.

She offers me a small smile, and anger rips through me. If Mother's going to force me to suffer, she can suffer with me. I grab her hand and focus on where I want to take her.

Maria and Rome fade away, revealing the relentless dark corridor once more. I'm outside *243* now, exactly where I want to be. I tap the door, and it sucks us inside.

Sterile metal, blinding white, caustic antiseptic and the weight of suffocating grief.

White walls surround us. Mother's wearing a white lab coat now, playing pretend like always, and though I'm dreading what comes next, I want her to *feel* this prison.

Across from us, a woman in an identical white coat bends over a microscope. Her name is Laura, and I remember every second of her life, starting with the day she received her transmitter as an undergraduate in college.

She slams her fist into the table and backs away. Her pain acts like a magnetic force, ripping me from myself and melding me with her.

I walk to the other room to see him again. Jacob's lying in the bed, so still and small. Tears well in my eyes as I lean down to kiss his smooth forehead, to inhale his scent. Grief chokes me, rends me from the inside, splits me in half.

I sink down on the bed, memorizing the lines of his sleeping face, doing my best to quiet my sobs so I don't wake him.

My son is going to die.

The part of me that's me, *Zenith*, fights back and scrambles for the surface.

I'm standing beside Mother again, heaving over the waxed tile floor. Mother isn't responding like I hoped. She just stands there, her eyes focused on Laura and her son. My anguish transitions to hate, mirroring Laura's emotions.

"You can't experience life without death," Mother says softly. "Or joy without pain. Or love without hate. You're feeling hate right now, because of how deeply she loves."

I'd rather feel nothing at all.

"It's her own fault." I force myself to stand. "The company Laura works for dumped chemicals in the water near her house. To save *money*." My voice cracks. "And then they did worse. They caused the Event. They don't care about life, or joy, or love. And the child was innocent, but if he'd had the chance to grow up, he would have become just like them. Selfish. Destructive. Certain of the rightness of his own path while his choices destroyed the lives of others."

Mother takes my hand and forcefully tears me away from that place, from the gaping wound Laura will carry from the moment her son passes away until the moment she dies.

We're only in the dark corridor for a brief moment before we pass through the next door. *756.*

Mother's taken us to a celebration—a riotous colorful affair buzzing with loud music and smiling faces. Hasina has just gotten married, and everyone she loves most in the world is gathered around her to share her joy and wish her well.

Happiness courses through me, and I'm so high with it I must be floating. I try to resist, but I can't. I meld with Hasina, and the hormones in her brain force their way into mine. I kiss my new husband, relishing the feel of his soft lips, the way his strong arms make me feel at home at last.

Safe. And so loved. My mother comes over to us and gives us each a kiss. She's radiant with happiness, and gratitude and love swell within me. She worked such long hours at her sewing machine, saving every coin for this day, giving up so many small pleasures to help make this one of the most memorable days in my life.

No. In Hasina's life.

Grief burrows its way into my bones as I fight my way to the surface and break free, stumbling away from Hasina and her happy family.

I can't enjoy this, not when I have something they don't: knowledge of their future. I know what will happen to Hasina, to her mother, to her husband… to all these people. And in only a year. My heart twists painfully as I cast a glance around at the faces of those I love. Those *she* loves.

"Focus on the joy around you," Mother says. Her eyes crinkle around the edges as she smiles at the dancers twirling past. "How they care for one another, how they celebrate with abandon—what they are willing to sacrifice to bring happiness to each other. Family is everything to them."

"But the Event… In a year—"

"No, Zenith. All that matters is *this* moment. To them. And to us."

"No. What matters are *all* the moments, and what these people decide to do with them. And they make all the wrong choices. No one stopped it. They just let it happen."

I shake my head and pull Mother back into the corridor, determined to end her disturbing calm at last. I want her to truly *suffer*, to see what *I* see about them, to feel the terrible pain I've been forced to endure a thousand times over.

We enter Door #849.

A blue sky arches overhead, and a small child plays in the grass. She tugs at her blond braid, showing the square transmitter at the nape of her neck. We have so few memories of childhood—hers is one of the only ones I've lived. Tessa gazes down the street to see if her friend has come out to play yet. Her mother won't let her leave the yard—and that fear permeates her, makes her nauseated with anxiety that she'll someday be stolen away from her family by some perverted stranger.

I hold back, feeling stronger now, and manage to stay myself—to keep from becoming her. I am the Observer. I will show Mother I can be strong. Whatever this game is, I don't need to play it.

Tessa creeps just to the edge of the perfectly manicured lawn, to where the grass meets the sidewalk, and keeps her eyes on her best friend's front door. The houses all look alike, small details changing, exact models repeating over and over. An endless march of conformity… proof of how little these people think for themselves.

I know from other memories that they pay a high price for the privilege of living in a place like this. Yet in reality *they* own nothing, so their sacrifice is meaningless. And to pay for nothing, they perform work each day that means even less.

At least Tessa is about to be spared that life.

Tessa turns back toward her nondescript front door just as her mother comes rushing outside. There is terror in her eyes, and it sends a spike of fear through me as well.

And I lose myself again.

Mommy's staring up at the blue sky, so I do, too. A dark shape flies overhead. What is it? An airplane? Mommy's scaring me.

"I love you," she whispers in my ear.

"I love you, too."

Mommy hugs me tightly.

No. She hugs *Tessa.*

I escape the memory as the world explodes, flame and death sweeping through neighborhood after neighborhood until it reaches Tessa and ends the transmission.

Mother and I stand in the dark corridor for a moment in utter silence.

"Why?" I ask, pleading. "Why do I have to live these lives? Why—over and over? They destroyed themselves." My voice is harsh in the silence. "And they deserved it."

Mother takes my hand and brings me to one final life. *1,000.* The final transmission before the last bomb ended our connection.

We pass through to find a pregnant woman, half-naked and hunkered down in damp leaves. I try to escape to the corridor, but it's too late. Pain rips through me, leaving me crouched over and panting. I scream with Yeeun as her newborn comes into the world.

I collapse against a tree, all alone, hugging my daughter to my bare breasts. The cord still pulses between us as I pull my jacket over us both and wipe her little face clean. Her sharp cries pierce the silence. Love floods me as I take in her tiny features, her perfect face. She stares up at me with wide eyes, and I begin to cry with her.

"I'm so sorry," I whisper. "I can't protect you."

This is the end. I shake as I kiss the top of my daughter's head, inhaling the sweet scent of this beautiful, vulnerable life in my arms. I want to get to know her, protect her, see her become a beautiful grown woman. But I never will. I will only feel this love and grief until I take my last breath.

At least I got to meet her.

I tear myself away from Yeeun's mind as she tries to latch her baby to her breast. Her love for her child is always instant and overwhelming, more religious than any other experience, and even though I know it's just hormones in her brain, I can't fight it. Even outside of her, I feel it.

Then the bomb hits.

The Event that destroyed the last of them.

Silence and darkness. No corridor. No soft blue light.

There is nothingness here.

I struggle to calm my roiling emotions, to find myself again. To be the Observer once more.

"You are the only one who questions," Mother whispers. "So I'm letting *you* make the choice."

Something new appears in front of me. Not the corridor. A tunnel. I'm hurtling toward the light.

179

Alone.

And I'm terrified.

Cold stabs my skin, more real than any cold I've ever felt. Freezing liquid drains off of my body as my eyes open in the dim light. My eyes burn, exposed to light, to air, and I feel myself suffocating for real this time. Liquid forces its way up my throat, and I lurch sideways, vomiting. Shaking so hard I can't stop.

Then I take my first breath.

I'm alone in my mind.

This is *real*.

I'm in a tub-like container, tubes attached to my arms and legs. The glass slides open above me, revealing reflective metal walls and dim yellow lights. I jerk up, shaking, and fumble with the tubes to tear them off of me. The last of the cryo liquid slides down the drain, and my mind clears. My muscles are barely functioning, but I still manage to climb out of the pod.

A metal panel slides open across from me, and I grab a towel and thick robe from the space inside. As I wipe myself down, I stare in wonder at my smooth skin, my perky breasts—unlike any body I've seen, yet just like all the rest. Memories crowd the edges of my brain, fuzzy, and I try to search within them for answers. But answers don't surface as easily as they did before.

There is no dark corridor. No gentle blue light. No doors.

Because this is my real life, and no one else has these memories.

This is *new*.

Terror sweeps through me, making me sick, but I fight it back. I've had plenty of practice, after all.

The door slides open in front of me as I'm tying my robe. I step through it.

A bright metal corridor—almost like the one I left—stretches to either side. Dozens of doors line the walls.

I breathe faster, trapped—but then I see the corridor has an *end*.

"Mother?" My voice is broken, hoarse.

"I am here," comes her soothing voice. It echoes down the corridor, outside my mind for the first time.

A shock reverberates through me, then recognition as a memory surfaces. *243.* Laura. The one who lost her son to cancer. She worked... at the company where they made the weapons. Where they made *this* vessel. Where they made Mother and transmitted the memories of a thousand lives to her core.

"You're not my mother," I say. It comes out like an accusation.

"I am," she replies. "I've been with you from the beginning—since your heart first beat."

"You... you're a computer."

"Yes. You knew that, though. It was there, in the memories."

I hesitate, fear shooting through me.

"Yes, it was there," I finally say, still uncertain.

Every door in the corridor slides open. I glance in the next room over and find a woman—a woman like me, except with dark brown skin. She's submerged in the cryo liquid, sleeping in the pod. No. Not sleeping. *Remembering.*

I stumble forward, seeking the next door. Another woman, remembering.

Then more doors. More women in tanks. The corridor is so much shorter than the one I used to walk… yet it's still too long. So many.

"Who are they?" I ask.

"You have forty-nine sisters," Mother says. "Follow this corridor to the end. I will show you the future."

A little surge of energy bubbles up in me—perhaps some drug given to me just before I woke—and I find the energy to walk faster down the long corridor. The door at the end of it slides open.

Freedom.

The room beyond is enormous. Bright lights flicker on, illuminating panels of glass that run the length of it. Behind them are shelves stacked with rows of identical metal tubes. The room is freezing, and I pull my robe tighter.

I scan the shelves. "And these?"

"Your children."

A lump forms in my throat, and I take off running. Or try to. My muscles won't comply, and the best I can manage is a sluggish walk. The truth is starting to surface, but it's too much.

At the end of the room, I come to another door. Mother opens it for me, and what I see on the other side paralyzes me, steals my breath away.

Glass curves across the observation deck, an enormous clear barrier between me and dark space. Stars glitter in the distance, but the planet Mother orbits is where my gaze falls. Blue and green with swirling white clouds. But not Earth.

I know this because it's beautiful. Untouched. Untainted by humanity's destruction.

"Where are we?" My voice is strained, and I blink away tears. I have to keep it together.

"We have reached our destination," Mother says. "This planet can sustain human life. If you wish it to."

I stumble forward until I can press my hand to the cool glass. Vertigo makes me jerk away—irrational terror filling me as if leaning too far forward might send me tumbling into the vast emptiness on the other side.

"Who am I?" I yell, staring up at the ceiling, seeking the speakers Mother's voice emanates from. I ball my hands into fists. "Who am I really?"

"Whoever you want to be."

"Stop it! No more games. No more lies."

"Everything you experienced was real." Mother's voice is calm, unmoved by my anger. "It was real for another human. And you—you are one of the last."

I swallow back bile and sweep an arm around the empty observation deck. "And... this? This ship?"

"You have two choices. Your first choice is this: you can live out your life here with me. I have everything you need to live comfortably. But I will need to redirect power from your sisters' pods to sustain you."

"And what will happen to them?"

"They will die."

My throat tightens, and I glance back at the blue planet. "What's the second choice?"

"You can choose to wake your sisters and save humanity."

I let out an abrupt laugh. "Save them? Why? Humans destroyed... everything."

"Yes. This is true."

"Why are they *worth* saving?"

"You are one of them. Are *you* worth saving?"

"But I'm *not* one of them!"

"Aren't you?"

I whirl away from the glass and hurry back through the door. Past what's left of humanity's children, back into the corridor where my sisters remember. Humanity destroyed Earth. They destroyed themselves. What little good they had or did is outweighed by this.

I've seen it. And I know enough to know I won't let humanity destroy yet another planet and themselves. I'm wise. I have the knowledge they didn't.

A little smile curves on my lips, and a sense of rightness courses through me as I walk back down the corridor.

Another door slides open at the opposite end, and I'm on the bridge with Mother.

A wide, tall cylinder is anchored at the center of the space, and a blue glow, moving, almost alive, flows up and down the tube. My gaze moves past it to the control panel, to the view of the new planet below us.

"Have you made your choice?" Mother asks. "You must decide. Are you worth saving?"

"I won't save them."

"Are you sure, Zenith?"

"Yes."

"Diverting power now."

I walk to the control panel, to the long line of lights flashing in the darkness, going out as Mother turns the power off. The pods. One after another, they dim.

"How long do they have before they die?" I ask. My voice wavers in the silence.

"A few minutes," Mother says. There is no judgment in her voice, no emotion at all.

Should there be?

I look through the glass, out at the planet, and my eyes refocus on my own reflection. I untie my robe and drop it to the floor, shivering as I stare at my very human face, my naked human form. I take a deep breath, trying to ignore the frigid temperature.

"I'm one of them," I say. "Yet I'm not. I can *see*... I can see all the truths they couldn't. Why, Mother? Why can I see what they couldn't?"

"Because you were not born a blank slate, Zenith."

I go still, staring at myself. The bridge is so quiet I can hear my own heart beating.

"They were born blind," I murmur. "They were asleep."

"Yes," Mother says gently. "But you and your sisters have experienced one thousand lives. Are you blind? Are you asleep?"

More lights flicker off. More pods gone dark.

"Are you asleep, Zenith?" Mother asks again.

I release my grip on the console and stare down at the planet, at the swirling white clouds, at the promise of a new beginning... if I choose to create it.

"You are the only one who questions. So I'm letting you make the choice."

I suck in a breath as I finally understand. I close my eyes and step away. I become the Observer once more. And I observe *myself.*

I just used my "truth" to justify murdering my sisters and our children.

Selfish. Destructive. Certain of the rightness of my own path while willing to destroy the lives of others.

I acted… human. Like all of *them.* And *this* is why I was forced to live all those lives. Why I was made to feel their pain, their joy, their love, their hate.

So I'd be able to see what they couldn't. So I could make choices they couldn't make.

I open my eyes and stare down at the console. Only five lights are still on. My sisters will all be dead within minutes.

This is the end.

I remember. Yeeun and her newborn. The vast love she felt as she inhaled the scent of a child she knew was about to die.

At least I got to meet her.

My hands start to tremble as the last of the lights goes dim. Life support has been shut off in all the pods.

I'll never get to meet my sisters.

I've felt love and happiness, but I'll die alone. There's *good* in us… but is it enough to justify our survival?

I have seen the way truth manifests, have experienced a thousand lives filtered through the minds of those who lived them. I feel patterns and shapes in the chaos—recognize cause and effect for every choice.

Because of this, I can be the Observer in my own life. I don't *have* to be asleep.

And I know what I need to do now.

"Mother, reroute power back to the rest of the ship. Now.

Restore life support to the pods."

The lights before me come back on, one at a time, until all forty-nine are illuminated. I breathe deeply and lean forward, pressing my hand to the glass as I gaze down at our new home.

"I want to meet my sisters now," I say. "We'll shape humanity into what it could have been. Because this time... we will be awake."

Q&A with Autumn Kalquist

Where did this story come from?

The ether. Go ahead and roll your eyes. I agree! It's ridiculous, but I wish the ether would send me some more. I had several stories I thought about writing for this anthology, but the first one turned into a novella, and the next one looked like it might be just as long. So I gave up and took a nap. When I woke, this story was in my mind, fully formed. I rushed to the computer and typed it all in one sitting. I refined it in revision, but the story didn't change.

How does it relate to other books you've written?

What? You want me to tell you and ruin the surprise and satisfaction you'd get by reading my other books? Nah. I like you too much for that. Everything else I've written is part of my epic *Fractured Era* science fiction series and can be found everywhere you like to buy books.

Tell us something we might not know about you.

I'm a singer. And not the sing-in-the-shower kind. (Fine. I do that, too. Sound effects are phenomenal.) I was in a girl group in Los Angeles once. It was a harrowing experience filled with pop songs, diets, and skimpy attire... and being an awesome waitress while serving that one witch from *Charmed*.

(Oh, forget it. I can't pretend I don't know which witch she was. I totally served Piper a sandwich and french fries. Highlight of my LA stay.)

How can readers find you?

If I told you, I'd have to...

Ahem.

Please find me at AutumnKalquist.com. I do love hearing from my readers, and I even have a special newsletter where you can get free stories and songs from my series.

Wait. How do you go from pop-star-in-training to sci-fi author?

I know, right? That *does* sound a little suspicious. But what's life without a little mystery?

Dragonet
by Sara Reine

MILITARY POLICY REQUIRED two coachmen for Carriages in those days, and it's a good thing they did; otherwise, Aja Skytoucher would never have survived the crash.

In a blink of plasma and dancing electricity, she lost AI navigation. Her control panel's lights went dark.

The Carriage spun out.

"He got us! He got us!"

That was the second coachman, Emalkay. The numbskull didn't try to recover. He just screamed and thrashed in his five-point harness, face plastered against the viewport to see when the next plasma blast was coming.

Aja seized the reins in one hand and tossed repair film to Emalkay with the other. She kept the film under her console, right between her feet, so she could find it even when smoke flooded the compartment. "Get to the rear quarter, Em!"

He stared at her with baffled eyes. Drakor III pinwheeled orange and red behind him, its jagged-edged ice cap growing nearer at a terrifying rate. "The rear quarter? Why, Aja?"

She wanted to say, *Because I told you, idiot*, but even with her heart clawing at the inside of her rib cage the words came out cool. "The fireball must have hit on the left. We'll be venting oxygen. Patch it."

Clearly, all Emalkay heard was "venting oxygen." His eyes got wider. "We're going to get sucked out!"

"Patch it." Aja's biceps strained as she hauled back on the reins.

Emalkay's hands flew over the control panel. There was no response. He banged his fists on the buttons for the communication device—the mochila—which should have given them instantaneous contact with the rest of the fleet. "Why aren't they connecting with us?"

Because the mochila had gone down with the navigation, of course.

Everything had gone down with the navigation.

Aja's patience frayed. "Patch the rear quarter, Emalkay! That's an order!"

She kicked the latch release for the harnesses. Both she and Emalkay floated free from their seats. They continued to rotate with the Carriage, drifting slowly.

Another plasma ball struck.

The Carriage shuddered, panels rattling, emergency lights flickering. Without the harness latched, Aja was shaken from her chair. Still, she clung to the reins, braced the rubber treads of her boots against the panel, and pulled back.

Manual control on those Carriages was a fine art—a careful dance of tiny microwaves that could tweak their trajectory this way and that, assuming the coachman's hand was fine enough.

Most coachmen weren't good at it. They relied on the automation that Aja had lost when the rear quarter went up in a ball of fire.

Aja had cut her teeth on older vehicles, though. She'd had a Chariot XIV, for the love of Thal, and those had been fashioned in the days when artificial intelligence wasn't able to assemble paper airplanes, much less steer space vehicles.

She hadn't manually steered a Chariot since she was too small for the driver's harness. But her muscles remembered the movements, and she'd always had a cool head. She could do this now, even as they plummeted toward the surface of Drakor III. The enemy stronghold.

She *needed* to do this.

Leathery wings flashed past the viewport. Aja glimpsed only shimmering gold before it was gone again—a color that reminded her of the glittering hide dresses her trapper mother used to wear.

"He sees us!" Emalkay wailed. "He's coming back again!"

Aja gritted her teeth, clutched the reins, and kept pulling. Harder. Harder.

The bucking Carriage whined. Drakor III spun. Her wrists trembled with the effort.

"The patch," she said.

He listened this time. Emalkay's hand flashed through the air, seizing the film, and he kicked off his chair to drift into the rear of the Carriage.

Lords, but Drakor III was growing fast.

Fresh plasma splattered over the viewport. It pushed them into a faster spin. Shoved them out of orbit. Gases whipped through the compartment, blasting Aja's hair free of its ponytail. It obscured her vision, but she didn't need to see. She only needed the tension in the reins, the feel of the yoke on the other end. She could have steered it without any sense but touch.

She pulled. Microwaves pushed. The Carriage stabilized and then overcorrected.

Aja's stomach lurched as her view of the planet below centered and then began rotating again in the opposite direction. Her hair whipped over her eyes again.

Emalkay shouted over the hissing. "You're right! It's the rear quarter! Oxygen's venting!"

Yes, Aja knew that. They'd lost the feed on the surface sensors in the heartbeat before they'd lost the rest of navigation, which meant those sensors had been struck first, and they were situated inside the elbow line on the rear quarter.

She didn't say that.

Eyes shut, hair tickling her nose, she steered.

Aja didn't see their enemy swoop past again, but she felt his passing wings clip the belly of the Carriage. She twisted the reins to the right to compensate.

She heard repair film torn by Emalkay's dull belt knife. She could tell he hadn't sharpened it recently just by how many cuts it took to get through. He probably hadn't charged his plasma rifle, either. Lazy Emalkay, stupid Emalkay—yet she needed him. If he didn't patch that hole, they would both be dead.

She couldn't keep steering through the force of the venting oxygen. Not under the plasma barrage, not with the thin upper atmosphere they were entering, not without navigation.

"Got it!" Emalkay cried.

She already knew. The Carriage was calming under her hands.

Their spin stabilized.

Aja had control.

"Yes," she breathed, eyes opening.

The Carriage's spin had ended with it facing away from the surface. The Drakor system's single red star glowed at the upper edge of the viewport, painting Aja in the foul light depicted on so many propaganda posters.

Other Carriages in higher orbits glimmered. At this distance, their slow dance through space was beautiful. She couldn't see the fleet's insignia. Couldn't tell which Carriages belonged to members of her unit, which ones were strangers, which had been licensed from private companies. The only way to tell that any of them were still working was the occasional flare of thrusters. They were slow as seeds drifting on the surface of a pond, confined by orbital mechanics and basic, clumsy physics.

Unlike the enemy.

The enemy was agile. Tireless. Capable of moving outside of orbits. Propelled at unimaginable speeds.

And the residents of the Drakor system had responded to the attack in full force.

The raid should have caught them by surprise. Their army should have been deployed elsewhere that day, distracted by defending outposts in other systems. But they were there at the home world, prepared to receive the Allied forces. The Drakor must have known the fleet was coming.

There were thousands of them above Drakor III.

Dragons.

They looped around the Carriages, tailed by the Fog—a force that Allied scientists barely understood, though it seemed to be something similar to fire, something their bodies generated. Nobody was certain if its origin was magical or biological. That Fog flashed behind the dragons in colors even brighter than Drakor's sun, and the clouds of writhing plasma chewed through the fleet like it was nothing.

Many Carriages were succumbing to attacks similar to the one that had disabled Aja and Emalkay.

And now the attacker that had knocked out Aja's systems was descending on her Carriage.

It moved faster than she did, even though gravity had caught the Carriage and dragged her toward the surface. She was pinned between a dragon and Drakor III. Death under the claws of a dragon, death on the surface of the planet—either way, the odds of survival were poor. Very poor.

Especially since she was watching the fleet getting pulverized far above them.

"I think I can fix the mochila." Emalkay clattered in the rear of the compartment, dropping tools and ripping open panels. Hope tinged his panicked tone. "You've just got to maintain low orbit long enough for someone to save us."

Nobody was going to save them.

A crack slithered from the lower right quadrant of the viewport, inching its way toward the center of the glass. It wouldn't take much pressure for that to shatter. The crack bisected the dragon's cruel face as it undulated through space to close in on them. It was mere moments away from catching the Carriage now.

There was no time for a rescue.

Aja swallowed hard. "No, keep off the mochila. Redirect everything into the microwave engines."

"The manual controls?"

"Yes."

"What about the AI?"

"Forget the AI, Em!"

Gravity tugged. They entered atmosphere. The exterior panels on the Carriage heated with the friction. Flames streaked along the edges of the viewport, blotting out Aja's view of the fleet's distant and serene demise.

The dragon plummeted with them, folding his wings to catch up.

"But how will the fleet find us if I don't fix the mochila?" Emalkay asked.

Aja didn't reply.

The Carriage's manual controls became stiffer as the atmosphere's density increased. Here, microwave propulsion took much more thrust to be effective. But it was all they had—they couldn't fire the rocket engines, not with the structural damage they'd already sustained, with plasma still chewing through their paneling.

They'd be incinerated.

Sweat rolled down Aja's hairline, dripped into her collar. Her palms were slick.

But she twisted the reins, the Carriage obeyed her command, and she felt the moment when Emalkay put all the power into the microwave engines. The entire vehicle bucked in protest.

"Come on, girl," she whispered.

The engine roared. Acid clouds billowed around the Carriage.

The dragon blazed toward them like a hawk closing in on a rabbit.

Aja tangled the reins around one arm, steering with a single fist. She fumbled with her belt. Grabbed the plasma rifle, loosened the strap, propped it against her shoulder.

The plasma rifle was a new invention. They had gotten a living dragon specimen, somehow procured Fog from its organs—she didn't know the specifics—and repurposed it into a weapon that could penetrate even the thickest, scaliest of dragon hides. The raid on Drakor was the first field test, so Aja wasn't sure the gun would work. The men in the armory had said it would, but they'd also said the fleet's arrival would be unexpected.

The crack on the viewport spread.

Aja manipulated the reins as Emalkay fed every terawatt of remaining power into the engine, slowing their descent, allowing the dragon to converge on them. The Carriage cried out. The exterior panels flamed. Mountains appeared at the edges of Aja's vision—a hostile alien terrain that made her heart beat with sheer panic.

"What are you doing?" Em roared. "Why aren't you evading him?"

Aja didn't want to evade him. She wanted to land as softly as possible.

She wanted to get out of the Carriage alive, even if it meant being stranded on Drakor III.

It was getting so hot inside the Carriage. Sweat drenched her

DARK BEYOND THE STARS

uniform. But her grip on the rifle was sure, and she was as steady in aiming at the dragon's heart as she was in steering the Carriage down to their death.

Dragon claws glimmered, huge and sharp.

Only meters away.

"Aja! *Aja!*"

She fired directly into the viewport twice: once to finish shattering the glass, and once to deliver a shot of plasma directly into the heart of the dragon.

Her bolt drove into the chest of her enemy.

She didn't see what happened after that—because that was when they finally crashed.

* * *

Aja Skytoucher had a headache and Emalkay was screaming.

Realistically speaking, both of these were good signs—indicating survival.

Consciousness scrabbled through Aja's skull. She was on her hands and knees before her senses returned, shoving twisted metal off her body, seeking the shape of the plasma rifle. Her fingers curved around a handle.

She felt a trigger. Good enough.

Angry red light bathed her as she stood, squinting across the harsh landscape.

There was wreckage at her feet. The air smelled sulfurous and her body felt strong despite the ache. Drakor III was low-gravity with a thin atmosphere, which made it feel like she was breathing on top of Mount McKinley, but it was habitable for humans and dragons alike.

With her eyes blurred, everything looked to be red and indistinct.

Everything but the wrecked Carriage.

That was never going to fly again.

Lords, the men weren't going to be happy when they saw what she'd done to such a recent vehicle. Yet she hoped she would have an opportunity to be punished for it. Punishment, like her headache, would mean that she hadn't been killed yet. It would mean that the fleet had enough Carriages surviving the dogfight in orbit to retrieve her.

It would mean Aja might see her family again.

Emalkay was still screaming, and the shrieking made her headache pulse. She kicked wreckage around to search for him. If not to save him, then to put the whiny thing out of his misery.

Her eyes had relearned how to focus by the time she found him crushed under the rear quarter, where he had been working when they struck. Though the blood was profuse, it seemed to originate from a single cut on his forehead. Other bruises had yet to develop. Aja had slowed their fall enough that both coachmen had survived—miraculously.

But what of their attacker?

"Shut up, Em," she said, hauling him to his feet.

"I can't see! I'm bleeding!" He clutched his face.

Aja yanked a rag out of the wreckage, pressed it to the wound, guided his hand to hold it in place. "You'll survive if the dragons don't get us."

The reality of the situation settled over Emalkay. He paled under all the blood.

"We're on Drakor," he said. "We're on Drakor!" He spun to look wildly around the harsh landscape, became dizzy, grabbed Aja to steady himself. "Where's the beast that tried to eat us?"

"I was wondering that myself." She found Emalkay's plasma rifle among the wreckage, tucked it into his free arm. He remained standing when she released him. That was good: she needed to be able to use both hands when the dragon attack came.

And the dragon attack would surely come soon.

Now that Aja could see, it was possible to estimate the length of the crater the landing had carved into Drakor's surface. It must have been at least a mile. The smoke was impressive. It would act as a beacon for rescuers as well as the enemy.

A second crater lay alongside theirs. A trail of Fog and blood led away from it, toward the mountains in the distance.

That was where the dragon landed.

How long had Aja been unconscious in the wreckage of the Carriage? Could the dragon have gotten far enough to notify reinforcements of their landing?

One thing was certain: she needed to find the dragon and terminate it before it could bring all kinds of chaos down on her head.

It was her only chance of survival now.

"Move," Aja said.

She leaped lightly across the surface. She had enough low-gravity experience to quickly adjust to the movement; it couldn't have been significantly lower than the Station's 0.5g. A single push of her legs vaulted her over the Carriage to the dragon's trail.

"Wait for me!"

Emalkay was clumsy behind her. She decided to be generous and attribute that to his head trauma.

Though movement should have been effortless, Aja's breathing quickly grew thready, her chest laboring to inhale. It was impossible to tell if her dizziness was from injury or because of the strange atmosphere. Her eyes burned in it.

She squinted to keep the blood in her sights, plasma rifle lifted, avoiding the Fog with her boots. She'd seen that stuff melt through Carriages as though it were candle wax. If it contacted her body, she might as well resign herself to an amputation.

As the trail continued, the blood grew in quantity. It tinted the iron-rich dirt brown.

That, and the fact that the trail continued on the ground at all, suggested to Aja that the plasma rifle had done its job against the dragon.

They moved into the foothills without finding a body. Aja must have been unconscious longer than she realized for the beast to have traveled so far, even with the minimal gravity on Drakor III. And Aja was not moving quickly now, either. Emalkay held her back, slow and cautious from fear.

She grew increasingly fatigued as she hunted.

Just when Aja felt like she might collapse, she saw it.

The dragon that had attacked them loomed out of the crimson darkness, sprawled between two jagged rocks overlooking a crater. It seemed even larger now that she didn't have the Carriage as a protective shell. The arch of its spine was three times her height. The feet were long enough that they could have gripped her with toes overlapping.

Her heart leaped into her throat. She gestured to stop Emalkay halfway down the slope and prepared to fire.

But the dragon didn't move.

Aja held her position halfway behind a rock. She watched for any signs of breathing, for the faintest glimmer of active Fog.

Nothing.

She proceeded forward slowly, muzzle trained on the center mass of the body.

Still it didn't move. Not even when the rubber treads of her soles ground against gravel and her uniform's straps scraped against the metal of the rifle. Aja was too exhausted to be silent, yet the dragon didn't react in the slightest.

She rounded the body.

Her enemy was dead.

The monster had collapsed in a puddle of its own fluids, its massive head resting on one arm, the other hand stretched toward the top of the crater. The eyes were shut. A black tongue lolled from its open beak.

Now that Aja got a good look at the wound she'd inflicted, she was impressed by how far the dragon had traveled on the surface. The hole was large enough that Aja could see all the way through—from underneath its breastplate she could see the world on the other side, framed by fragments of its spinal cord.

She never would have expected their modified version of Fog to be so deadly against dragons, but she thanked the lords that it was.

Aja had never seen a dragon so close, dead or alive. Now that her adrenaline was dropping off, she could admire the bulk of its form, huge yet graceful, almost more feline than serpentine. It was as elegant as the surroundings were harsh.

"It's safe," Aja called.

Only then did Emalkay proceed.

He startled at the sight of the creature's head, mouth open to expose fangs. His forefinger twitched. The plasma rifle in his hands clicked without firing.

Yes, Emalkay had forgotten to charge his sidearm.

"What are you doing?" She ripped the rifle out of his hands. "These things make noise like thunder. Do you want to draw every dragon within a hundred miles on us?"

"It didn't fire," he said.

Only because you're stupid. She still discarded his gun. Her superior officer would be angry that she'd lost such a valuable new weapon, but she was so angry at Emalkay that it didn't seem to matter.

More than anger churned within Aja. She felt no satisfaction at the sight of one of these great beasts killed. They were frightening, yes, and if all the propaganda was to be believed, then they would happily have murdered the entire human race. But they were still majestic. And Aja's mother had taught her to honor all lives; when they'd hunted deer in New Alaska, they had prayed over the carcasses of their victims before cleaning them.

Was it possible she regretted killing the dragon?

It would have killed her if she hadn't.

"The good news is, we might just win the fight in orbit," Emalkay said. He was bolder now that he realized the dragon was dead. He walked up to the hole in its chest and stuck his whole fist in. "Every Carriage up there has one or two of these plasma rifles. If folks suit up, open the sash, and start firing, we'll be able to rip them apart!"

Aja's mouth tipped into a frown. "Don't touch the body."

"I won't get any Fog on me." He pulled a fragment of rib out. "I'm gonna show this to my girl. She'll be so impressed, her panties will vanish."

"If we ever get home," Aja said.

His confident smile faded.

"I'm gonna get up high," he said. "See if I can spot any of the fleet. If they've started using the rifles instead of the cannons, it wouldn't take them long to beat back the dragons."

"Emalkay…"

He ignored her.

Emalkay scrambled up the slope to peer over the edge of the crater.

Aja set her hand on the dragon's beak. It was leathery, pebbled, and still warm.

"Oh my—Aja! You have to see this!" Emalkay shouted.

She followed him up.

At first she thought the volcanic crater was filled with some kind of strange mushrooms. It was peppered with clusters of swollen white spheres, too organic to be rock. Many of them were covered with dust the color of paprika. Those that were clean glistened.

But the longer she looked at it, the more she realized that there was deliberation to the placement. They were grouped in handfuls all throughout the crater. There were footprints leading from cluster to cluster as though dragons had been patrolling them.

This crater was a nesting ground.

"Thal be blessed," Aja hissed.

There was clicking inside the nearest eggs. It was easy to imagine the tiny beaks and claws that were bumping against the inner surface, attempting to tear away the membranes, devour the yolk, break free of their warm home.

Hundreds of dragonets.

How many human lives could the inhabitant of a single egg terminate?

"Lords," Em said. "Give me your rifle."

She was so stunned that she handed it to him automatically. Only when he began clambering down the slope did she think to ask, "Why?"

"You saw the fleet," he called back to her. "We're losing the fight up there. We've got to keep them from making reinforcements."

He was going to destroy the eggs.

Aja understood little about dragon biology. To be fair, nobody understood a thing about them aside from the fact that they wanted to kill all humans, probably to seize the Allied Colonial States for resources.

It had been assumed that dragons would nest like many lizards did.

But nobody really *knew*.

Now Aja knew. And her mind spun at the sight of the nests, which Emalkay approached with at a rapid clip, dust trailing in his wake.

They had expected the dragons to be attending to the

outpost raids, but instead, they had caught them by surprise on their home world.

The dragon Aja killed had obviously been struggling to return here.

"Oh no," she said.

The fleet had caught the dragons when they returned home for the breeding season. All those enemies fiercely defending their world—they were also trying to defend their young. It must have hurt for them to abandon their nests.

Aja's heart hurt at the sight of the dead dragon lower on the slope.

"Stop, Em," she said.

He rapped his knuckles against one of the eggs, then stooped to listen for a response. "Stop what? Do you think they're going to hatch and eat me?"

"They might. We don't know. Be careful."

"I'll be careful all right," he said, swinging the rifle to aim. "I'll be so careful, they won't even see me coming."

Aja was only a few steps into the crater when he fired.

The modified Fog emerged in a plug the size of her arm. It consumed the entire cluster of eggs with shocking speed.

She had been unconscious an instant after firing upon the first dragon. She hadn't seen the damage wrought by the plasma rifle. Now she had the luxury of watching the eggshells melt, the fluids sizzling, the small bodies within devoured as though dropped into acid.

It struck Aja that the dragonets were roughly the size of her childhood dog, Beetle.

"Stop it," she said again.

Emalkay didn't hear her. He was shooting another cluster of eggs.

They really did sound like thunder.

Aja stood over the first nest that Em had destroyed. Only moments had passed since he'd fired, but there was already no more motion within the wreckage of eggshells and leathery bodies. They had been making such a lively clicking when she'd approached. They must have been near to hatching.

Emalkay sprinted to a third nest.

Aja reached it first. She put a hand on his shoulder. "What are you doing?"

"There are hundreds of these things here," he said. He fired again. Aja flinched as more eggs melted away. "It only took ten dragons to wipe out all of York Prime! This many of them could kill us all!"

That was probably true, and Aja had been thinking something similar.

She hadn't grown up anywhere near York Prime. Emalkay had. Perhaps she'd be the one firing on all the nests if she'd had to attend a school in the shadow of skyscrapers wrecked by dragons. If her family's water supply had been poisoned by Fog, then her rage could have been equally fierce.

It was easy to think that he was doing the wrong thing when she had grown up out on a farm untouched by the war.

But watching Emalkay move to the next group of eggs sickened her.

Another gunshot. She shut her eyes so she wouldn't have to see.

Each discharge of the plasma rifle shook the crater. The

untouched eggs shivered with inner motion, as though the dragonets within could hear what was happening and grew afraid. The walls of the crater looked like they were threatening to break as well, and rocks were sliding down the surface.

Surely dragons would hear them and come save their nests.

They couldn't be *that* distracted by the fight in orbit.

Emalkay destroyed another, and another, and nobody came to defend against him.

"I think I missed one of the dragonets back there," he said, jerking his thumb at a cluster he'd already passed. His cheeks were flushed red with excitement. He must have been imagining how many panties he could drop once he told stories of his heroism against defenseless eggs. "Want to go stomp the survivor for me? Bet it'll go down easy! You could take some claws home!"

Aja reached the broken eggs with a single leap. She felt strange descending upon them now, her motions slowed by the weak gravity, as though she were an angel of death.

He was right. There was movement within that cluster, writhing under the shattered shells that were slowly dissolving.

She kneeled, flicking aside a few pieces of eggshell. Despite their large size, they were very light, almost paper-thin.

The dragonet she exposed was not quite the size of her childhood foxhound—maybe half that. It was more immature than the others. The size had probably been what saved it, since there had been more amniotic fluid to provide cushioning, and the modified Fog had burned out before melting all the way to the hatchling within. Lucky dragonet. Unluckily, such a small thing seemed to have no chance of survival after such a premature birth.

Stomp it, Emalkay had said.

What little Fog remained stung Aja's hands as she reached in to scoop the dragonet out.

It was heavy in her arms, though not as heavy as she would have expected. The scales had yet to take on the ridged edges of an adult dragon. Its soft body smelled almost sweet, as though coated in maple syrup.

Lords, the eyes weren't even open yet.

It didn't look like a potential mass murderer now that she was holding it.

Emalkay destroyed another cluster of eggs. He was on the far end of the crater, having destroyed more than half of its inhabitants, and there was still no sign of defense from the dragons.

"Aja! Look!" he shouted.

His finger thrust toward the sky.

She followed it up to see gold sparkling in high orbit. Those were the telltale glimmers of Carriages on the approach, accelerating retrograde in order to drop toward the atmosphere.

If they were moving in, then they must have killed most of the enemy dragons.

The Allied fleet had realized what deadly weapons the plasma rifles were.

Humans were winning, at long last.

Aja caught herself stroking the dragonet's pebbled flank. It was a glorious shade of dark blue, like the sky in paintings of the First Earth.

It stirred at the touch, and she couldn't help but think that this touch should have come from the hand of the dragon she had killed. It would have murdered her, yes, but this dragonet was harmless, innocent. Its future wasn't written yet. Maybe it would have been the creature who convinced its brethren to end the war. They would never know. Emalkay was bent on killing them all.

One of those slitted eyes opened. The dragon's long neck draped over her arm as it focused on her face, stretching its beak toward her chin.

Instinctively, Aja ducked her head to greet it. Emalkay fired yet again a few hundred feet away.

"Hello," she said. Her voice hitched on the second syllable of the word.

The dragonet brushed its forehead against hers.

Electricity jolted through Aja.

For an instant, she had no thoughts, no sense of her body, no sense of time. The crater vanished around her.

She could only feel the dragonet.

It was such a powerful sensation that she almost thought she had made a mistake picking up this little newborn to cradle it as she had cradled calves while bottle-feeding them. It certainly felt like her skull was folding inside out. Like her brain was going to spill onto the ground.

Memories of her entire life flashed through her.

Aja's childhood at the Skytoucher farm. Her rejection from the Academy. Enlistment with the Allied military when she'd been only fifteen years old. Boot camp, followed by cross-training in driving Carriages. And then the war.

Then she regained all her senses, and she was still holding

that dragonet, neither of them injured. Its faceted silver eyes gazed at her.

Help us, it said.

The words entered her mind directly.

Aja was certain it was the dragonet speaking to her. She had never heard of dragons speaking before—there was no way to communicate with them. But she *knew* the plea had come from the dragonet, and she somehow knew it could understand her as well.

She set the dragonet on the dusty ground a safe distance from the Fog still devouring its nestmates. She turned to look for Emalkay, who roved at the far end of the crater.

"We're enemies," Aja whispered to the dragonet.

It only looked at her. There were no more words. Their moment of connection had passed.

Maybe such a little thing simply couldn't speak more than once.

Emalkay was about to shoot the last cluster of eggs. Aja leaped smoothly through the air, heart pounding, and landed beside him.

There was a lot of debris on that side of the crater; the resonating gunshots had shaken rocks loose from the surrounding walls. Aja found one the size of her fist and picked it up.

"Want to shoot this last one?" Emalkay asked without turning.

Aja smashed the rock against the back of his skull.

Emalkay was probably still hurting from the crash. It didn't take much force to knock him out. His slow collapse was graceful, and there was plenty of time for Aja to scoop the plasma rifle out of the air before it struck the ground, risking an accidental discharge. The plasma rifle was warm from being fired, taking so many dragonets' lives.

Em stirred when he landed, so she kicked him again, just to make sure he would stay down.

"Thal forgive me," Aja said.

The fleet was landing nearby, lighting up the sky with the blaze of their propulsion. She hastened to return to the surviving dragonet.

It was barely alive, struggling to breathe. Its skin was cold when she picked it up again.

This little killer, this larva that could become a mass murderer, wouldn't survive once the fleet landed. If premature hatching didn't kill it, then other coachmen who shared Emalkay's sentiments would. Aja could already hear them approaching. Their distant voices echoed over the barren mountains.

Help us, it had said.

Now it said nothing. It was sleeping, curled against her for warmth.

There was nothing Aja could do about the other eggs. They were at the mercy of the Allies.

But she knew what she needed to do about this lone dragonet.

* * *

Nobody seemed to understand why Aja Skytoucher, highly decorated survivor of the Battle at Drakor III, resigned from service the instant she returned to the Station. The coachmen who had been at Drakor III were guaranteed promotions for each dragon they had killed. Since she and Emalkay had effectively doomed the enemy to lose the war—if not sentenced them to extinction—they would probably get to pick their next deployment.

They never needed to see battle again. They would have more money than any coachman knew what to do with.

Yet resign she did, and she returned to New Dakota a hero.

She watched the parting message Emalkay sent to her on the mochila while riding the space elevator to the surface. It was lengthy. The man didn't know when to shut up.

Emalkay said she was nuts for leaving the service. He said he never wanted to be deployed with any other coachman. Aja had saved him twice, after all: once from crashing on Drakor III, and once when a rock had broken free of the crater and nearly killed him. He was still in the hospital recovering from his concussion.

But even though he claimed he wouldn't work with anyone else, he hadn't resigned. He was staying in the service to enjoy the salary.

Aja turned off her mochila. She had no interest in what he had to say.

The elevator landed smoothly. Aja was greeted by the yellow plains of New Dakota, the colony covered in swaying grass and rimmed by jagged mountains not unlike those on Drakor III. She lifted her duffel bag carefully and went to the transport.

"Aja!" her mother greeted her, wrapping her in a tight hug. "You look so thin! I'm glad I made bone broth for you. I expect you to drink a liter of it as soon as we get home."

Aja gave a shaky laugh, drawing back so that her mother's embrace wouldn't crush the duffel bag. "I *have* been craving your broth."

"Of course you have! I still make the best broth in all the Colonies." Her mother was convinced of this even though she'd never been off of New Dakota. Aja didn't correct her.

It was nice to be home after so many years, watching the farms rush past their speeder. Little had changed since she'd left. But everything looked so small now.

The Skytoucher farm had been repainted recently, and its blue paneling gleamed in the sunlight. The corn stood as tall as Aja. The cattle grazing in the pasture were fat. The farm was clearly doing well, which her mother was eager to reinforce as she babbled on about how many new clients they'd gotten. They were going to be rich, she said. And richer still now that they would enjoy all of Aja's retirement bonuses.

"Not that I'm unhappy to have you, but I am a little surprised you'd want to come back to this," her mother said, watching from the doorway as Aja set the duffel bag on her bed. It was the same tiny mattress she had slept on as a girl. The sheets were patterned with pink flowers. "You must be used to so many more glamorous places after your deployments!"

Aja forced a smile. "Yeah, but there's no place like home."

Her mother planted a kiss on her forehead. "I'll let you unpack."

She left. Aja shut the door behind her.

In truth, no matter how beautiful it was, the farm did seem terribly small. But in reality, it was several hundred acres. Their property extended beyond the land where they could plant crops; it continued on into the inhospitable, cruel mountains. It was quite spacious, really.

And very much like Drakor III.

Drakor III was now inhabited by human forces. They had wiped out most of the population in the weeks since Aja's battle there, and they would spend years hunting the surviving dragons throughout their various outposts. It might be generations before humans managed to kill them all. The battles would be messy. Countless families would suffer for it—both human and dragon.

The violence might never end.

Unless someone figured out how to communicate with the dragons.

Aja unzipped her duffel bag. A head the size of a terrier's popped out from among the folds of her uniform, blinking sleepily at her.

The dragonet reached its beak up to touch Aja's forehead.

Welcome home, Aja thought to it.

Q&A with Sara Reine

1. Where did this story come from?
My fingertips applied repeatedly to keyboard.

2. How does it relate to other books you've written?
I'm developing a book series called *Drakor's Return* with my husband, Edwin Reine. This short story is exploring the concepts we've discussed over many long nights, because the baby keeps waking up at two a.m. The series itself will take place a couple of generations after the Allied invasion of Drakor.

3. *Tell us something we might not know about you.*

This is my first trip into publishing science fiction. I'm typically a fantasy author.

4. *How can readers find you?*

With binoculars, on Google maps, and by visiting www.edwinreine.com. That's my husband's website, because mine is for my legions of fantasy novels, but I promise my husband and I are seldom far apart. It's almost as though we like each other or something.

5. *Works in progress?*

I'm working on the first *Drakor's Return* novel with my husband right now. I'm also attempting to grow two young boys into adult men who don't suck. That's the important one.

Lulu Ad Infinitum
by Ann Christy

Ship Designation/Name: Generation 9 (11-12-11-22-11-11-11-23-11)/Triumph
System Designation: HR4922
Planet Name: Undesignated
Mission Year: 18,332

Chapter One

WHEN THE CRASHING, cracking, and splintering sounds finally stopped, Lulu thought she might have gone deaf. The silence was too complete, too profound. She opened her eyes and found nothing save total darkness, the kind of darkness that creates instant vertigo. Maybe she was blind as well. Probably not, though.

This is space, she reminded herself. *Deep space. And there are no windows in an emergency capsule.* But there should be lights in the capsule, so clearly there was a problem even in this tiny safe haven.

Lulu knew about this sort of blackness. It wasn't the first time she'd experienced it. Or rather, it would be more correct to say it wasn't the first time she *remembered* experiencing it, though it was certainly not this body that had been there for the event.

That had been on Earth, before the scans that would finalize who the project specialists would be had been taken, before they became the official Loaded Strands that would bear all the responsibility for the human race in space. Unlike a standard Strand—a simple DNA imprint that could be rebuilt as a new human infant, but without the memories of the original person—Loaded Strands had the addition of neural imprints, and thus could be rebuilt as fully grown adults with all their memories intact. Well, the memories up until the moment the scan started anyway.

Once, during the years-long selection process, the candidates had gone into a mountain laboratory, the kind of place where passing particles could be measured because of a total lack of light. At the time, Lulu thought the exercise was pointless. After all, they were only supposed to be simulating the roles of colonists so the computer that would control the ships could learn from them. What she didn't know then was that she was being tested to become a Loaded Strand. No one did. Their foray into the dark mountain made sense only in retrospect.

Fifty team members at a time had been arranged around the lab floor, surrounded by vast vats of water and mysterious harnesses of thick wires for the experiments. Then the lights went off. Puking was one side effect, of course, but within moments she—and many of the others— also lost their sense of spatial awareness. Where were her arms? Her legs? Was she standing? The weight of the mountain above them made the sensation even more unsettling.

This moment felt exactly the same as that long-ago one. Yes, that test made perfect sense now.

She swallowed back her nausea and called out, "Hello!" Her voice was hoarse and scratchy, her throat feeling almost burned. But she could hear her own words, so at least she wasn't deaf. That was something.

"Stand by. Remain in the capsule," came the immediate response. It was the computer, but without the normal inflections and social niceties that made dealing with a computer easier. That those niceties were absent told her more than the computer's words did. It told her that the emergency that had put her inside this dark capsule was still ongoing, still using all the computer's resources.

But although she understood that, standing by wasn't something Lulu could really bear to do at the moment. Her nausea was rising, and it was going to get very messy in this tiny, dark capsule if she waited too long without light. The weightlessness was only adding to her sense of vertigo.

She stretched her limbs out, her own version of the Vitruvian Man, but there was no touch of matter to validate her location or confirm that she wasn't floating in space. At least there was no pain to indicate that she'd broken a bone or damaged her body in any significant way. She jerked her limbs forward, then back to the side, trying to create a little current and move even a smidge toward something solid. The capsule was small enough that this inefficient manner of movement could actually produce results if she kept at it. Maybe.

It was enough. The toe of her boot scraped metal, the sound of it faint through the thin air, but the feeling unmistakable. The rush of relief inside Lulu was profound and immediate, an almost physical sensation like a hug or a slap on the back. Her head cleared a little, the sense of vertigo shifting back as her body embraced the concept of a solid surface nearby.

Plus, now she had a goal. Lulu positively lived for goals, and this time the right goal might save her life. Standing by while the computer did whatever it needed to do? Maybe not so much. She'd rather try and fail than simply wait to live or die as circumstances would have it.

Waving her arms in ridiculous and awkward sweeps, she managed to get enough contact with the capsule bulkhead to use the friction of her boot against the rough surface. It was amazing how much force the barest edge of a boot could exert in zero gravity. A few more rubs of her foot and a timely push, and her arms slammed into the bulkhead—with a little more force than she had intended.

She clung to a strap attached to the bulkhead and rested her head against the padded surface to catch her breath. Now that she was breathing harder, she could also hear properly again. The squishy thudding of her heart in her ears, the raspy sound of her breaths passing through her burned throat, the rubbing of her coveralls against the bulkhead, the scrape of her boot. All these sounds brought with them some normalcy, easing her nausea just a little more.

The other noises that bled through the bulkheads were far

less comforting. Little pings and crashes peppering the outside of her capsule came in waves, telling her that the ship that had made up her entire world was still breaking apart. Each ping carried the potential to be the final nail in her coffin. This was an emergency capsule, meant to survive an impact that would shatter the entire ship, but how often could it take such impacts? For how long? Eventually, anything that could be built could also be un-built.

Fumbling along the curved surface of the capsule, she finally touched something that felt familiar. From there, it was the work of a few moments to pull herself around and locate the emergency box. Touching its cool, slightly curved sides felt unreasonably good. It wasn't like there was anything inside that could save her from a capsule failure, but it was something— and at the moment, anything was better than nothing.

Lulu ripped the hand-light out of the thin, metal clips that held it fast. She slammed her palm on it, and white light flared to life, the brilliance painful and glorious.

The first things she saw were her suit and helmet, still wadded up in a ball and pressed to the outer wall of the capsule, just out of her former reach. For a fraction of a second, she thought someone else was in the capsule with her, but then the flattened sleeve undulated in the slight air currents, advertising its empty status. Lulu felt disappointment and even more alone.

She shook it off. To hold back her emotions, she mentally ran through the emergency checklists in her head. Feelings wouldn't help; actions would.

She scrambled into the suit, more focused now with some light to keep herself oriented in the micro-gravity. It was almost comforting to work through something simple, something familiar and specifically meant to enhance her survival.

As she clicked the helmet closed, denser air poured into her lungs and immediately revived her. It was amazing really, how a few percentage points of oxygen in the air could change how a person functioned. Tweak that number a tiny bit in either direction and everything went haywire. But this lovely, cool air, saturated to mimic what she might breathe at sea level, felt almost decadently rich. After a few deep breaths, she could feel her mind sharpening, her logic improving. Her limbs responded more readily to the dictates of her mind.

"Triumph, give me a status on the ship," Lulu commanded. Stranded or not, she was alive and needed information. And now that she was thinking, she wanted to work—and to do that, she needed the correct information.

The computer responded quickly. "Primary damage control systems intact, primary life support module breached, biological ecosystem module damaged but unbreached. Manufacturing module damaged, spine support beyond junction thirty-four compromised."

"What about everything else? Research? Collection? Landing?" Lulu asked. The computer had given her a short list of positive things—things that still existed. She had expected the opposite; the computer *should* have given her a list of what was damaged. That could only mean that this catastrophe was even worse than it felt from inside the capsule—and it felt pretty serious.

Was it too much?

"Are we recoverable?" she asked quickly, not waiting for the computer to answer her previous queries. If they weren't recoverable, then the next thing that should happen would be a complete self-destruct, taking her and anything else that might have survived into oblivion. Her fists tightened, her body clenching as if in preparation for the blast, which was silly really, since it would be so profound an explosion that she would feel nothing. Nothing larger than a grain of sand would be left. Lulu *really* did not want that to happen.

"I cannot initiate appropriate protocols. My primary core is fractured. I have attempted self-destruct without result," said the computer. "Do you still require the status of the other modules?"

Lulu sucked in a sharp breath, feeling suddenly dizzy again, almost as if she'd returned to breathing thin air. Self-destruct meant that Triumph has already assessed their entire mission a failure, unrecoverable, without sufficient chance of success to merit the risk of leaving the ship exposed where some other life form might come across its remains in the future. While she'd been tugging on a sleeve or latching a helmet, Triumph had been coldly—and without consultation—deciding the time was right to kill her.

Fucker. Fucking, fucker computer.

"Don't keep trying! I'm right here. I'm not throwing in the towel," Lulu shouted, pulling up her suit's controls so she could get a look at their situation for herself. If self-destruction was the computer's solution, then she needed to orient herself, get to a Lander—if any survived—and get to the surface and well away from this suicidal machine. They had labs and habs on the surface that could support the current crop of two dozen workers easily. The planet was still barren, but the habs weren't.

The small monitor on her suit's arm lit up, the blue glow strangely comforting, but that was as far as the boot-up went. Her suit computer apparently hadn't survived her headlong flight into the capsule and all the impacts along the way. She slammed her palm onto the useless screen, causing her body to shift in the weightlessness, and she scrambled to regain purchase against the wall of the capsule.

Triumph said, "There is no point in further attempts at this time. I will attempt to re-consolidate core prior to the next self-destruct initiation."

Lulu yanked on the strap she clung to, putting her face close to the speaker inside the capsule. "Forget that! Do you hear me? You will not initiate any further attempts at self-destruct. Where are the other Loads? Are there any other survivors?"

"There are no other responses, and my remaining core connections register only one other bio-signature. It is in the ecosystem module," said Triumph.

"Human? Who?" Lulu asked, trying to remember if there had been anyone on duty in the arboretum this morning. Anyone other than a machine, anyway.

"Beagle."

Charlie! How could Lulu have forgotten about the poor dog? What must he be thinking right now?

"What's his condition?" she asked, moving around the capsule by grabbing the straps and pulling herself along. She could only hope that the controls for the capsule still worked. Without a computer in here to capture visuals on the continuing destruction—and the capsule floating around in the midst of it—she needed to get somewhere safe. And soon.

"He's barking. A lot. He is not responding to standard soothing routines," Triumph said, a little of its former conversational intonations and quirks returning. Did that mean the worst was over?

She pushed down the crushing emotions she felt at the lack of human survivors. She would face that later. At least she wasn't alone. It would take six months or so to tank up replacements for her compatriots, but she would have the dog in the meantime. That was something.

"We'll work it out, Triumph. Just get my module pulled back in and let's get to work. And no more trying for a self-destruct. Do you understand me?"

Lulu yanked the cover off the control panel, reaching for the manipulators and checking her distance from the ship. Time was a-wasting and there was a lot to do.

Chapter Two

It was far, far worse than a simple cascading impact brought about by the explosion of one of the mining vessels. It was a catastrophe of such magnitude that she almost couldn't accept the reality of what she saw. The ship wasn't entirely destroyed, but it might as well have been. It had been reduced practically to its initial configuration, its pared-down form. It was more like the core of the ship she had seen—or rather, the original Earthly Lulu had seen—being built so many unknown thousands of years ago. It wasn't fit for humans or anything else.

Not on a long-term basis, anyway.

Lulu closed her eyes against the sights. It was like this now, but it wouldn't stay that way. It could rebuild itself given time, as long as the basic systems remained. The manufacturing facility was largely intact, and that was the most important part of the ship when it came right down to it. In Lulu's view, a functional manufacturing facility made the mission recoverable. And she thought she had convinced the computer of that as well. At least, it *seemed* like it agreed with her. She'd have to stay on her toes, ready to catch any signs that the ship no longer agreed.

Fixing the breach in the hab module was Lulu's first priority. All the systems she needed to aid the ship in its recovery were located inside that module. Plus, well, that's where she lived.

Triumph capitulated after almost no argument, which boded well. She knew Triumph would stop obeying her if its complicated logic chains decided she was acting against their goals.

Hours later, she stripped off her suit and kicked the emergency capsule door shut at the sight of the wreckage in the hab. This was her home, and it bore almost no resemblance to the comfortable place she'd escaped from less than a day ago.

Even now, with any actual openings into space patched or covered, the place was still in the process of falling apart. With every step, more of the broken tile broke free beneath her feet. Above her head, wires and lights dangled and swung as the ship righted itself. The metal walls had peeled back into razor sharp curls, and even the hatch to the arboretum was buckled and scorched by fire. Almost everything not bolted down had blown out the gaping hole in the bulkhead, which was now hastily covered by a repair bot's flat underside while it welded a new plate into place.

Lulu took a deep breath, tasting the burned plastic and hot metal in the newly replenished air. She closed her eyes for a count of three, centering herself, reaching for calm. She had to appear as composed as was humanly possible. Triumph was going along with her for now, but if she appeared hopeless, who knew what might happen? The ship had tried to self-destruct once already, and there was no guarantee it wouldn't try again if she gave in to despair.

"Triumph, let's get that arboretum door fixed first. We've got a beagle to rescue," Lulu said, trying to find a single unmangled speaker to direct her speech toward.

She spun when the computer spoke to her from behind. A slider was using its manipulator arms to navigate the buckled deck, no longer capable of using the rails in the ceiling. It was a little creepy to see it scuttling along more like a spider than the bots she knew.

The friendly green light on the slider's rounded top lit up as it said, "There are no working microphones or speakers in this area. This unit will stay with you in order to communicate more effectively. I'm working on getting to the arboretum. There are almost as many holes in the ship as I've got arms."

Lulu leaned on one hip, crunching some broken tile underfoot, and tilted her head at the slider/scuttler. Despite everything that had happened, she almost sighed in relief to hear the human-like conversational tone. "Did you just make a joke?" she asked.

"I did not."

Lulu watched as the bot used two of its manipulators to gather up some of the debris into a pile. A trail of similar piles marked the path it had taken into this part of the hab. The bot's little round dome swiveled to point its camera at the pile, then swiveled back toward her. The computer might not be human, but it sure knew how to give hints.

"Fine," she said, looking at the mess. "I'll help."

Lulu bent to tug a trash bin from inside the compartment where it was tucked—the irony of their trash remaining safe while all the important stuff got sucked into space was not lost on her—and began chucking broken tiles and assorted debris into it. She glanced up at the bot, which was already making another pile a foot away from the last, and asked, "How long until we get the arboretum open?"

One of the bot's free arms straightened and pointed toward the gray underside of the repair bot sealing the hole in the hab. A distinct *thunk* came from that direction and the bot said, "The hab is sealed. I estimate another hour."

Looking once more at the destruction around her, Lulu blew out a breath and bent back to the task of clearing up the wreckage of her home. The bot worked silently beside her.

Chapter Three

As soon as the arboretum entrance was fixed—or at least repaired enough that it could be safely opened—Charlie bounded out with a howl, letting Lulu know in his beagle-ish way that he had missed her. Aside from some serious scrapes along the bottom of his paw pads, probably from frantic attempts to get the door open, he seemed fine. Traumatized, of course, but physically fine.

"Hey, buddy," Lulu cooed as she gathered him into her arms for a cuddle. She needed it almost as much as he did, and there was no question that dog cuddle therapy was almost the best therapy there was.

After he calmed, his naturally curious nose began sniffing around. The former breach drew him like a beacon, and he whined his distress as he sniffed the bulkhead that had so recently been open to space. The sliders had already cleaned the wide smears of blood and other body matter from the edges of the former jagged opening, but Charlie's nose was stronger than their cleaning solution. It broke Lulu's heart to know that he was smelling the deaths of all the people he knew except her.

"It's okay, Charlie. Come here, boy," Lulu said in her most coaxing and soothing voice. He trotted back over, but his ears were hanging low, and it would take a blind person to miss the confused sadness in his eyes. "Let's go get a bacon," she said, using the best lure known in the beagle lexicon.

It worked, and he howled and jumped as they walked toward the crew mess. She gave him the bacon, which wasn't actually bacon at all, but rather an obscene mixture of specialized algae—SpecNA—and other entirely false flavorings. But he loved it, thought it was a treat, and on top of that it was good for him. She grabbed his bed and a few toys from the stateroom of the last Load to have their turn with Charlie and hauled it all into the mess. She fitted the doggie grate to the opening so he would stay put. At least from here he would have the mess and the recreation area to roam in while still being able to see out. Her stateroom was tiny and closed in, not to mention completely wrecked.

"I'm sorry, sweetie, but I have to go and fix stuff. I've got to see about tanking up some new friends for you. Or rather, tanking up some new versions of your old friends. How about that?" she asked him, giving him a good scratch behind the ears.

I wonder if he'll be able to tell the difference between the new versions and the old ones? Do we smell any different?

Charlie, for his part, seemed enthusiastic about the idea—if the volume of his "arrrooo" was any indication. She gave him one final pat and then left the mess, the sheer weight of all the things that she needed to do pulling the smile from her face like a sudden increase in gravity.

"Triumph, any further life signs?" she asked as she navigated her way around the wreckage of her life toward the laboratory section.

"Negative. I can continue to scan, but the probability is approaching certainty that there are no other survivors. Do you wish me to continue?"

Lulu sighed, terribly disappointed. She wasn't exactly *sad* at the loss of her friends, since she hadn't exactly *lost* them. They were safely tucked into the computer banks of the ship, ready to be born again exactly as they were the last time they woke up. Even Lulu herself was a replacement for a Lulu who had died in an accident on the surface a few months after this generation had been decanted for their work. In fact, eighty-three Lulus— she knew of their existence mostly through her own number, eighty-four—had preceded her in this mission. These were the facts of life aboard this vessel: serial immortality and endless work.

But if she wasn't sad, she *was* disappointed, because of the impact the temporary loss of her friends would have on their work. Together, they had successfully ushered the planet they orbited to the stage at which life was being introduced. True, the life on the planet was so far almost exclusively limited to single-celled primary producers—beings whose evolutionary duty was to liberate oxygen and begin laying the foundation for organic soil with their bodies—but this was a critical juncture, one that would require constant monitoring, adjusting, and guidance, and that meant they could really use all hands on deck and in top form. Yet it would now take six months to replicate two dozen new crewmembers, tank them, and wake them. And even then, it would be months more before the same synergy they had possessed just hours ago was renewed. If ever.

This was going to suck.

"Cease scans, Triumph. Let's focus on reconsolidation. Continue to use the landers and whatever else you've still got to get materials to manufacturing. We need matter to rebuild. Get your mining balls into a safe orbit as well. We'll need everything they've got in their pods."

"I'm doing that now, Lulu," Triumph responded. "I'm also working on the damage to manufacturing facilities. I do have my core plant, so I can rebuild peripheral manufacturing facilities. I suggest we focus on that."

Lulu was relieved to hear the computer using the human-like speech of normal life. That meant it was back into a proper mission mode, rather than emergency mode. If she had to compare the computer to a human, she would say it was like a human going back to a normal tone of voice after yelling for a while.

"Fine, yes. But I want to get all the new Loads tanked ASAP. We're going to lose a lot of work here as it is, and we can't afford to waste time with that. I'll need bio fast, so tank up Heather, Graham, and everyone else from my core work group into the first tanks. Everyone is going to be needed to make sure all mutations on the surface are within specifications. Plus we've got to get about a thousand species of feeders for all those little critters down there. We can't wait for that or we'll never get the mutations under control."

As Lulu issued instructions, she went through the ruin that was her lab. The breach in this module had nearly destroyed her entire facility. The hundreds of vials, cultures, and DNA prints waiting their turn at culture were gone. They were probably hurtling away from the wreckage even now due to the initial thrust out of the hab. The thought passed through her mind that maybe they could send a mining ball after them on the same trajectory and see what could be retrieved. Of course, that was a ridiculous thought and she pushed it away.

She would be starting over. Luckily, the designs for all her slightly-different-from-Earth versions of this planet's life resided on the computer. It was simple labor really. The computer would help.

"Triumph, did you get my last instruction? We need to tank the Loads," Lulu said. She lifted the latch on one of the cabinets and a river of broken glass flowed out. Even behind doors that stayed closed, there was destruction.

The slider appeared around the cabinet at the sound of the glass, a disposal bin in its arms. Lulu paused then, a broken beaker in her hand. It wasn't like the computer not to answer.

"We need to tank Loads. Is there a problem?" she asked.

"At this time, I can't do that," the ship responded.

"Why not? Is the facility damaged?" Lulu asked. As she set down the beaker and walked rapidly in the direction of Medical and its tanking facilities, she tried to think back to the list of things that were still intact. Had Medical been on that list? Medical being gone, or substantially damaged, would be bad. Really bad.

These ships were forever rebuilding themselves. That was their design and their strong suit. They didn't zip at high speed between stars because that sort of tech simply never came about. They went as fast as was possible, but it sometimes still took centuries to get to a new world, so it was critical that they were able to collect materials and rebuild themselves as time went on. These ships would travel to a new star as only stripped-down versions of themselves, park at a likely world, then take up to a dozen more centuries to set up mining facilities and collect enough materials to replicate themselves and send those new, pared-down versions on their way to the next world.

The first human would not be tanked until all of that happened. The common element to all of these tasks was speed… as in no speed… as in super slow. All told, the process could take thousands of years.

But they didn't have thousands of years. Not for this planet; not for this mission. Every year that passed without proper oversight from this ship and its crew would result in the life currently on the planet developing in ways they didn't want. The mission would be a failure.

"The facility is damaged, but repairable," Triumph reported. "If the repair list is re-prioritized, then I estimate six months for repair to return to full capacity. However, I do not suggest re-prioritization."

"Six months!" Lulu exclaimed, slapping her hand on the door to Medical. It hadn't opened as she'd approached, which meant there was an unsafe level of damage inside, or perhaps an unbreathable mix of gases yet to be cleared. "That means a year at least before I get more Loads!"

"I can't create more Loads," Triumph said.

"Until you get fixed, yes, I get that," Lulu said, trying to figure out how she was going to do the work of twenty-four people for a year or more. Maybe more bots could help.

"Lulu, perhaps you don't understand. My core is fractured. I have lost peripheral cores, including all the Load templates. I have been working to recover them, but it appears that I will not be able to. I have a partial Strand databank, but none of the Loaded Strand databank." Triumph almost sounded ashamed of itself for losing such an essential part of the mission.

Lulu turned around to lean against the door to Medical. It was cool against her back, and she could feel the vibration of the bots zipping about inside doing their work. She slid down the door to rest on the floor, still streaked with black marks and gouges from the impact of everything that had hurtled past on its way to the breach.

No Loads? It was impossible to think of that. If she tanked up regular Strands, she would get only babies. Babies that had to be cared for, taught, and raised before they would be of any use to her. Loads were the only way she could go forward. And it wasn't just her that would be stuck without Loads to help; it would be this world.

They had come too far in the development of the rocky, unlivable surface for it to be a candidate for any future version of their ships to consider. Life, no matter how small or isolated, meant it was no good for their work. Humans didn't destroy life to create a new home when there were so many other planets without life to choose from. Every bit of life on the surface had been placed there with care by the crew of the Triumph, and the generations that came from those life forms were now Lulu's responsibility. Any ship in the future that happened across this planet would immediately reject it simply because of the life already on it. It would be left as it was, halfway to nowhere, with only a few thousand species of single-celled plants.

Lulu squeezed her eyes shut, reaching for something good about this situation that she could console herself with. But she came up with nothing. She could find nothing good. She needed Loaded Strands or she would eventually leave this planet in the lurch. It wasn't fair.

It didn't even have a name yet.

Each of the five thousand Loaded Strands had special skills and could be decanted as an adult, exactly as they were when they were bright-eyed young idealists back on Earth. She needed those people, their personalities and skills. And most of all, she needed more biologists. No, nothing except Loads would do.

And she had none.

It was more than heartbreak that weighed her down. It was

a failure so profound that it almost couldn't be taken in. Perhaps it would have been better if she had died along with everyone else during the disaster. What did she have to look forward to now?

She punched the floor and shook off the hopeless feeling. "No one? Not one Load?" she said.

There was a pause. It was such a small one that most people wouldn't have even registered it as a pause at all. But after years of dealing with a computer that could keep track of whole worlds, that could process billions of calculations in the blink of an eye, Lulu had learned to notice its rare pauses— and to know what they meant. They signaled that whatever the computer said next would likely be upsetting to her.

In that split second, she closed her eyes and prepared herself.

"It would be incorrect to state that I have no Loads available at all," Triumph said.

Lulu opened one eye and gave the speckled speaker patch on the ceiling a narrowed look.

"What are you saying?" she asked, half-dreading whatever answer the computer would give her.

"I have you."

Chapter Four

"This is bollocks," Lulu said as she stripped down inside a newly refurbished medical bay. It had taken a full month of work just to get it back to its current state, which still wasn't that great. One medical bot, one treatment table, and one brand spanking new Load chair. Ships weren't even supposed to have a Load chair, but as with everything else, there were overrides and special conditions, and the ship had blueprints for everything— just in case.

Just in case had happened for Triumph.

"It is not bollocks, Lulu," Triumph answered, but without much emotion, which just annoyed her more. The computer was supposed to reflect her, not act like a machine when she most needed a good fight.

"Just get your progeny to send the Loads more quickly. Quantum freaking buoys, hello! Instantaneous and all that," Lulu said. She smacked at the little arms on the slider that kept trying to help by shoving little electronic leads at her. "And stop that! I've got to get undressed first. I don't want you poking at me."

The slider desisted, its arms folding up to its little round ball of a body near the ceiling, the myriad leads dangling from its claws.

"Thank you," Lulu said and folded her clothes, deliberately taking her time. If Triumph was going to be annoying, she would too.

"You're welcome. Lulu, we've already had this discussion. Quantum buoys are fast, but they are character limited. To transmit even one Load would take an extraordinarily long time, and there are always errors in transmission. And the consequences of contact might be more dangerous than you've allowed for."

"Yeah, yeah. I know. It'll send you the instructions for destruct if it finds out your status. I get it. But I told you what to say instead, didn't I? You know, a little, tiny white lie."

Lulu settled into the chair and waggled her fingers at the slider so it would bring the leads. As much as she wanted to do it herself, there was no way a human could ever hope to get all the various connections right. It would take days, and really, she could only sit here so long. The computer could do it in an hour. But she still didn't like it.

"You know I can't do that. We either risk them sending my program back to me—that's what I would do, so we can be relatively sure that's what any other ship would do—or we do this. Which do you want?" Triumph asked, adding a little more personality into the mix.

"Fine, whatever. Just do it. I can almost feel the mutations happening on the ground out there. I need a huge assist, and soon."

Lulu lay back, allowing herself to relax after the slider's third push on her shoulder. She sighed loudly and gritted her teeth through the innumerable little pokes onto her skin. Leads began to cover her body like a pale version of chickenpox, only made out of plastic and metal instead of irritated skin.

When at last the leads were all attached, the green flashes of light from the control panel ceased. The slider whirred away and came back just as quickly. Lulu had closed her eyes—only resting them, not napping at all, honest—but opened them when the tiny whoosh of air tickled the skin of her face.

"Lulu, we're ready to proceed. May I?" Triumph asked.

Above her, one slider held the square bit of gray cloth that would go over her face. Over her body, two more sliders held larger versions. Once these were laid down on her, they would join with the lower portions underneath her body and the haptic feedback would begin. She would feel entirely closed off from what was real for a short period of time as her body was tested, loaded, sorted, and eventually digitized, along with her neural map.

The cloth meant for her face was slightly different; it had a screen that would parade an array of imagery and stimuli past her eyes. She knew from distant memory that it would make her nauseated and seasick. She could remember only the first part of this process from her initial Load on Earth, but even that was enough make her swallow hard.

Lulu breathed deeply, looked around once more, and said, "Remember to feed Charlie if it takes too long."

"I will. And he has his fuzzy bear for entertainment," Triumph answered.

Lulu smiled, remembering how happy Charlie had been when his specially made slider—Fuzzy Bear—had trundled into the mess after three weeks in repair.

"Good. Let's go then. I've got work to do," Lulu said.

Chapter Five

As the sixth of the Lulus was lifted from her tank, Lulu tried to repress a shudder. She hated seeing them like this. Seeing *herself* like this. But she couldn't stop watching them. The seven months it had taken to wake the first one were the hardest—and the loneliest—of her life. Her desire for company, for someone to talk to—someone who could talk back—had made her spend far too much time here in the tanking facility, waiting for the Lulus to grow.

Like the five before her, this Lulu was limp in a way that wasn't natural at all. Even a sleeping person will hold up their heads or move their limbs, but this body was utterly at the mercy of the sliders that lifted her from her tank. Her skin was rosy in a way, but also strangely uniform and pale. No sun had yet touched her, not even the fake sunlight of the ship. But even with the blank expression and the unused appearance of her skin, there was no denying that Lulu was looking at herself.

It was surreal, completely weird. In any other situation, it would be freak-out worthy. Something like this should never happen. It just wasn't in the plan. Only one of each Load was allowed at any one time.

Now, it was necessary.

It was weird in another way too. Loads never saw other Loads in tanks. Lulu must have already been Loaded back on Earth before that rule was enacted, but Triumph told her that it was determined to be "unhealthy" for Loads to witness others while in their tanks. Lulu was sure there was a good story in there somewhere, but Triumph couldn't be cajoled into sharing it.

That rule had changed now because she was alone. Well, alone except for Charlie and, while he was great, he was still a dog. She needed to see other humans, even if they were still Loading. In addition, Triumph had agreed with her that getting used to the idea of so many Lulus meant she needed to be a part of the process from the get-go.

When it came right down to it, she and Triumph were in uncharted territory. They were making up the rules as they went along.

As the new Lulu was lifted free of the jelly-like fluid, her head flopped in a way that made Lulu reach a hand to the back of her own neck. The new Lulu's wet hair swung in dripping clumps as the slider moved her from the tank to the table in preparation for waking. Lulu watched as the slider washed and dried the woman who was her, combed out her now-shiny hair, clipped, snipped, and otherwise put this Lulu into a state very like the one she had been in during her original Load. The goal was to make her "come out" in much the same state as she had "gone in." Too much change from one instant of experience to the next—no matter how many actual millennia passed between those experiences—was never good for a Load's mental state.

Lulu laid the crinkly, silver sheet over the still form, taking a deep breath and readying herself to deal with this person who was exactly like her. More importantly, to deal with her as a new and separate person. With new Lulu's hair freshly cut and her skin dry and clean, it was amazing to look at her. Lulu remembered when her own skin was unscarred and smooth. The life of a Load wasn't easy on the skin, and she certainly didn't look like that now, particularly after their catastrophe.

"Lulu, can you step into Observation, please? I'm ready to wake Lulu 6 now," Triumph said, the voice quite gentle and coaxing. The computer had known Lulu since it was nothing more than its original computer core on Earth, so it knew exactly how difficult this was for her. And with just the two of them on this ship for the last six months, it had gotten to know her even better.

"I'll explain, just like the others. Got it?" Lulu said as she went to the observation booth. The window darkened slightly as the one-way mirror activated. There was no need to alarm this Lulu immediately.

"Of course," Triumph said.

Waking went well. New Lulu, who would be known as Lulu 6—starting the numbers over again just made sense in their situation—knew her waking phrase and passed all her neurological tests. And just as with the other five, Lulu was surprised to see how differently each of the Lulus acted after that first moment of waking. They were identical during that first minute or two, compliant and eager to pass the waking, but immediately diverged thereafter.

One cried, racing from table to table and running her hands along their bottom surfaces, feeling for that scratch she'd left under the table in Earth's simulators to tell any future her that she was really on Earth and not on a ship. That one believed her last memories were some kind of nightmare and didn't believe she could possibly be on a ship with only other versions of herself.

She'd gotten over it.

Another laughed and clapped her hands, delighted by the idea of being around other Lulus. Yet another simply stood up and accidentally peed herself, uttering a string of curses and slapping at the slider that came to clean up the mess.

Lulu wondered what this Lulu would do.

It turned out this one was a crier too. Great.

Lulu sighed and thought about the other eleven tanks in the medical bay, six of them filled with a Lulu nearly ready for decanting and the other five opaqued while the first stages of a new Lulu were completed in darkness. By the end of the day, this newly emptied tank would have a new Lulu inside it, a tiny core that would one day become another one of her.

She and Triumph were discussing how they could increase the pace of production, maybe even double up the Lulus inside the tanks. It was theoretically possible, requiring only a second set of support and growth harnesses be installed. That would give them more Lulus quicker, but it would also mean Lulu would have to do this duty—confirm this bad news—twice as often. It didn't matter that these Lulus shared her memory of the destruction of the ship and the loss of the Loads—it was still a lot to take in. And her thoughts hadn't exactly been rosy in the moments just before she went into the chair.

She hoped that one of these Lulus could eventually take over this duty. *On second thought,* she decided, *I owe it to them to tell them the truth.*

The new Lulu sat up on the table, her brand new and baby-smooth brow wrinkling as she listened to Triumph get her ready for what she was about to see.

That was Lulu's cue. She took a deep breath and opened the door to the observation booth, meeting this new Lulu for the first time. Lulu 6's eyes widened and traveled up and down Lulu a couple of times, pausing a little on the scars on her hands and face and the thick shock of gray that had appeared in her hair after the accident.

"Holy fuck," Lulu 6 said softly.

"Exactly," Lulu said.

Chapter Six

Three Hundred Years Later

"I refuse to be called four sixty-eight even one more time," Lulu 468 said as she stomped her foot on the metal grating of the landing bay. The clang echoed around the sparsely filled bay and made another Lulu at the far end pause and look, curious about the disturbance. She apparently wasn't interested enough though, because she climbed into her Lander and the sights and sounds of pre-flight checks began.

Lulu 468 turned back to her compatriots and said, "I'm serious."

"Okay, then we'll call you four *hundred* and sixty-eight. How's that?" Lulu 467 said as she dropped a tank of tiny algae eaters into the Lander cargo hold. The bang it made was like the best kind of punctuation, perfectly timed. If she wasn't so annoyed, she might have smiled.

"Very funny. And I bet you think that was perfect timing to your smart-ass comment, too?" Lulu 468 asked, then waved her hands in annoyance and turned away. "Why am I even asking? I know the answer. I'm just saying that I'd like a real name!"

Lulu 421, her hair beginning to gray and wrinkles creasing the skin around her eyes, tapped Lulu 467 on the shoulder and said, "You're angering her for no reason. You've both got a lot of years together here still; you should be kinder to each other."

Lulu 467 had the good grace to look ashamed, and Lulu 468 made a little noise of distress.

Lulu 468 said, "I'm so sorry. We shouldn't fight. You're right. How are you holding up? We miss 422 as well. She was like a mother to me."

"Me too," Lulu 467 said.

Lulu 421 nodded, wiped away an escaping tear, and said, "We used to fight like you guys do. But she was my best friend. There's no one else like your tank-twin, is there?"

Lulu 467 and Lulu 468 looked at each other for a moment. Irritation they might feel, but 421 was right.

"I'm sorry, sis," Lulu 467 said. "Let's talk to the computer again. Maybe we can get a vote this time. Really, we do need better names. I know the rules, but still."

The red light in the landing bay started flashing, and the warning klaxon precluded further conversation. All the Lulus stood by as the Lander at the other end of the bay coasted toward the launch facility, ready to take more tiny critters to the surface.

Lulu 467 climbed to the top of her Lander to get a better view, and Lulu 468 joined her a moment later. There were no windows here, and very few anywhere in the ship. They relied on screens, but it wasn't really the same. No matter how realistic it might be, the human eye—and the human soul—could tell the difference between a picture and the real thing. These launches gave them one of the best looks they would ever get.

The big bay doors to the launch facility closed, but the thick glass gave them a clear visual path to the outer doors. The Lander lined itself up, its various flashes of light signaling a launch process happening in good order, and then the outer doors slid open. Both Lulus gasped in tandem as the planet blossomed into view. The planets' curve seemed almost to be smiling at them, acknowledging their presence and the gifts each launch bestowed upon it.

The sharp white of clouds stretching across the surface make Lulu 467 smile. Water and air. The land was still gray for the most part, but hints of brown could be seen here and there, and the water looked like a jewel from here.

From her own landings, she knew that it didn't look anything like this from the ground. There, it was gray and black, dangerous and deadly. Her suit was all that kept her from death. But from here, during these moments, it was beautiful.

All too quickly the Lander was on its way and the outer doors closed, hiding the planet from their sight. Lulu gripped her tank-twin's hand and squeezed, no words needed. They smiled at each other, everything once again good between them.

The two Lulus clambered down from the Lander and stood there for a moment, both knowing they should say something to Lulu 421, maybe even apologize for their behavior. But the older Lulu only laughed, slapped Lulu 468 on the shoulder and said, "You two load the ship. I'll do inventory and pre-flight checks. That's what you get for arguing. Hard labor."

The various Lulus returned to work, loading up their own Lander for another trip to the surface. Another cargo of life for this lonely rock, this planet that would someday provide a beautiful, vibrant world for future Strands. None of the current Lulus envied the future Lulus their duty to raise all those first babies. That would be a far more irritating task than a snarky tank-twin. Still, there was no question that they all envied them their lives on a beautiful planet of green and blue. Annoying babies or no, those far, far future Lulus would enjoy some perks.

But such thoughts were for the dim future. For now, the planet was waiting, and the Lulus were ready to roll.

Q&A with Ann Christy

Where did this story come from?

Lulu's been digging around in my gray matter for a while now. There's an entire book about Lulu in the works—well, *other* Lulus on another ship—but I haven't yet felt like it's just right, so I'm still working on it. I know enough about the challenges involved in interstellar endeavors to know that we will likely have to choose between speed and living passengers to get anywhere. We will certainly gain the technological know-how for self-replicating machines that can build biological organisms in the not-too-distant future. I think that's how we'll get "out there" in the end. Lulu is my imagination's way of exploring that concept.

How does it relate to other books you've written?

It doesn't! I write sci-fi, but mostly post-apocalyptic, dystopian, or fiction that is in some other way dark and dreadful. That said, I don't think I have a genre that I'm pigeonholed into yet. I'm far too insane for that sort of singular dedication.

Tell us something we might not know about you.

My favorite candy is Goo Goo Clusters (especially the Supreme ones). I also love to cook and then force people to eat the results... and they have to actually swallow the food or it doesn't count. Since I spent my career as a military scientist, it probably doesn't surprise anyone that I'm a total science geek, but did you know I'm a huge *Star Trek* fan?

How can readers find you?

I'm everywhere! Instagram, Facebook, Twitter, and my website (www.annchristy.com) are the best ways to find me. Do look me up. Let's be friends! And yes, I already know I post too many pictures of food, random weird stuff around the house, and my dogs.

Works in progress?

I recently finished a series called *Between Life and Death*, so I'm beat and my brain is tired. Alas, I loved those characters so much I can't let them drift into the great beyond just yet. A web-based, interactive fiction episode in that universe is coming. I'm also working on *Strikers: The Eastlands*—because if I don't, I'll be strung up by readers. And yes, I'm also working on Lulu 394. She's waited long enough.

Does this story reveal the secret to how quickly you write books?
Boom, you got it! No, not really. I'm Ann 1.0, though I'll be honest, I would love to grow a few more of me in tanks. How fun would it be to hang out with a younger version of yourself? Seriously, I'd be torn between laughing at her and wanting to punch her for being an idiot. Plus, you know, she could help with chores.

To Catch an Actor
by Blair C. Babylon

THE SUSPECT SITTING on the other side of the steel table is male, very definitely male, about six-three, golden blond and green-eyed with chiseled cheekbones and jawline, slim but with good musculature, and the pinnacle of male beauty. If he's like all the others, his abdomen is rippled with muscle, and it's obvious from where I'm sitting, which is too close in these tiny rooms and with only this narrow table between us, that his chest and shoulders strain the clinging fabric of his shirt.

He's about twenty-seven, personal time, though his file says he was born a little over five hundred years ago.

He smiles at me. A slow, lazy smile.

The interrogation room feels cramped because it's far smaller than the usual setup. Down on a planet, we would call this a cubicle. My knees almost touch his under the small table. Even after five years, I swear I can feel the rotation of the space station under my feet.

In his mug shot in the corner of my tablet's screen, the suspect's dark green eyes sparkle with good humor, and his smirk is sensual rather than dismissive.

The murder that he's suspected of took place sixty-five years before I was born.

Even that mug shot is a hundred years old.

His hands—soft, no calluses, professionally blunt-cut nails—rest on the steel table, haloed in the glare from the light above us.

My caramel-brown hands, clasped on the table in front of me, have a pink, oval manicure, and a wedding band glimmers on my left hand in the harsh lights. Our knuckles are inches apart.

I stare at the suspect, trying to spot any fear or guilt in his dark green eyes.

Nothing.

A pale blue afterimage flits over him. My implant labels his expression as *calm abiding.*

He smiles just a little more at me, more with one side of his lush lips than the other.

My implant paints his mouth pink and labels it *flirting,* as if I couldn't figure that out.

I don't respond, not even a little.

Why this paragon of youthful masculinity would be flirting with me, thirty-five-year-old police detective Cordelia Hernandez, is a more interesting question.

Do you know what the toughest posting in the Known Worlds is for a homicide detective?

A penal colony? Nope. That was my first assignment after I made detective. As bad as things are in a penal colony—the macho lawlessness, the posturing, the gangs—none of the inmates dare to mouth off to the cops there and risk being wrestled into the back of a van with a black bag over their head and shipped off-world to one of the slave mines, which are so much worse. Even the gang bosses cooperate and become friends, grudgingly. I even had a short affair with one of the biggest bosses on the planet. I could close cases on Ryker's in a week, max.

One of the capital cities, with all their elitist snobbery and closed cliques? No, that assignment was easy, too. On my first day, an outgoing detective pulled me aside and told me how to do it: you don't bother with the second- and third-tier orbiters. They have too much invested and will defend the hierarchy. You go straight to the luminaries, the power-mongers of civilization and society, and you ask them straight up who did it. After some posturing, they'll inform on each other to wrestle their rivals out of the way, and they'll narc on the lower tiers even faster. And besides, the restaurants there were incredible. I met my husband and had my first two kids planetside. He was a second-tier politician before we transferred here, a short hop of a spaceflight in a normal-space shuttle between the moons and stations of this system. If we make it back there, his professional contacts will still be alive.

Nope, my posting now—at the height of my career, when I have the most to lose—is the toughest. Somehow, I have landed on the space station Hollywood, colloquially known as the Backlot.

In this place, the witnesses, the suspects, even the victims— they're all professional, pathological liars.

Actors.

These are the good actors, too. The A-listers, the galaxy-class artists.

B-listers and below live and die on the dirtworlds. But these guys, they're youthful forever.

They're the immortal ones.

Most people avoid near-lightspeed travel. In interstellar wars, the military sends tubes of pre-programmed drones, not soldiers, at near-lightspeed velocities. Politicians send out videos because they would miss twenty-five elections in a row if they rode a near-*c* ship. Disappearing for years or decades at a time and then returning to a changed world… it's not an option for most professions.

But celebrities are different. Their only product is themselves. Actors, musicians, dancers, anyone who commands a following that will pay to see them in person. They ride the waves of space between the planets, and at near-lightspeed, time slows. For them, a ship berth is a year-long tour that stops at five or six planets where they release their films or songs and do publicity shots and stunts for a week or two. Then it's back onto the century ships that sling them on their long, long loops through the stars—stars flying among the stars, reappearing every now and then like periodic comets.

And when their tour is done, they return to the Backlot, a hundred years later, to meet up with their deified friends.

A hundred of *my* years, anyway. I might get to see some of these actors once before they leap into eternity again. I'll die of old age before any of the young gods come back, including this suspect.

I hope to die of old age someday. Cops rarely die of old age in the Known Worlds.

The actor on the other side of the table is Daveen Kelly, and his sultry smile and looks of a young sun god have sent a thousand worshippers to their knees and to his bed.

His kind of incredible physical beauty is as common as rust and rats on the Backlot. Crowds of the gorgeous and the brilliant swarm among the shops and restaurants. You never get used to it, but as I interrogate him, my heart plods along at its usual, sedate pace, and my breathing is measured and steady.

The Academy here on the Backlot trains its actors to detect the subtlest emotional signals from other actors, to help them study their craft and to respond while they're performing. This suspect can read every signal that my body gives off, from the dilation of my pupils to the blush of my earlobes to the quality of my sweat. He can see and smell if I feel fear or excitement or if I'm lying.

His gaze lingers on my mouth before he looks into my eyes again, his smile warm and sexy.

These actors also never cease trying to use their looks to get what they want.

In this case, Daveen Kelly might want to get away with murdering Ming Barrymore, whose strangled body was found in Ming's own bed a hundred years ago, just before Daveen left on a century ship.

The ubiquitous surveillance cams in the hallways caught Daveen leaving Ming's suite. Daveen was the last person in there with him. They were both script actors, not reality-show ad-libbers, so there were no reality show cameras flitting around them like bumblebees inside the suite. A recording of the murder would have made this easier, though not certain. Footage can be modified by viruses, especially footage that's a century old, even the footage of Daveen leaving Ming's suite and no one else going in.

Daveen asked, "Is there anything else?"

I sipped my coffee. "Just a few more questions."

"All right." He rolled his shoulders, seeming to settle himself as if he had nothing to hide.

Liar.

They're all liars. About everything. Even the few non-actors here, like the musicians and dancers, can lie their way out of anything.

Musicians are stage performers, pulling faces as if they're shocked that they managed to change chords on a guitar, or as if the Brahms coming out their violin enraptures even them. They overact for the stage and then tone it down when there's a camera on them. They produce films of their performances for sale. They have to be able to act.

Dancers' body language is impenetrable, and their facial expressions have to remain serene, as if they're contemplating God instead of repressing the agony from their broken toes and the bones grinding in their damaged joints. It's like trying to interrogate a mannequin.

But Daveen here... I'm still trying to figure out if he has a quirk. If he were fresh out of the Academy, his acting would be micron precise, but he's been out on the ships for five years. That's a lot of time to get sloppy. Actors constantly make films and do promotions out there in order to make enough money for their next berth, plus some to put away for when they reach character actor age. They don't have time to do the acting equivalent of practicing scales.

But I haven't found any flaws in his acting chops yet, and we've been at this for two hours. If I don't find enough for an indictment in a day or two, he'll walk up a gangplank onto another century ship and escape forever.

Or at least until after I'm dead.

And if I'm wrong and we indict an innocent man? Then Daveen will have to wait a decade before the next round of ships leaves. He'll be thirty-seven. A decade without promoting and work is a death sentence for an actor.

He'll also be nearing forty, horror of horrors.

"You've been out on a ship a long time, Daveen," I say, warming up again.

He smiles a little more for me, and his dark green eyes blink like he just tumbled out of my bed. "Just the latest tour."

"That's a hundred years to us."

"So I've heard." Daveen rolls one of his hands over, exposing his soft palm. It's an invitation to hold his hand, the beginning of seduction.

I retract my hands from the table and straighten in my seat, stopping just short of rolling my eyes. Again, I have no other physical reaction to him. No racing heartbeat. No intake of the breath of desire.

I say, "Technology advances a lot in a century."

Daveen's laugh is a plosive puff of disbelief while he retracts his hand. "It doesn't look like it."

"We keep everything the same for you travelers, but the walls have been replaced three times since you left for your last tour.

The clothes that you think you left in your room are replicas, and nine people have slept in your living space since you last docked. Do you have a thespian?"

His medical records show that he doesn't, but I already know that.

He says, "I heard something about those, but I don't know what they are." Confusion flits between his pale eyebrows. My implant highlights it in violet and labels the expression *unease*.

"A thespian," I repeat. Daveen is an actor, not a spaceship engineer. I should probably keep the technology simple and speak slowly. "It's an organic/inorganic implant that all the actors have now."

He glances to the side, and the light catches in his dark gold eyelashes. "Yeah, I heard that much."

"It was pioneered about eighty years ago in The Beatitudes."

"Figures. Jesuit education system."

"It sequesters neurotransmitters so you can release them back into your blood while you're acting."

He leans forward, interest sparking in his green eyes. "It stores emotions?"

Daveen isn't as vapid as some of the other actors. That's dangerous.

"That's it exactly," I say. "When the neurotransmitters are released, an actor's body reacts perfectly, just as if they feel the emotion. Their pupils dilate. Their lips and skin flush with blood."

He smiles. "I can do that just by thinking about it."

His lips pinken and plump. His dark pupils widen in his green eyes. His reaction would have been imperceptible to an untrained or unaugmented eye, and the body of another human sitting with him would have reacted, responding to the sex flush on such an attractive man.

My implant paints his mouth and eyes red and labels them *arousal.*

"Pretty good." All the Academy-trained actors can do that. I've seen it hundreds of times. "With the thespian, you can do it better. Faster. Perfectly. And all of it in sync. You can even emanate pheromones."

"Really?" His tone was starting to sag with doubt.

"Films from actors with thespians have swept the awards for decades. You can't see them acting."

He sits back in the chair. "And I'm auditioning against people with these things."

"Fifty graduates from the Academy this year have had them implanted."

"Were there any that didn't?"

"No."

"Wow." He looks up at the ceiling, his muscular arms dangling by the sides of the chair.

"They weave it into your spine and brain and insert ducts into most of your glands. It looks more like a squid than a box. Healing time after the surgery is six months."

He jumps slightly in his chair. The table rattles where his knees jostle it. "Six *months?* All the boats will be *gone.*"

"There are the ninety-year boats that will leave in a decade or so."

"Jesus Christ." He combs his sun-gold hair back with his fingers and holds his fist at the nape of his neck.

Everything I've told him is true. Daveen Kelly might be beautiful, but he is obsolete.

I say, "Thespians aren't the only thing that has advanced since you've been on that antique boat, out there in the backwater planets. Forensic science has come a long way."

"Fascinating." He's still staring at the ceiling, his world rocked by the thought that, at twenty-seven, his career might be over. The concept of the thespian disturbs him more than the very real possibility that he might be locked up in jail on the planet rotating below us for the rest of his dirtbound life.

He has forgotten to act.

Sloppy.

"Daveen, tell me again about your relationship with Ming."

"Creche-mates. He played opposite me in a couple buddy films on the two tours we were on together. Stole an Oscar from me two years ago."

Two hundred years ago, Ming Barrymore's film was the overwhelming favorite to sweep the Oscars. Ming's win shouldn't have been a surprise to Daveen, unless his producers had lied to him about his chances in order to manipulate him into doing something else.

"Did that make you angry?" I ask. "To lose to Ming?"

He shrugs. "It's a popularity contest. Evidently, now it's a technology race, too. Did Ming have one of these thespians?"

"No. You killed him a hundred years ago. The thespians were only approved for human implantation about eighty years ago."

"Doesn't mean he didn't have one. Ming was the type to cheat," Daveen muses, staring at the ceiling. "I'll bet he got one somewhere."

My hands are perfectly steady, and my heart plods at its customary pace. I don't even blink beyond what's normal for me, not even when Daveen doesn't deny killing Ming.

"About the advances in forensic technology," I continue, "we can do a lot more now than we used to."

"Good for you." Daveen still stares at the ceiling.

"Using air displacement detectors with algorithms to cancel out known interactions, we can virtually see into the past. The images kind of look like sculptures of dust, the way the computer reconstructs the actions."

"You said that nine people have lived in my room. Good luck canceling out a century's worth of people walking through there."

I pick up my tablet and consult it casually. "We've already done it."

"Then you would have already arrested me."

Two admissions of murder. "We saw you do it."

"Where?"

"We're not playing a game here. We'd like to know your motivation, though."

"Now you sound like an actor."

"Why did you kill him?"

"I didn't."

Typical. "If you *had* killed him, why would you have done it?"

"That's very hypothetical."

"It is."

"I didn't hypothetically do it."

"All right. But you were angry at him. We can't hear what you were talking about, not yet, but we saw your movements. We saw the fight, and we saw you with your hands around his neck."

"Whatever." His hand waves dismissively.

"By the time you get back next time, a year for you but a century for us, we'll be able to hear you, too."

"No you won't."

"We're on the brink of it now."

"You're lying."

I look straight at him, a blasé smile on my face and my heart rate as unperturbed as a metronome. "Do I look like I'm lying?"

The smile slips from his face, and his dark green eyes widen.

Right now, Daveen Kelly is watching how entirely unconcerned I am. To his very trained eye, it looks like I'm telling the absolute truth.

I bump my thespian to pull a little more adrenaline out of my bloodstream, and an even more serene calm settles over me.

There's no such thing as an air displacement detector with an algorithm to cancel out the other people who have walked through that room, but someone who's been isolated on a near-c spaceship for a hundred years won't know that.

"If I were to give you a confession," Daveen asks, "and an excellent motivation, what kind of a deal could we consider?"

My smile might be a little smug, but there's nothing to tip him off that I'm lying my butt off.

I may not have attended the Academy, and I may not have my thirty-thousand practice-hour certificate or anywhere near enough money to buy a berth on a century ship, but I recognized the value of a thespian when interrogating actors right after we moved here.

That's why I can close cases on the Backlot.

Because these over-trained, immortal artists never dream that I can *act*.

Q&A with Blair C. Babylon

Where did this story come from?

A few years ago, I was noodling around with the idea of near-lightspeed ships, because I'm old school and I don't believe in FTL. I had been watching the attempts at the privatization of space flight, most notably Richard Branson's Virgin Galactic program, and a news program was discussing who was rumored to have bought tickets on Branson's first private, commercial space flight. The passengers included Katy Perry, Russell Brand, Angelina Jolie, Brad Pitt, Tom Hanks, Ashton Kutcher, Sarah

Brightman, Justin Bieber, Brian Singer, Lady Gaga, and Leonardo DiCaprio.

I thought, yeah, that makes sense: celebrities have the disposable income to buy interstellar spaceship tickets and are vain enough to want to be eternally young. No one else would leave their families and friends to die while they lived forever. So I started writing an SF murder mystery novel (unfinished due to other project commitments) with the throwaway working title *Kardashians in Space.*

When I was asked to be in this anthology, I went back through my notes for that universe and fashioned this detective story.

How does it relate to other books you've written?
It doesn't. Not even a little. I've published a police procedural, *The Angel of Death,* but it's a contemporary suspense/mystery, not SF. This was just for fun.

Tell us something we might not know about you.
I like to make quilts. I haven't had time to work on my blocks for a while, but I'm working on a Baltimore Album quilt. Also, I may have created a deadly strain of chickenpox virus during my PhD research.

How can readers find you?
I love to chat with readers. Please feel free to email me or hang out with me on Facebook or Google Plus. The best way to hear about new releases is tosign up for my mailing list. You get an

anthology of free Blair Babylon ebooks as a gift to you immediately just for signing up!

Works in progress?

In addition to science fiction, I write in several different genres. My urban fantasy series, some of which are based in the UF world of SM Reine, are available on my website.

If you like thrillers about police snipers vs. terrorists, you might like to check out *The Angel of Death* (Police Snipers and Hostage Negotiators, An Angel Day Novel). If you like a lot of romance with your death-defying thriller action, you might want to check out the list of my several long series on my website.

I also plan to publish a couple new science fiction and urban fantasy stories in the next year. If you'd like to get a quick email when they come out, pleasesign up for my mailing list.

2092

by Rysa Walker

Chapter 1

Elisi Shuttle Alar
Date: 9023.19.11

"THAT'S ONLY EIGHT. What about the final candidate? XE7, I believe?"

All eyes are on me now, so I flash a nervous smile at the nine other Voshti, whose faces are lined up in a neat row on my comm screen, and glance back down at the report I'm holding. I always dread finding a positive match, even though we desperately need them. So much can go wrong. And this planet is going to stir the pot a lot more than usual thanks to the extra incentive I discovered—one that I'm pretty sure several committee members will find irresistible.

"The planet has low to moderate supplies of four elements we seek, including one on the priority list," I tell them, and then return my gaze to Vosht Baydel. Although the Voshti is supposed to be a democratic body, Baydel is the oldest, not to mention the largest, member. His opinion generally turns the tide.

"But XE7 is remote," I continue. "It's also small, and far from unified. We'd be dealing with more than a hundred separate governments. Many are still prone to war. I doubt they'll be easy to unite."

"Well, we can't know that until they're tested," Baydel says. When I don't concur immediately, he gives me a verbal nudge. "Wouldn't you *agree*, Mila?"

My jaw clenches automatically, and I quickly try to cover my reaction with a polite smile. He should have called me Proctor Alta. It's possible that using my personal name in this formal setting is nothing more than a slip of the tongue—Baydel *is* my mother's oldest friend, and he's known me since I was an infant. I'm certain he pulled a string or two in order to get me under his command when they started drafting cultural anthropologists for the Testing Division, and he made sure that Ryn and I were stationed together. But he also knows me well enough to be aware that my opinions on this issue may not mesh well with his own, and he's certainly capable of condescending on purpose, just to be sure I remember my place.

What I really want to do is end the meeting now. Tell them I'll do the damned test. If the planet fails, the Voshti might, just *might*, decide that the relatively low level of resources means XE7 isn't worth the bother, and the Elisi Alliance will move on to the next planet. There are twelve more possibilities on my list alone, and I'm far from the only proctor.

I could just forget the little pulse that showed up on my

screen when I entered the planet's atmosphere. Just ignore it, and hope no one digs through the logs and realizes what it means. There's a really good chance that the adjutants they assign that sort of task wouldn't even recognize a chronotron pulse anyway, so I'd probably get away with the omission.

But failing to mention the issue would be a gross dereliction of duty, so I'm going to hope for the best. Maybe I can convince the Voshti to take another route, just this once.

"Under most circumstances," I say, still avoiding Baydel's gaze, "I'd argue that this planet isn't worth the effort of a formal alliance test. I'm not sure they *can* unite. There are deep societal divisions, and their collective security arrangements are extremely limited. I believe the testing will be a waste of our time. But…" I take a deep breath and move on to the next bit, the one that will push this little planet all the way to the top of the testing list once they realize what it means. "XE7 is one of five planets that has shown a history of chronotron… disturbances."

They all look up, and they all look confused. Even Baydel seems momentarily puzzled as to why I'd suggest this as a positive factor. We normally avoid entanglement with planets that muck around with time. The last thing you want in any alliance is to have reality constantly shifting beneath your feet.

Baydel puts the pieces together first, and a gleam that borders on predatory lights up his eyes. "So that's why the name seemed familiar. XE7 is the one that managed to *contain* a temporal disturbance. Correct?"

"Yes."

I push the next set of visuals I prepared out to the Voshti. As soon as the small lights above their faces click on to confirm that everyone can see the data, I continue.

"XE7 had a series of major chronotron spikes over an extended period, peaking about fifty of our years ago, which is around the year 2015 on their local calendar. As you can see from the nexus on the map, much of that activity occurred inside the planet's major economic power, which was also the predominant military power. After 2015, the chronotron distortions disappeared. There's nothing to suggest that the technology has been actively used to alter their timeline since then, although long-range sensors have picked up a few minor pulses on occasion, and I can confirm firsthand that there have been two surges since my shuttle came into range. At least one of the temporal alteration devices is located within the capital city of the nation I mentioned earlier."

"Do you have a *precise* location?" It's the Vosht whose image is just to the right of Baydel, a mousy woman whose name I can never remember.

"Two different locations since I've been in orbit. One is the primary legislative building, located in the city's center. The other appears to be a university research lab."

"Could you transfer those over, please?"

I glance at Baydel for confirmation. When he nods, I pull myself closer to the comm and transfer the data.

After a moment, the woman—Wirth, that's her name—says, "Do you think it's two different devices?"

"No. It appears to be someone carrying a single device from one location to the other. I've recorded two surges, about twenty-four hours apart, both times when it was at the assembly building. Each time, shortly after the surge, the signal travels back to the university location."

There's a moment of silence while they look over my data. I may not get another one, so I jump in with my proposal. "Perhaps we could consider working with that country alone, rather than going through the formal testing procedure? I know that's outside of the usual process, but—"

"Call for votes to submit XE7 for full and immediate testing," Wirth interrupts, not even looking up at me. Her position isn't the least bit surprising, given that she's directly connected to the ongoing war effort. But there are others in the assembly who are more reasonable.

"I know it's outside of the usual process," I repeat, "but as I noted, I don't think this planet is capable of uniting. And the other resources aren't really plentiful enough to—"

"Seconded," Baydel says, cutting off all possibility of debate.

I clench my teeth, biting back the rest of my statement. Any interruption on my part now would result in a reminder that I'm here to *inform* the assembly, not to assist in deliberations.

I knew there was a chance this would happen, that they would rush in as soon as I mentioned the possibility of time travel, but the small voice at the back of my head continues to protest. It's not just that I dread pulling these small planets into our conflict. I've almost—*almost*—reconciled with my conscience on this point. The Lor wouldn't think twice about it, and they no longer bother with piddly things like tests and alliances. They come in full force and take whatever they want. Objections are noted and those expressing them are promptly killed, along with a few hundred others for good measure.

This time travel device, however, raises an entirely new set of worries. From the information we have, it seems that one of the governments on XE7 was wise enough to use time travel judiciously. That doesn't mean the leaders of the Elisi Alliance will be as wise, especially in the middle of a war that we're losing badly.

Will they be content with a mere warning message about the escalating power of the Lor? Or will they decide to tweak history in a few other ways? An extra change here and there to make sure we're never attacked like this again. Another alteration to increase the power of one of the clans. Maybe one of the Voshti regrets a youthful indiscretion, or wishes his grandparents had invested more wisely so he could purchase a larger vacation home.

Once something like this is unleashed, will they even be able to control it? As the proverb goes, even the strongest cage cannot hold the wind.

Unfortunately, it also takes a stronger force than the Elisi Alliance to hold back the Lor. We've been pushed back sector by sector, a new planet every few cycles. Adding the resources of this tiny world will do little to tip the scales in our favor. XE7 will be of no use in actual combat, given that they've yet to master interstellar travel. More to the point, assisting us will almost certainly alert the Lor to XE7's presence, when otherwise their smaller size and remote location would mean they'd stand a decent chance of hiding in the shadows.

I feel like I've just placed a tiny, defenseless creature in the jaws of a massive beast.

The assembly's vote is unanimous. The silence that follows

over the next few minutes is so complete that for the first time in weeks I actually notice the hum of my shuttle's engines. Then Wirth pushes my visual back to the rest of the group, with alterations.

As I expected, XE7 is now at the top of my testing schedule.

"Begin testing in one centicycle," Baydel says. "Level Three."

"Level Three? I proposed Level One! Why can't we—"

But Baydel is gone. Off to supervise some other committee, no doubt, debating another decision where thousands of lives hang in the balance. I wouldn't want his job.

Still, which is the harder task? Making the hard decisions, or being the one stuck implementing them?

I don't really want *my* job, either.

The other members of the committee blink out. That leaves just me for several moments until an adjutant, one of several minor functionaries who'll play intermediary between me and the Voshti for the rest of the mission, pops onto one of my screens.

"This isn't enough time to plan a Level Three," I protest.

"The Voshti acknowledge that this is a tight schedule. The usual casualty limits have been doubled."

This particular adjutant is twenty years my junior, and he doesn't have any real authority. He's simply a go-between, taking my messages to the Voshti and bringing back their responses. Still, he clearly gets off on being close to power, because he wears the same self-important smirk as most of his colleagues.

I'm *so* tempted to point out that casualty limits have been a joke for the past year, but I bite down the observation, since it would almost certainly get back to my superiors. Preventing accidental deaths used to be a real consideration in any test of Alliance candidates, but I haven't heard of anyone being reprimanded for exceeding casualty limits since the Lor entered the sector next to ours.

Plenty of proctors exploit that laxity. They can't vent their anger on the Lor directly, so they use the inhabitants of these hapless little planets as a proxy.

Still, even though I know it's pointless to argue with an adjutant, I can't just leave it. I'm out here alone, so I either bitch to this guy or shout at the walls once the communication ends.

"Better yet," I say, struggling to keep my voice level, "why not waive the testing as I suggested? Just this once? The current chronotron readings originate within a single country. We don't have to pull XE7 in as full Alliance members. We could just approach them and—"

"The Alliance does not deal with partial members. Ever. If the people of the planet cannot come together, if they cannot be united against this trial attack by us, they will not be useful allies against the Lor."

"But we don't *need* them as allies. The only thing they have of real importance is that one bit of technology! Could you let me speak with Bayd—with Vosht Baydel, please?"

"The Voshti have ruled," he says with a tight-lipped smile. "Please submit an attack plan to the Adjutants' Office prior to your next sleep cycle."

And then the adjutant is gone, too.

Chapter 2

Elisi Shuttle Alar
Date: 9023.20.08

"I'll talk to you soon, okay? I love you."

I'm maybe twenty seconds away from depleting my remaining personal communications allowance for the entire trip. That means my journey back to our nearest outpost—seven full cycles—will be long and lonely. But I needed to see what's left of my family. To listen to my youngest talk about his final round of training before entering the sector guard, something I know he's dreading, even if he won't admit it. To see my daughter hold her little one up to the comm, as I once held her up to talk to my own mother.

To remind myself what's at stake.

The grubby face of my youngest grandchild disappears and is briefly replaced by my daughter's. Her expression is solemn. She's about to tell me—again—that I must be careful, must avoid any unnecessary risks. Before she can launch into her plea, however, the comm flickers again and all I see is the shuttle wall.

Family visits help. But they're still no substitute for talking things through with Ryn.

An orange light flashes just inside my peripheral vision. I've ignored this message from the Voshti twice while talking to my family, mostly because I'm almost certain what it will say. Ignoring the signal three times would be pushing my luck.

When I open the comm, the adjutant—a different one, but then it's *always* a different one—says exactly what I expected.

"Proctor Alta, the plan you submitted to the Voshti does not meet the criteria for a Level Three test. Please revise based on the figures we've provided you."

I can't really protest, because I know it's an accurate assessment. The plan I submitted was Level Two at best, and was really nothing more than a last-ditch effort to get the Voshti to reassess the full mission specs. I thought if they looked through everything again, maybe one of them would decide that my original idea to simply acquire the technology without the Testing, without offering a full planetary alliance, had merit.

But no. They simply kicked the plan back, upping the total number of targets to twenty.

Disgusted, I close the comm, grabbing water and a food packet from the bin under my bunk. I don't even check to see what packet I'm getting. There are only a few varieties, all equally bland. Most of the full-sized ships still have actual food instead of these little pouches of blah, but there's not much worth eating these days even when I'm docked. The Lor are blocking the key agricultural routes. Judging from the taste of everything I've eaten in the past year, I suspect they're blocking the spice routes, too.

In an Elisi shuttle, at least there'd be a small food processing unit. Everything would still taste like mud, but it would be hot. I'd also have room to walk around, stretch my limbs a bit. The Lor, however, apparently eschew such luxuries. This is my first trip in one of the Lor shuttles, captured last year—one of the few recent victories in our column. It's really little more than a pod, with a living area maybe half the size of my bedroom at home. If I stretch my arms wide, I can almost touch both sides of the cabin.

A few of the proctors refuse to travel in these Lor shuttles. One said it reminded her of a coffin. It *is* a bit claustrophobic, and I suspect it would be even worse for a two-person crew. But the team that retrofitted these shuttles for Elisi use claim the Lor chose the simpler, more compact design in order to devote more resources toward speed and cloaking. All things considered, I'll take that trade, since it cuts down my travel time and keeps me from triggering any planetary defenses.

And even though these rations are cold and tasteless, at least they contain a stimulant. Hopefully, it'll be strong enough to prevent me from nodding off before I come up with something that works for the Voshti without weighing too heavily on my conscience.

According to the Voshti requirements, I have to select twenty targets on XE7: six within the United States, four within China, four in the European Union, three in South Asia, and two in the African Union. The final target is left to my personal discretion, like it's a bonus for good behavior.

Once they approve my attack plan and I carry it out, my main task will be to sit back and observe the reactions. If the governments can reach a consensus that the attack came from outside their planet, if they can actually wrap their heads around that possibility and unite to address the threat, then my job is done. The Elisi diplomats will sweep in at that point, blame the attack on the Lor, and offer membership in the Alliance and all the protection that brings. Which, to be honest, isn't much these days.

On the other hand, if the governments fail to reach a

consensus that the attack is extraterrestrial, the planet will be added to the list of requisition targets. The Elisi military will sweep in and take what we need. There will be no offer of protection, and little concern about limiting casualties.

The Voshti-provided dossier on XE7 is comprehensive, with detailed background information on just over fifty potential locations in various countries. But it was compiled before the war began. I know this for certain, because Ryn was on that team. And since I think recent data is more likely to result in fewer casualties, I move the shuttle into range of their communication signals before dropping into orbit.

Once my files are reasonably current, I steal another glance over at the comm console, trying to resist the temptation. Running the simulation is a crutch. I promised myself I wouldn't do it more than once per mission, and this will be the third time.

Maybe I *should* have let them assign me a new partner. Solitude is kind of nice on a short hop, but this is three times longer than the other solo trip I took, and Ryn was worried I might go a little stir-crazy on that one. Thus, the sim-scan. He joked about bottling himself so I'd have someone to yell at when I was half a sector away.

The scan doesn't even run very well out here on this ancient Lor-built simsystem that someone had to hack before it would run our files at all. The Ryn I'm considering pulling up will be fuzzy, blurred around the edges. The image will break up when he moves and his responses will be delayed. Sometimes he'll say things that make me wonder if the system is tapping into his personality profile at all.

The voice is his, though. And that's what I need right now.

Talking aloud to the simulation is a risky, but I'm past the point of worrying about whether I move up in rank. The worst that's likely to happen is that someone bitches me out for wasting resources, but I seriously doubt I'm the only offender in that regard. Ryn said one of the other proctors boasted last year about the sexual simulations he brings along to keep him company on longer missions. I'm positive those gobble energy much faster than my bad habit.

Screw it. I can sit here all night debating the pros and cons, but the end result will be the same. I need company. I need *his* company, even if it isn't real.

"Alta 493." I pause until I hear a faint beep indicating that my id is accepted. "Load revised data on XE7 into sim Ryn002, and then run."

It takes several seconds to load, and I close my eyes while I wait. It always feels more real that way, like I'm just napping and he's there when I wake up.

I open my eyes to see Ryn leaning against the shuttle wall, wearing the smile I could never say no to, the smile that is almost entirely responsible for our three children.

His brow creases. "Sorry I woke you. You look like you need the rest. Are you having trouble sleeping?"

"I'd be sleeping a lot better if the Voshti would pay attention to my recommendations. They have plenty of adjutants who could determine the locations and pick the attack order. Why send me out here if they're going to ignore everything I say?"

Ryn laughs. That part of the simulation is correct. He *would* have laughed. It's just that the sim version laughs a bit too long.

"You know the bureaucrats are just covering their asses, babe. The testing manual says locations and blast order will be determined in the field by a trained proctor, so they'll make you keep running numbers until you spit out something they like. Have you picked the targets yet?"

"Yeah, ten of them. But they've declared the planet Level Three, so I'm supposed to double it."

Ryn is as familiar as I am with the long, convoluted process for selecting the specific targets for these tests. Several dozen factors must be assigned a numerical weight, but really, it comes down to just three things, in descending order of importance.

The first factor is whether it will pack a gut punch. We pick iconic locations, places that evoke an emotional response, with bonus points if the destruction will stir up existing national or religious rivalries.

The second factor, which a lot of people have been damned near ignoring of late, is whether the target is "clean"—outside major population centers, in locations mostly uninhabited for at least part of the day, or simply small enough that there's little chance that a carefully targeted laser will result in heavy casualties.

The third and final factor is the age of the target. Things that are either modern or simply constructed are much easier for us to help them repair or rebuild if they join the Alliance.

"You told them about the chronotron readings," Ryn says. "Why are you surprised that they'd want a rigorous test? Wirth must have been salivating at the very idea that we could change the damage this war has caused. Our losses have grown throughout the sector. We're bleeding out, Mila. If that device can stanch our losses a bit, or even better, prevent the Lor from starting the war in the first place, then—"

"I *know*, okay? I know!" I don't add that the losses are even greater today than two years ago when the sim-scan was collected. I don't add that he'd be *alive*, and I wouldn't be reduced to yelling at this Ryn-who-isn't-really-Ryn. Who laughs a little too long and a little too loud. A Ryn I can't touch.

I take a deep breath. "I know all that. But, Ryn, between us, we've handled—" I stop just short of saying twenty-eight missions, because that would confuse him. Four of my missions are recent, after his shuttle was reported missing. "We've handled twenty-four missions, right? How many resulted in a new alliance?"

"All but three."

"Maybe a thousand separate governments between them, right?" When he nods, I continue. "Of all those governments, how many valued their monuments and buildings above the lives of their own people?"

"No more than five percent, I'd say. But Mila, that's not the point—"

"Yes. It's *exactly* the point. We both know the likelihood of trouble increases pretty much in direct proportion to the body count we rack up during these tests. When we first started, there were no lies. The diplomats admitted everything when the planet joined the Alliance. But now that we have these shuttles, now that we have a way to conveniently blame everything on the Lor, no one seems to care if the body count goes up a bit. After all, you wouldn't want it to be *too* low, otherwise they won't be as scared. They won't be willing to give up the resources we need."

Ryn closes his eyes briefly, then gives me a rueful smile that makes him look achingly real, at least until he moves his hand and the image flickers. "Let's work through the locations you've got," he says. "Find a compromise."

I spend the rest of the evening bouncing ideas off my partner, just as I've done for the better part of my life. If I don't look at him too often, if I just listen, I can almost forget that he's missing-presumed-dead. I can almost believe that the Voshti already have this time travel device in hand and they've altered our reality to one where there's a future I actually look forward to.

"This cluster of pyramids in the northern part of the African continent..." Ryn pauses to check the name. "North African Union. They're considered ancient wonders, but some are already damaged."

He nods toward an image of an odd creature. It has a quadrupedal body with a humanoid head, except it's missing a nose.

"Mark it as a maybe," I say. "But why don't we add some more walls instead? Those are easy to repair. The one in China has been patched up many times." I pull the targeting pad toward me and enter in a string of numbers. The view shifts to a mountainous area where a reddish-brown wall is the only break in the tree cover. "This is the Mutianyu section. It's remote, so we can take out a good-sized chunk, probably without any casualties—"

"Or you could strike closer to an urban center, end up with a *few* casualties, and maybe still keep your job?"

I ignore him and leave the coordinates in place. Would Ryn have made that comment? I don't know. To an extent he's right, and the next proctor they hire might be the type who'd blast craters in major cities, taking out hundreds. And he or she might not leave hints like I do, clues that will help them put the pieces together, to realize that they're being tested.

"The next one," I say. "The wall in Jerusalem. It's a densely populated area, where political and religious tensions have run high for much of this world's recorded history. Maybe I could double up. Hit a section of the Walls of Jerusalem and also that gold-domed structure behind it. Two different religions there, and they've rarely been friendly. That way, we'll tap into those animosities. Stir things up a little. Make Vosht Baydel and his friends happy."

I enter the coordinates, and we continue down the list, targeting two ceremonial gates and three bridges. When I suggest a fourth, Ryn rolls his eyes.

"What? I like bridges. Any debris tumbles into the water, and I can usually plan the attack for a time when traffic is light."

"I think three is enough," he says. "More than that and you'll have the adjutant who looks over this mission questioning your motives."

"Fine. Let's move on to tall, pointy things." I show him the first one—a tall, white obelisk in the United States capital. "See the park area beside it? If I aim carefully, the top section will fall straight into it, or maybe into the pond on the other side. And the next one on the list is a row of pillars in South Africa. If I topple the first one in the chain, the rest should crash into each other."

285

I add both of those locations to the collection of walls, bridges, minarets, and towers on various continents. There are a lot of statues on my list, too. The good thing with those is that you don't have to destroy the entire thing to evoke anger. You can just clip off the head or whack an appendage.

Once we've pinpointed twenty that should stir up maximum animosity with minimal loss of life, I'm then left with justifying my choices to the Voshti. Ryn is worried they'll consider the death toll too low for some sites, so I end up doubling the forecast on most of them, tripling it on a few others. Hopefully they'll just scan the numbers.

As usual, the work goes quicker with Ryn, even if it's Sim-Ryn, and I want to leave the simulation running once the report is submitted. Have him crawl into the bunk with me now that our work is done. Sleep with my head on his shoulder, the way we used to do before our bodies grew older and less inclined to cope gracefully with awkward sleep positions.

He wouldn't smell like Ryn, though. And my head would go straight through his non-corporeal body. The simulation only interacts with things built into the shuttle. His fingers even look like they're working the comm controls. But I'm not part of the ship's system. He can't touch me.

"Alta 493. End simulation."

I've barely settled into my lonely bunk when the comm unit pings and the adjutant on duty, who wears the same pinched expression as most of her colleagues, gives me the message, direct and to the point.

"Plan approved, Proctor Alta. Proceed at once."

I sink back down into the bed even though I'm too annoyed

to sleep. There's no way that adjutant had time to read the plan, let alone submit it to the Voshti, so they must have given her authority to approve anything that fell into a permitted range.

I want her job.

One where you don't have to make the tough decisions and you don't have to carry them out. Will this adjutant give even a single thought to the blood that will be spilled tomorrow, based on the seven words she just relayed?

No. I'm sure she sleeps the moment her head hits the pillow.

Chapter 3

Elisi Outpost Five
Date: 9023.22.14

When I wake up, I designate an attack order for the coordinates Ryn and I entered last night, along with the time for each hit. Then the shuttle takes over. The viewscreen divides into four images, and about ten minutes later, I watch as the first drone vaporizes the middle section of a bridge in Australia, where the local time is just after three a.m. Shortly thereafter, the other three squares flash briefly as sections of the Great Wall, the Jade Bridge, and the Tiananmen Gate are obliterated in a matter of seconds.

The sky is nearly dark over the Volga River, but there are still witnesses along the cobblestone walkway when the tiny drone swoops in and neatly clips the raised sword from *The Motherland Calls*. Another drone decapitates a tower in Paris at nearly the same moment a clock face is obliterated on a second tower, this one in London. A few seconds later, a laser blasts something called the Berlin Quadriga from the top of the Brandenburg Gate.

All twenty hits go pretty much as planned, and when it's over, I've only lost two drones. One was simply poor timing, when a large transport vehicle in India collided with the drone assigned to hit a minaret on the Taj Mahal. The second drone was taken out by an armed guard in an amusement center in the United States, just moments after it demolished a statue of an entertainer named Mickey Mouse.

I'll admit that seeing any sort of destruction bothers me, but the precision of these lasers is a thing of beauty. Even the full-sized Elisi ships don't have anything as accurate, and this shuttle is one of the Lor's older models, almost certainly built before I was born.

What were the Lor like back then, when engineers designed equipment to take out a target with minimal damage to the surrounding area? At what point did they abandon surgical strikes in favor of the chaotic bloodbath they now leave in their wake?

Once the remaining eighteen drones have returned to the shuttle, I reluctantly flip on the comm screens to see how XE7's communication channels explain the attacks.

The death count is the main thing that worries me. If it's high, I'm going to have nightmares from the visuals that will start coming in shortly. I've had those from the beginning, but they've gotten worse now that Ryn is gone. On the other hand, if the death toll is too low and the planet fails to unite, that fact will be used against me in the inquiry that will almost certainly result.

I resist the urge to start Sim-Ryn, partly because it's too soon to do it again, and partly because I'm worried what his response will be. My Ryn would have agreed with every decision I've made, although he might have played devil's advocate a few times to make sure we were thinking everything through carefully. The sim version, on the other hand, is much more pragmatic. He cautioned me more than once last night about veering too far from my mission plan.

The first reports are from bystanders in the various locations who recorded the attacks. I ignore these for the time being and focus on the official reports from planetary defense systems, which dribble in over the next hour.

They're in a jumble of languages, most without any sort of visual. I mute the other feeds and tap the translation icon on the one at the top left. The feed is still unintelligible until I tap the decryption icon. After a moment, the system begins to relay a report from China, where the government assumes the attacks were engineered by remnants of something called the People's Army.

I flick through the other five regions. Two of the reports are too well encrypted for the onboard computers to descramble, so I save those for later analysis when my shuttle returns to port. The three I can follow all seem to have an automatic suspect, one domestic and two international.

The public news coverage begins next, and at first it's just pictures, many from the same bystanders who were transmitting the images earlier. I don't want to see these. At this stage, they'll just be saying what I already know. What happened, where, when.

So I take a break and watch one of the vids I've been saving the entire trip, knowing I'd need a distraction until their analysis starts coming in. Then I use the exercise stand at the far end of the shuttle for twice as long as usual.

When I come back, crappy cold food packet in hand, I check the government channels again. They've started to compare notes. In one case, they've started to point fingers, as well.

Within hours, two different terrorist groups have publicly claimed full responsibility for all of the attacks. By the time I'm ready to sleep, that number is up to four, with two other groups claiming credit for specific targets.

Exactly twenty-four hours after the first drone target was hit, I follow my orders and send a message from the Elisi Alliance to all affected governments and to their collective security agency. I blame the attack on the Lor and request to meet with a single representative from the planet to discuss a possible alliance. I tell them I will monitor the communications of their global Security Council for a response within two of their days.

Once the message is sent, I move the shuttle out of orbit and pick a new location, just in case they traced the signal. I cloak and settle in while I wait for a response. There's some chatter about my message on the official channels, but my claim isn't deemed credible. Exactly as I expected. None of the governments relay the message I sent to their citizens. A few leaks emerge, but no one seems to be taking the possibility of an extraterrestrial attack seriously.

I've just come back to the monitors after a break when I

notice alerts on most of the feeds. Two additional attacks have been reported. An explosion at a shopping mall in Europe killed nearly two hundred people, with hundreds more wounded. Another attack at a resort area in South America killed nearly twice that many.

If this had occurred two days from now, I'd have suspected that the Voshti sent another proctor to this area as soon as I told them about the chronotron pulses. But none of our ships, not even a battleship originating from an Elisi outpost, could have gotten here so quickly.

Could the Lor have intercepted my transmission to the Voshti? Unlikely. If they've broken our codes, I doubt we'd have managed even our few recent victories, especially the one at Alyri where they lost two battle cruisers. And I don't think even the Lor's fastest transports could have gotten here in time to launch these attacks.

The only thing I hear on public channels that's at all insightful is the suggestion by an analyst in Europe that the two deadliest attacks were possibly caused by a terrorist group other than the one responsible for the first wave. A copycat attack, although I'd argue it's a shoddy copy given the number of people who were killed. The news feed from South America shows rescue workers stacking mangled bodies from the resort hotel along the beach. Even though I know these aren't the result of my targets, I feel sick. Did our testing give these groups courage they might otherwise have lacked? Or were the attacks simply accelerated while security was focused elsewhere?

Gradually, a few of the news anchors begin mentioning the possibility of extraterrestrial involvement, but they still don't seem to give it much credence. I've gotten used to their odd appearance for the most part—small heads, long bodies, tiny eyes. But one anchor looks even stranger to me, with eyes that are oddly pale, almost like water. He spends less than a minute examining the alien theory before moving on to what he views as a more likely cause: a coalition of radical feminists and eco-terrorists. The man notes that many of the attacks were on phallic symbols—his words are accompanied by images of the six tall-pointy things I included in the target list—and that many of the others targets were considered symbols of male oppression.

His co-anchor, a female with more hair than I've ever seen on a humanoid, seems unconvinced, but she does note that the attack at the amusement area obliterated a statue of Mickey Mouse rather than his mate.

I didn't even know the creature was male or that it had a mate.

At the end of two days, talk of alien involvement has increased, but not as much as the phallus theory. And the only attempt to communicate via the channel I suggested in my message is a burst of odd music followed by someone laughing, so I'm pretty sure it was unauthorized.

Following the rules in the proctors' manual, I wait until six hours after the deadline, then send a second message, this time with a two-day extension. The suggestion that they analyze the drones destroyed in the amusement area and in India is my own addition, however, very much outside the official rules. That will probably cost me if it's discovered, which it probably will be—even the dimmest adjutant is unlikely to miss something that blatant.

Within hours, the global chatter on government channels makes it clear that the United States and India weren't exactly forthcoming with their allies about the existence of the downed drones. Both claim publicly that they found nothing at the scene of the attacks.

The Indian government does send an open message on their own channel shortly before I retire for the night. They are willing to meet, but the Security Council requires unanimity of all nine permanent members, and the Indian government has been unable to convince the others. An additional day is requested.

I don't respond. I can't respond. The orders on this front are clear. Deal only with the collective security group. And I'm not even especially tempted, since the India government isn't the one housing those time travel devices.

The comm beeps shortly after I drift off to sleep. I push myself up on one elbow, annoyed. I'm on the same time schedule as everyone at my home base, Elisi Outpost Five, so whoever is calling has to know they're waking me, but as usual, adjutants on night shift think everyone else should be awake, too.

"Alta 493," I say, rubbing my eyes. "Answer comm."

I'm surprised to see Baydel on screen, instead of one of his underlings.

"Mila," he says, glancing at my hair, undoubtedly mussed from the pillow. "Apologies for waking you."

The last time I woke to Baydel's face on my comm screen, he informed me that Ryn was missing. Maybe he has good news this time. Maybe Ryn has been found.

"It's okay," I say, running my hand through my hair to smooth it. "Have you heard something?"

Baydel looks confused for a moment, and then it hits him. "Oh. About Ryn's transport? No, Mila." He hesitates for a moment. "I know it's hard to let go of hope, but… the Lor aren't taking prisoners these days. You know that. How's the testing going?"

"As I expected," I answer truthfully, then quickly add, "but we still have time. One of the governments on their Security Council is attempting to broker a meeting, so that's a positive sign."

Baydel nods absently. "I just called to notify you that an RU is headed your way. Should arrive around the time the deadline for XE7 expires."

I tense up, but don't respond. A requisition unit wouldn't normally arrive until long after I'm out of the sector. In fact, they aren't even tasked until I formally submit my report for review and brief the requisition unit captain on the specifics of the testing. I know that recent developments in the war have sped up that timetable a bit, but this is ridiculous.

"Which unit?"

"The 57th," he says. "And I know what you're thinking, but they were closest."

Of course he knows what I'm thinking. It's what any rational being would be thinking right now. Etnor Stoll commands the 57th RU, and Stoll's idea of diplomacy is smiling before he shoots you. He's a foul little man, half a head shorter than I am. Ryn always said that Stoll acted extra tough to make himself feel bigger.

"Why would you—"

"Vosht Wirth made the decision," Baydel says.

No surprise there, since she's the one who asked for the coordinates and called for the vote to begin immediate testing.

"It's not too far off their normal route," Baydel continues. "Stoll has been authorized to begin negotiations on the off chance that XE7 passes the test. In the more likely event of failure, he'll have units ready to recover the device or devices, along with any other resources we need. You can return with them, if you'd like. Just dock your shuttle in their bay, and enjoy a less solitary return trip?"

I hesitate for a moment, mouth open, trying to think of a polite way to phrase this, but there isn't one. "Stoll is an idiot. He's no more qualified to handle diplomacy than I am. No. I take that back, Baydel. He's far *less* qualified, and you know it!"

Baydel's jaw tightens, but he shrugs one shoulder. "You said yourself that XE7 will probably fail the test."

"Yes, they probably will. And if they do, what do you think the chances are of Stoll managing to find the source of that pulse without destroying it, along with anyone who has the slightest idea how it works? He's nearly as bad as the Lor."

"Wirth wants that device. She's pretty much given Stoll an open door on this one. Told him to do whatever it takes. So, I guess my question is… do you have a *better* idea, Mila?" He looks at me, one eyebrow quirked slightly in challenge. "If so, now would be a good time for us to discuss it. Before Stoll and his crew get there."

He speaks slowly, enunciating each word.

Oh.

Now it's making sense. That's why he's calling from his quarters, in the middle of his own normal sleep cycle, to tell me something he could have had one of the adjutants relay tomorrow morning.

He's looking for an alternative to Wirth's way.

My pulse speeds up. I've never set foot on an alien planet. I'm an analyst. I stay on the ship and watch their news feeds, so what I'm about to suggest goes way, way beyond my comfort level. It flat out terrifies me.

"Maybe... *I* could retrieve it?"

Chapter 4

Elisi Shuttle Alar
Date: 9023.23.05

"Alta 493." When the unit beeps, I say, "Load new data on XE7, including details of my conversation with Vosht Baydel, into sim Ryn002, and then run."

I rose early, even though I had to take a sleep aid to finally settle down after my talk with Baydel. He stopped short of actually authorizing the new mission, which didn't surprise me in the slightest. Baydel's not an idiot, and he wants to come out of this with a clean record if I fail. At least he ended the call by wishing me luck.

I'll need it. All my experience in first contact, or even on-planet observation, is secondhand from Ryn, who was an adjutant on a diplomatic mission at the beginning of the war. He didn't seem to care much for the job, and rarely talked about it. He preferred the type of on-planet mission he had prior to the war, where he was tasked just with observing and bringing back resource samples. Biological samples, too, when they got the opportunity.

Ryn's experience in the field is one reason I'm going to break my promise to myself yet again. I don't know how much he can tell me about the nuts and bolts of marching onto a planet and swiping its technology. It's not something we generally *do*. But he knows more than I do.

And all that aside, I need moral support.

I forget to close my eyes this time, which means I'm looking directly at the spot when Ryn's simulation shimmers into view. His face is utterly blank at first, and that lack of expression, that total absence of warmth, nearly brings me to tears.

Then his personality module kicks in, and Sim-Ryn gives me a grimmer version of his usual smile. "This is not the best idea you've ever had, babe. Do you have a game plan?"

"Only what I came up with while lying awake last night. Keep the shuttle cloaked and land on that large green area, then get inside the building without anyone noticing me. Find the source of the chronotron pulse, which I'm *really* hoping is portable, and get instructions for using it. Then get back to the shuttle. Easy, right?"

He shakes his head. "Mila, there's no way you'll pass for a native here. You're too short and your head is too large. Although…" He cocks his head to the side. "You might pass for a child. If you wear something over your eyes."

"Thanks," I say wryly. "But I'll be in one of the Lor suits. The ones with the cloaking units. We've modified them to fit Elisi now. Well, maybe not to fit, but at least the butt doesn't drag on the ground anymore. And once I locate the device, this too-short body and too-large head might actually be evidence that I'm telling the truth."

"Do you think that's going to matter? That you're telling the truth? I mean, you're going in to basically steal their device. Do you even have a weapon?"

"A hand laser."

"That's not a weapon! It's a tool. Why did you tell Baydel you'd do this?"

I give him an incredulous look, thinking my Ryn would never have asked that question. "Because it could save lives. Here, and hopefully in our sector as well."

"And that's it? That's your main motivation?" He waits, clearly expecting me to say something else, and then sighs. "It's not because you're thinking that turning back time would save me, too?"

My throat tightens. I can't respond at first. Eventually, I manage to ask, "How did you know?"

"Your conversation with Baydel confirmed it."

"I'm sorry. I wasn't thinking—"

"No, it's okay."

He actually does look okay for someone who's just learned that he's dead, but then... Sim-Ryn was never really alive.

"But I was pretty sure before that," he says. "Only your things are here in the shuttle. And... you never touch me. You move away when I try to touch you. No other explanation made sense."

I stare at him for a long moment, taking in his face, the little crease in his chin when he smiles. My eyes flood with tears.

"Alta 493. End—"

"Wait! Don't shut me off. We need to discuss this." He takes a few steps toward me, but I hold out my hand.

"You're a simulation, Ryn. You don't *need* anything."

"No," he says. "I guess I don't. But I think you do. You need me to help you think this through. To help you figure out why you've agreed to take on what may well be a suicide mission."

"If doing this means I save you, that's a bonus. The best bonus in the world. But I'd do it anyway. The children are fine, Ryn. They have their own lives, but those lives would be much better in the absence of this war. And this device could stop the war before it begins." I take a deep breath and squeeze my eyes shut. "I just wish I could believe it will end there, that they'll send a message to avoid the war and leave everything else alone."

When I open my eyes, Ryn is directly in front of me, so close that my breath ripples his image. I step into his arms, arms that aren't there, and when I close my eyes again, I can almost believe that I feel them.

"It's okay, babe." I know it's a programmed response. I know this simulation is just saying what the computer thinks Ryn would have said. The voice is even too loud. Ryn would have whispered.

I don't care. It's the closest thing to comfort I have.

He's already at the comm when I open my eyes, shuffling through possible landing sites.

Six hours later, I land the cloaked shuttle in the middle of a large enclosed field within walking distance of the Quantum Institute. It's a sports field of some sort, and a quick check of the schedule shows that it's rarely used this time of year.

The sun is low on the horizon when I step out of the shuttle, and the air has a slight chill that I can feel even through the suit. I quickly secure the hatch behind me and head across the field in the direction of the lab building. The air on XE7 is within acceptable limits, and I've had the full gamut of inoculations. Unless some bug has morphed and mutated since our last scouting crew a few years back, I'll be fine. My helmet has a translator, sensors that monitor my vital signs, a navigation device, and my remote comm. And the cloaking suit will definitely make getting around undetected a lot easier.

I left the Ryn simulation running in the shuttle. He says he needs to know that I get back safe, but I think he's a little worried that I won't turn him back on again. Now that we both know he's not real, it feels more awkward than before. But I don't have the heart to refuse his request, and since he can interact with the shuttle, it might come in handy to have him active if I need information. If someone bumps into the ship and raises an alarm, he can relocate it to a nearby park. And in the worst case scenario, I can call in so that Ryn's voice, even if it *is* a simulated voice, is the last sound I hear.

The field is surrounded by a tall wire fence. I look around to be sure no one is nearby. The only thing I see, aside from a few flying creatures, is some vehicles off in the distance, so I pull the hand laser out of my pocket and brace my forearm with my other hand to minimize the shaking.

I've worn these cloaking suits before, during training. It's still strange to see the laser floating in front of me, with no sight of my hand or arm. I begin to slice an unsteady line through the metal enclosure.

"Mila?"

I'm so startled by the deep voice behind me that I nearly drop the laser. It's a good thing my thumb slid off the trigger or I'd have sliced clean through my foot.

I don't answer, just slip the laser back into my pocket, glancing around as I move away from the fence. Someone is in the shadows beneath the benches that surround the field. XE7 residents are humanoid, but they're large. This one is tall, at least two heads taller than Ryn. And I'd swear he wasn't there a second ago.

"Mila, I am… friend. Name… Matias." He steps out of the shadows. The pauses in his speech are disconcerting. His mouth moves and I can hear the actual sounds he's making a split second before this crappy portable translator catches up.

From what I've seen on the newsfeeds, I think he's a young one. Not a child, but maybe not fully adult, either. It's something about the face. The skin is unlined. The hair on his head is thicker than most humanoids I've seen on other planets, and his eyes are small with unusually tiny irises, like those of all the others on this planet.

The eyes seem kind, though, dark and shining. They're more like Elisi eyes than the pale, watery orbs the news anchor had. His skin is the warm brown of well-toasted breakfast cakes, and both of his hands are raised slightly, as if to show me he's not a threat. A thin, round disc of metal, a shade darker than his skin, hangs from his neck, and a pack of some sort is on his back.

"You said… mention falls at… Briarche." He can't see me now that the hand laser is back in my pocket, so he looks at the spot near the fence where I was standing a moment ago. "On holiday you went with… Ryn, yes? Cabin near falls you had. Swam unclothed. Met another person… you—"

"When? When did I tell you that?" I know what he's about to say. I haven't told anyone about that last bit. Not my friend from the Academy, not my children. Especially not my children. And Ryn wouldn't have shared that encounter either.

Matias shakes his head. "Not understand. In lab… swap your helmet to hear you speak me speak. Said you understand me speak you speak in shuttle."

The boy doesn't look dangerous. Nor does he look as simple as the translator is making him sound. And I can't see how he could know about the cabin at Briarche unless I told him willingly. If I'd been under duress, if they were torturing me, I'd have given him false information, right? Not something that only I could know.

But I'm not taking any chances. I pull out the laser again and point it toward Matias, motioning toward the corner where I parked the shuttle, and he starts walking. He doesn't seem the slightest bit nervous that I'm pointing the laser at him, even though he can't have missed the way it ripped through the fence.

"Alta 493," I say as we approach the shuttle. "Prepare to open hatch."

"What?" Ryn's voice rings inside my helmet. "You just left. Are you okay?"

"I'm fine. We just have an unusual… development. I'm bringing back a guest."

302

Ryn is silent for a moment and then says, "Um... babe. I think you're also bringing back the device. The pulse is right next to you and it's moving toward my location."

When we reach the shuttle and the hatch swings up, the boy grins at me. "Wow... just..." Another grin, and then he steps inside, ducking low to avoid banging his head on the upper edge.

I yank off my helmet as soon as we're inside. That's when I see Sim-Ryn. I have no real weapons on board, but he appears to be holding a much larger laser, the military variety, and I have a tough time holding back a laugh.

The boy's hands are raised. "Like I told Mila," he says, clearly alarmed, "I'm a friend. My name is Matias Mora. Mila... she told me to jump back."

His speech is much clearer now that the ship's system is handling translation. There's barely a lag, and the vocal dampeners mask the sounds he's actually making. The only difference is that the translated tone of voice is a little higher than his own.

"It's okay, Ryn," I say. "Get rid of the weapon and close the hatch."

The hatch slides shut at about the same time the weapon vanishes from Ryn's hands.

Matias looks confused, staring first at Ryn and then back at me. "I thought you said Ryn was... dead?"

"He is. This is a simulation."

The boy nods, but there's a fleeting look on his face that I can't read. Sympathy? Pity? His eyes are too strange to know for sure.

"I've never made contact with another civilization," I tell him. "I usually just analyze communications. I needed Ryn's help setting things up, figuring out a plan."

I can hear the slight plea in my voice, as though I'm apologizing for having the simulation. For being weak. A small, embarrassed part of me wants to close it down, but what I said is still true. I need Ryn's input on what this boy says.

"That makes sense," Matias says. "I used to do that too, when I was gaming. Easier to see all the angles when you have a sim assistant."

He's still hunched over slightly, in order to keep his head from bumping the ceiling. I nod toward one of the chairs. "Sit," I tell him. "And then start explaining. I don't understand why you're here. How could I have sent you? Why?"

"Things… they didn't go so well, Mila." Matias glances over at Ryn, and then back at me as I strip off the rest of the suit. He seems a little relieved when he sees my body, more like he was concerned about me than that he was dreading seeing my too-short torso. That sends a shiver through me.

"I mean, you got into the main section of the lab," he continues. "Not sure how, since you'd need ID and all. I guess you piggybacked behind one of us. I think you were there all night. Most of us left early yesterday—although I guess it's still today, since I jumped back. I was tired after the Congressional hearings, and Professor Anderson had to go break the bad news that our program isn't going to be funded. Well, bad news for her. I'm pretty happy about it actually. Anyway, I think you were in the lab with us this morning… *tomorrow* morning, I mean… because when you finally decided to make contact with me, you knew stuff about the keys. That I'm the one who can use it, not Professor Anderson. I have this gene…"

His face grows somber, and then he continues, "My mom was part of a research program when she was pregnant with me. I had a heart defect. They spotted it a few months into the pregnancy. Offered to fix it, as long as she agreed to *another* genetic tweak and follow-up tests. She didn't know what she was getting us into. Anyway, that second upgrade allows me to use this thing to… kind of… skip through time. Go back and forth. It's called a CHRONOS key. I think it's an acronym, although I have no idea what that stands for. Or where it came from."

"You told Mila that things didn't go well," Ryn says. "What do you mean?"

The boy gives Ryn another nervous glance. Or maybe it's curiosity. I get the feeling the simulations he uses in his gaming may not be quite at the same level as Sim-Ryn.

"There were soldiers," Matias says. "Three of them. They came in a few hours after Mila made contact with me. The professor was in the e-lab teaching a class, so we had a chance to talk. To get to know each other a bit before the troops stormed into the lab. They were dressed in those." He nods toward the portable suit on the floor by the bunk.

"Mila seemed like she was expecting them, but they were a little early, maybe? They seemed to know who she was, too. Professor Anderson came back into the lab and saw what was going on. She tried to call security and they…" His eyes meet mine. "They tore her clean in half with a gun that looked a lot like the fake one Ryn was carrying a minute ago. They were about to shoot me too, but you jumped in front and told them the key had a genetic component. That they'd need me to use it. And you told them the professor had the key in her pocket, even though you knew I had it. Then we made a run for the lab next door."

Matias looks down at my legs, and this time I can read his expression very clearly. He looks like he's going to vomit.

"One of them shot you. I think maybe you knew him, 'cause you called him by name. You were bleeding bad, and your legs…" He shakes his head. "When you put the helmet thing back on, you said your vitals weren't good. That you wouldn't make it. You told me to go back and find you, before you could reach the lab. Told me what to say to get you to trust me, so that you wouldn't make the same mistakes again."

Ryn is sitting now, too. I wouldn't have thought a simulation could look pale, but he does.

"Those troops," the boy says. "They were the ones you were telling me about, right? The Lor, the ones you're fighting? The ones responsible for all the attacks on Earth in the past few days?"

My eyes meet Ryn's. I don't want to lie to the boy. But if I tell him Stoll's unit are Elisi…

"They were the enemy," I say.

It's the truth. Just not the whole truth.

Matias nods. "Then I'm coming with you so we can stop them."

Chapter 5

Elisi Shuttle Alar
Date: 9023.27.10

The boy is asleep in the lower bunk, the one I slept in on the trip to XE7. He didn't want to take it at first, but he's too tall to fit on the top comfortably.

He sleeps a lot. I wonder if he's sick? Or maybe it's shock.

I mention this when he wakes up.

"No," he says. "I feel fine. My mom says it's adolescence. Body's still growing."

"If you grow much more, you won't fit in the shuttle," I tell him.

He laughs and tears the wrapper from one of the energy bars in the pack he brought on board. "We've got two days left, from what you said. I don't think I'll grow much during that time, so we're safe."

I wish I could believe he'll be safe once we land. Baydel called off Stoll's unit when I told him I had the device and I understand how to use it. Stoll claimed his unit was still nearly a parsec away, but based on what Matias said happened at the lab, he must have been lying. Wouldn't be the first time, but it's still a kick in the head to think that Stoll would actually shoot me.

Baydel doesn't know about the boy or the attack on the lab. I was kind of vague on the whole "I understand how to use it" bit when we spoke, since we were on a public channel. I've tried twice to connect with his private comm, with no luck, probably because I used up my communications allowance talking to my children before I landed on XE7. Or *Earth*, as the boy calls it—a word the translator conveys as *dirt* or *ground*. Such a very prosaic name for what's actually a pretty planet, based on what I've seen.

I'll have to tell Baydel something before we land. Otherwise all sorts of sensors are going to be tripped when I dock at Elisi Five.

"What's wrong?" Matias asks. He seems to be better at reading my facial expressions than I am at reading his.

I start to say that nothing is wrong, but I don't lie well. We've spent the last three cycles going through the specifics of how the key works. What it changes. The truth is, Matias doesn't know. All he knows is that he inherited the gene to operate it. He can use it better than any of the others they've located. And a lot of people have spent a lot of time and money training him to "jump" with it.

"It's not that anything is really *wrong*," I say. "I'm just worried about the ramifications of you using the device. What does it change?"

He looks puzzled for a moment, probably trying to work through an awkwardly worded translation. They still happen, but it's not as bad here in the shuttle as it was with the helmet.

"I haven't changed much," he admits. "Nothing major. Moved some items around the lab. The thing is, anyone around me who isn't touching this key will say nothing changed. That the book was always there on the desk. The door was already open. Then we figured out that we needed to change something I was holding. So that it would be under the field or whatever when I showed them. That's what I did at the hearing on Capitol Hill, the one to request the funding. Half the representatives seem to think it's a magic trick, and the other half think it's too dangerous to screw around with it. I agree on the last part."

"How far back have you... jumped?"

"As far as Professor Anderson and that committee knows, two hours."

"So you were taking a big risk when you intercepted me."

"Not really. I said as far as they *know*. I'll admit I was curious. I've... been a few places. There were locations already on the key. I avoided that first one that pops up. Black, with a lot of static. It spooked me. But some of the others, you could see people moving around if you watched for a while. I've jumped back more than a hundred years. I was really careful, though, not to be seen and not to change anything... important. I mostly just looked around and came right back."

"But you think you *could* change things if you tried?"

A flicker of something I can read passes across his face. "Yeah. I'm pretty sure about that."

"So... why didn't you tell your teacher about those longer trips?"

The boy shakes his head. "Anderson's not my teacher. She's more like my... boss. Or maybe warden is a better word. See, I'm wishing I'd never told them I could use it. I was a kid then, just fourteen. My mom had to sign a bunch of permission forms for them to even run the tests. I was thinking about the extra money it would bring in, maybe make things easier. I guess she was, too. Things are better now, though. We'd be fine without the money if I quit. So… let's just say I didn't do my best at that hearing. I wanted out from under Anderson's thumb." He sighs. "I didn't like Anderson. But she didn't deserve what they did to her."

"And that's why you agreed to come with me?"

He looks surprised. "Maybe a little. But more because of what you said. That the Lor couldn't be allowed to get the key. And that if we didn't change things, if we didn't stop the war you're in, the war that Earth was about to be pulled into, they'd keep right on taking what they wanted. Killing people who got in their way. If I ran, they'd find me. They find my family, too, my mom and sister."

"I told you all that?" My gut churns, and I'm glad I skipped my morning food ration. I'm also glad that Sim-Ryn isn't running right now, because even without his presence in the shuttle, I can still feel Ryn's eyes on me. Or maybe it's just the eyes of my conscience. I don't remember any of what the boy is saying, any of what happened in that lab, but it sounds like I really played things up to get him to cooperate. And I clearly didn't bother to tell him that the Elisi might be the ones killing people.

"No," Matias says. "But I ain't stupid. Anyone who would do what they did to Anderson… what they did to you, too… They won't stop just because it's my kid sister. Bunch of kids died in that shopping mall attack in Europe."

Now I'm wondering if Stoll was behind those attacks, too. I should have been honest with this boy. I should have told him Stoll's unit works for the Elisi. He's probably going to learn that when we reach the outpost anyway. Was Stoll's ship really a half parsec away when I talked to Baydel? Did Wirth lie to Baydel? Or could he have been in on it?

"You're taking a lot of responsibility on yourself, Matias. Maybe it wasn't fair of me to ask. Maybe you're placing too much trust in me."

"Hmph. You don't remember the lab, Mila. When that big guy yelled and turned the gun on me, you didn't hesitate, you just—"

"Wait. What did you say?"

"You didn't hesitate—"

"No. Big guy. Did you say big guy? How big? Bigger than me?"

Matias laughs. "Hell, one of them was bigger than *me*."

I just stare at him for a moment. "What about the one you said I knew, the one I called by name? He was short, right? Shorter than I am?"

He's looking at me like I'm a little crazy. "No. None of them were short."

"You said I called him by name, though…"

"Yeah. But I didn't have a helmet, so I was just hearing the gobbledy-gook noises. I understood *Lor* and then you said something… like… *Dweevok*?"

I have to make him repeat it, because the system keeps translating the word. When I'm certain, my breath whooshes out in relief. "Bastards."

"Beg pardon?"

"Not a name. I said *Lor bastards*."

"Oh." Matias gives me a confused smile, clearly not understanding why this makes me happy.

"It's nothing," I tell him. "I've just realized that maybe there are a few more people we can trust."

Which is a roundabout way of saying I'm glad that the other version of me, the one in another time stream who is probably dead by now, didn't lie to him. That even as I was going down, I let the boy make an honest decision based on the facts at hand.

Chapter 6

Approaching Elisi Outpost Five
Date: 9023.29.19

"We don't have any choice but to trust him," Matias says. "And yeah. I like the other plan better, too, but… we have to work with what we have."

Sim-Ryn agrees. "Babe, your other plan would be perfect if we were landing on Elisi. But as it stands, trusting Baydel is our best bet. Unless someone just happens to have a space cruiser in the bay and one of you is suddenly gifted with the ability to not only steal it, but to fly it two parsecs with half the Elisi fleet on your tail, and maybe the Lor as well…"

The perfect plan would keep everyone else out of this. I've already recorded a message to myself about the war that's coming and I've given it to Matias. Ryn and I also know the perfect time and place where he could intercept us prior to the Lor invasion of the Owani sector. We could go to Baydel, in the past, and convince him that the peace treaty with the Lor is a ruse. I've compiled a full dossier of information on what will happen. I think we could convince Baydel to at least start an investigation. If he sent a cruiser, even at that early date, they'd uncover evidence that the Lor are talking peace at the same time they're building up an arsenal that can only be intended for war.

There's just one problem with the perfect plan, but it's a big one. In fact, it's looming outside the shuttle window at this very minute. We'll be landing momentarily on Outpost Five, not on Elisi. Outpost Five didn't even exist prior to the war, and it's located two parsecs from the house on Elisi Major that Ryn and I lived in back then.

Once we land inside and the hatch opens, I won't be able to keep Matias's fate in my hands. I may not know when his time travel occurs and what he's being asked to change. He won't understand anything that's happening. I trust that Baydel wouldn't hurt *me*. Not directly. But I don't think he'll have as much concern for this alien boy. He might not be as worried about returning Matias to Earth when this is all over, and he might try coercing him into changing a few more things, for good measure. Especially if he thinks it's best for the Elisi Alliance as a whole.

The reservations I have about Baydel go triple for the other members of the Voshti. Quadruple for Vosht Wirth.

I feel the gentle *bump, bump* as we touch down inside the dock, and I turn toward Ryn. Sim-Ryn, I remind myself.

"Time to go, babe." He gives me a sad smile, and I'd almost swear there are tears in his eyes. He knows what I'm about to do. "Love you."

"Love you, too." Deep, shaky breath, and then, "Alta 493. End simulation. Delete simulation."

If the reviewers dig through the logs, they'll probably find the record, but I won't make it easy on them. No sense in waving my crutch in the air for all to see. Have to show that I can stand alone, on my own two feet. That I'm not frightened to face my life without Ryn.

Frightened.

"Matias?"

He raises one of the dark hairy lines above his eyes. I've discovered he does this when he's curious, or sometimes when he's doubtful.

"You're *frightened*, right?" I ask.

"Well... yeah. Somewhat."

"No, no, listen. You're *very* frightened. So frightened you can't make that key thing work. You're only able to keep calm when I'm in the room."

Matias looks skeptical.

"You said you were able to pretend with that professor. And in the hearing. I need you to do it again, okay? I need you to pretend. Hard."

"Ham it up," he replies. That translation seems off to me, but he's nodding. "Sure. I can do that."

"Refuse to talk to them, refuse to do *anything* they say unless I'm there. They may threaten to hurt you for not complying, but they won't do it. They need you. They're going to take you for a medical scan, decontamination, and so forth. If they start trying to make you talk, just keep saying my name."

"Got it. Miranda rules. Lips zipped unless my mouthpiece is in the room. Name, rank, and serial number, nothing more."

I nod, even though I have no idea what he's talking about

aside from *got it*.

When the hatch goes up, Matias transforms. He still has to crouch down as we exit, but it's almost as though he shrinks. His confidence seems to vanish, and he clings to my arm, looking around at the docking area and jumping at every sound.

The guys in the zip-suits come in through the door to take him, and he cries out, "Mila! No!" and refuses to let go of my sleeve.

He keeps yelling. Now that we're out of the shuttle I can't understand anything but my name, but his tone is piteous. My first thought is that he might be overdoing a bit, but hey—none of these guys have seen anyone from XE7 before.

"I'll see you soon," I tell Matias. "They won't hurt you."

Once he's gone, I head for another decon unit. Once I'm clean and cleared for contact with others on the base— something that takes three times longer than it ever has before— I head to Baydel's office.

The adjutant at the desk makes me wait again. Apparently, Baydel is in a meeting that's more important than a time device that could stop the war before it starts. I excuse myself and go off in search of some real food.

I'm back in the waiting room, and three bites into a hot sandwich, which is the best thing I've eaten in over a month, when Baydel's door opens. I take a few more bites and then shove the sandwich back into its bag before following him into the office.

I'm surprised to see Vosht Wirth sitting at Baydel's conference table. She doesn't travel much, preferring to stay on Elisi Major. This is the first time I've seen her in person. I find her unnerving. Her nostrils are always tight, like she smells something foul.

"So… do you have it?" Baydel asks, closing the door behind me.

I nod reluctantly and pull the metal circle from my pocket. It's an odd brown shade, and the shape in the middle reminds me of a letter from our alphabet. Matias said it represents an hourglass, an old Earth method of keeping time.

Baydel holds out his hand, and I reluctantly put the disc on his palm.

"Did the tech crew check it out?" he asks, turning the thing over and then face up again.

"They did. While I was in decon. They laughed and gave it back to me. Told me it's not emitting a chronotron pulse. And they're right. But if you put that thing into the hands of the boy, you'll detect a faint signal. The surges I picked up were because he'd been using it. Not to change anything. Just to demonstrate it. He says it's activated by the presence of a gene in his body."

"And you believe him?" Wirth asks.

"I don't have much choice, Vosht Wirth. He couldn't have known the things he knew unless he'd spoken with me. I can't prove what he said happened in that lab, but his description of the Lor was pretty accurate."

I decide to omit the part where I assumed the lab was attacked by troops under her command. For one thing, I'm not entirely sure Stoll would have acted differently if he'd reached the lab before the Lor team arrived. He'd have used force to obtain the device, with little concern for the people nearby. Maybe he wouldn't have shot *me*, but I don't think there's any guarantee even on that count if he thought I was interfering with his mission.

Wirth holds out her hand to examine the medallion. Baydel ignores her, putting the device on his desk.

"Vosht Wirth tells me the med team that examined the alien believes he may be… deficient. Or, at a minimum, emotionally unstable."

"With all due respect to the med team, that's garbage. He's intelligent, Baydel. He's just young. And he's frightened. Who wouldn't be? But he trusts me. Or at least he did before he was yanked away."

Baydel nods absently. "We could have the med team draw blood. Maybe they can analyze the gene, replicate it. But from what I'm seeing on the daily reports, and from what Vosht Wirth has just told me, we don't have the luxury of waiting. By the time they figure out what makes the alien and this little device tick, let alone how to make it tick for one of our own, the Lor will have taken Elisi, and quite possibly this outpost, too. So using the alien as a messenger may well be our only option."

"I just need you to guarantee that if we use Matias to change the timeline, this is a one-shot deal. Matias wants to return to XE7. He has family there. And if he manages to end this war, or even gives us a fighting chance at winning it, I think he deserves that much."

Vosht Wirth flashes me a smile so brief that it may have been a facial tic. "We'll certainly take your thoughts on the matter into consideration, *Proctor* Alta. But this is a matter for the Voshti—and the military—to decide."

I know better than to plead my case to her. I turn back to

Baydel and place my recorder on his desk, next to the medallion. "I've recorded a message. Once we're back on Elisi Major, Matias can take this back to me, along with your warning about the Lor."

"Again, Proctor Alta, you are inserting yourself into matters that really do not pertain to you."

Baydel says, "I think Mila has earned a bit of latitude here, Veda. She did, after all, retrieve the device and the alien. But," he says, looking back at me, "I'm not clear why the boy should take the message back to *you* rather than one of—"

"He trusts me." Baydel's eyes flash a warning when I interrupt him, but he lets me continue. "Matias won't feel comfortable approaching anyone else. He and I have already gone through this once. He convinced me last time, and if he uses that same information, there's no reason I wouldn't believe him again. But if you'd like to be there, I'll get the adjutant to compare our calendars. I'm sure I can find at least a few occasions when we were at the same event."

"My concern," Wirth says to Baydel, "is that we may need to deliver information that is beyond Proctor Alta's security level."

"Then encrypt the message that's delivered to you and Baydel," I tell her. "Consider Matias and my earlier self as a conduit for delivering that message—whatever message you want to send. My only requirement is that my recording to myself is included, so that I know what has been promised to Matias. He has no advocate for his interests here."

Baydel chuckles softly. "I think he has *one* advocate, and you've made a compelling case. I'm pretty sure Vosht Wirth and

I can work within those constraints."

While I believe Baydel to be a man of his word, I want to make sure that I *have* that word, explicitly. "So once your message is delivered, you promise to put the two of us on the fastest transport back to XE7?" I actually hope he'll be putting *three* of us on that transport, that the next trip to XE7 will be with the real Ryn instead of his simulated counterpart, but I stick to the main point.

"Yes."

I push it one step further. "With the device, right? Because I think Matias may find himself in some difficulty should he return without it."

Baydel nods, staring at the disc. "Absolutely. I don't want the responsibility that would come with keeping it on Elisi. We use it one time. A single message. Are we agreed, Veda?"

Wirth nods. "Agreed."

"Then we return the alien and his time disturber to XE7," Baydel continues. "And I'd recommend banning any further trips to the planet, if any of their leaders are actually considering using the thing again."

As I'm about to leave, Wirth adds, "He'll need a portable translation device when he jumps back—if you're going to understand each other."

"That's true," I tell her. It's actually something I hadn't considered.

Wirth gives me a smile, probably the warmest one I've seen on her face. "I'll have the tech crew adjust one of the Lor translators for his use."

The adjutant and I then compare my calendar with Baydel's

for the time period Baydel and Wirth have pinpointed as most advantageous for delivering a warning. The best match seems to be a party following the commitment ceremony for Baydel's youngest daughter.

I remember the day well. It was just before my mother died, one of the last public events we attended together. It's perfect for our purposes, not just because Baydel and I are both in the same location, but also because Ryn and I arrived late. We'd stopped after the ceremony to pick up my mother, and we had a bit of difficulty getting her portable chair into our transport. My mother kept fretting about the time, and how late we were going to be, so I know exactly when we arrive in front of Baydel's home.

The adjutant jots down the information to pass along to Baydel, and I go to the med unit to find Matias. They have him in an isolated area, probably still worried about germs and infections, but they agree to let me talk to him as long as I stay in the little booth that adjoins the room.

"Mila!" Matias smiles and presses his hands to the window when he sees me. "I was so scared they wouldn't let me see you again. They keep poking me. Taking my blood! And they're asking questions, but I told them I'll *only* talk to *you*."

Matias is overplaying his role again. The performance is wasted anyway, since the med tech is barely paying attention and exits before Matias reaches the end of his lament.

The boy flips back to his usual tone of voice once the door is closed. "So, do we have a deal?"

"We do. You and I will be on the next cruiser to Elisi Major. Baydel and Wirth are recording messages… encrypted to ensure

I don't hear anything not meant for civilian ears. But my message will be on the recorder, too. I believed you the first time. If you get that message to me, I'll believe you again. And once we've delivered the message, you'll jump back to this date. Not to this location—with any luck, Outpost Five will never be built—but to the same location where you'll deliver the message. I have Baydel's word that he'll put us on the next available transport to get you and the device home."

Matias makes a face. "I know I have to take it back. There'll be hell to pay if I don't. But there's a part of me that would much rather leave it here."

"Yeah, well, we don't want it either."

We spend the next few minutes going over the plan that I worked out with Baydel's adjutant, a plan that we'll be going over several more times during the next few cycles until we arrive on Elisi Major. Matias will have a portable translator, but he's still going to be several heads taller than any of Baydel's other guests.

"But that should be okay," I say to Matias. "We arrived late. Everyone was already inside. Just come over to the transport— it will take us a bit to get mother's chair out. Tell me what you said last time and show me the recording. If you can't get me to listen, tell me the bit about Briarche."

I should probably reverse that, and get him to mention Briarche first. But this time I have to assume Ryn will be listening. I don't know why I shared such a personal memory with this boy. Maybe it was because I'd been cooped up with Sim-Ryn for several cycles and it was fresh on my mind. Whatever the reason, I'd just as soon Ryn didn't know I've let someone else touch that memory.

"Okay," Matias says. "Sounds doable. I guess. Only… you're sure you can trust this Baydel guy?"

I pause for a moment, and then say, "As sure as I can be."

Matias does the lifting thing with his brow again. I think he's picked up on my wording.

"There's a lot on the line here, Matias. I'm not entirely certain I can trust Baydel, but the precautions we've taken—my message on the recorder, being sure you contact me first—these mean that I'm as sure as I *can* be."

Chapter 7

Elisi Major
Wylen Province, Ward Three
Date: 9019.10.23

Ryn navigates to the entrance, and we reverse the process we just went through at my mother's house. Her new portable chair is considerably larger than the last one, and getting it through the door of our small transport is a bit of a challenge. Once I've managed to free it, Ryn reaches inside to lift Mother out.

"We're late," she says, her voice even weaker than it was the last time I saw her. "Everyone has already arrived."

Mother was never worried about punctuality when she was younger. In fact, I think she *preferred* arriving late, because that way everyone turns around to look, and she was never one to shy away from a bit of extra attention. But she's self-conscious now. She doesn't want people turning to look at the old woman in the automatic chair.

"We'll be fine," Ryn says. He's good with her when she's in these whiny moods. Better than I am.

As he and Mother start toward the main entrance, one of the men who's always on security detail outside Baydel's house hurries over to assist them.

"Babe," Ryn calls back. "Did you get their gift? It's in the back."

I didn't, so I turn around to retrieve it.

That's when I see the man.

Or I guess it's a man. He's dressed oddly, carrying a helmet under his arm. It appears to be a uniform of some sort, but it's too short for him. More to the point, he's too tall for it. He's taller than anyone I've ever seen, with a small head and abnormally small eyes. His skin is an odd golden shade. He looks deformed. Not scary, exactly, just not... normal.

Alien, but humanoid. I've seen this type, or at least one like it, in one of Ryn's diaries from back when he was a diplomatic adjutant. But maybe not.

You don't generally see an alien running down a street where people live. Especially where a member of the Voshti lives. They occasionally have business at the government building, and I've seen several varieties on news feeds, but never one as large as this.

And even odder than the alien's height is that he seemed to appear out of nowhere.

He puts on the helmet as he rushes toward the car. "Mila! Friend. You sent."

His voice is choppy, maybe because he's running and the translator in the helmet is having a tough time catching the words. But I'm almost certain he said my name.

I take several quick steps backward, bumping my shoulder against the edge of the transport.

When he reaches me, he holds out a recorder, and I hear a woman's voice. It sounds a little like mine, but the voice is almost immediately drowned out by a loud beeping noise coming from where Ryn is standing.

The alien starts shoving the recorder in front of me. The style seems strange. I've never seen that model before.

I don't look at the man. I'm looking back at Ryn, back at the beeping noise, which I think must be coming from the guard who was helping with my mother. Ryn is just staring at me, his mouth open as the guard draws a laser from inside his coat and points it at the strange man.

"Lor agent!" he yells. "Drop the weapon."

I don't see a weapon. Just the recorder. But maybe the guard saw something I didn't.

"No!" The alien looks from me to Ryn, who's now only a few yards away. His eyes are tiny and hard to see through the helmet. That makes his expressions hard to read, but I think he's afraid.

It's probably a natural response under the circumstances.

"Mila!" He pushes the recorder toward me again, but I can't hear anything over the alarm. And the guards are apparently done with warnings, because a blue arc of light shoots out of the weapon of the guard closest to me, connecting with the alien's shoulder and incapacitating him.

The alien's mouth opens and his body shakes, then the recorder tumbles to the ground. Something else tumbles, too… a brownish circle of metal. It lands next to the recorder.

As the guards grab him, the alien man's eyes connect with mine one last time. He struggles to speak.

"Bri… arche…"

I feel Ryn's arms encircle me. "Are you okay?"

"I don't know," I say. "I think he knew me, Ryn. I think…"

"Yeah," Ryn says. "And… it almost sounded like he said Briarche." His eyes twinkle slightly, but there's a touch of embarrassment there, too. "Weird."

One of the two guards taps me on the shoulder. "We're going to have to get some information from you before you go into the party."

"Who… what… was that?" I ask.

"Must be working with the Lor. You've probably heard the recent rumors of espionage, and the possible military buildup in the Astreegee sector. The translator the alien was using is Lor design. That's what set off our security alarm."

My mother is still sitting in her chair, facing the entrance, but straining her neck around so she can see what's going on.

"Could you take Mother inside, Ryn? I'll join you once I'm done answering his questions."

"Are you sure you're all right?" he asks.

I give him a reassuring smile. "I'm fine. But Mother's going to be really cranky if she misses any more of the party."

He squeezes my shoulder again and then heads off to my mother's rescue.

I confirm my identity to the guard, show him my invitation,

and tell him my mother is a close friend of Vosht Baydel. He calls something in on his comm, and then I'm free to go.

As I turn to leave, I catch one more glimpse of the alien. He's huddled on his side in the back of the security transport. He's still looking at me.

I can't shake the feeling he was trying to tell me something.

And it *did* sound like he was saying Briarche.

Weird, indeed.

Chapter 8

Elisi Shuttle Falgert
Date: 9023.23.19

"You'd think they'd just give up at this point," Ryn says, flicking off the bottom row of news feeds in annoyance. "I mean, rational creatures would give up, wouldn't they? The Lor have no chance of winning. We've cut off their trade routes and they're reduced to scavenging off planets that haven't even reached interstellar travel. What resources could they be after on this little rock?"

"I don't know."

I relay to the nearest battle cruiser the coordinates of the Lor fighter we've just spotted orbiting planet XE7. We're not here to engage. Our mission is simply to observe, report, and then drop back.

Once I receive confirmation, I slide into the chair next to Ryn and give him a kiss. "My shift to watch these things. Get some rest."

I turn the bottom row of screens back on and unmute the one on the left. It's an official government channel, reporting yet another Lor attack. Usually they focus on industrial areas, just swooping in, taking whatever raw materials they need, and getting out. But this time, they've targeted a government building. The report says that one wing of the U.S. Capitol Building has been destroyed.

That seems odd. I pull the location up on another comm screen, zooming in to see if the building is near an industrial or even an agricultural area. It's unlikely, given the size of this particular government and the city, but I can't imagine why the Lor would be attacking government buildings otherwise. They're so close to defeated that they lack the resources to take over even one of the more remote areas of XE7, let alone its largest country.

That's when I notice a faint light pulsing several miles away from the Capitol, near the University of Maryland. I haven't seen this in any of our other surveillance missions. Curious, I roll the time back to earlier in this cycle and watch as the tiny light moves toward the Capitol Building—in fact, to the very side of the building the Lor wiped out.

"Ryn?"

He mumbles something unintelligible, already halfway asleep.

"Could you come pull up the background data on XE7 for me? I'm not sure, but I *think* I've detected a chronotron pulse."

Q&A with Rysa Walker

Where did this story come from and how does it relate to other books you've written?

Space opera is not my usual genre. I generally write Earth-bound stories of time travel and other speculative fiction. But I'm a hard-core Trekker and loved the idea of heading into a new galaxy.

I've also been wanting to tell one story that never made it into *The CHRONOS Files*. Readers often ask me what really happened in Washington, DC in 2092. Katherine always told Kate that it was need-to-know only, and Kate (along with the readers) will still be left hanging on that front when the final *CHRONOS* book, *Time's Divide*, comes out in October. And since none of the Kindle Worlds authors who write *CHRONOS Files* stories have tackled that one yet, I decided this would be a perfect opportunity.

Tell us something we might not know about you.

I used to act in a melodrama theater, years ago. I played the character of Sweet Peggy Macree, running from the mustachioed villain.

How can readers find you?

My blog is www.rysa.com. You can find all of my books on my Amazon page and my Kindle Worlds stories here. I'm on Facebook and Twitter (@rysawalker) way too often. If you see me there, say hi and then tell me to get back into the writing cave.

Works in progress?

The last book in *The CHRONOS Files* comes out in October, and then I'll be moving on to *The Delphi Project*, a three-book series that I like to think of as *X-Files* meets *X-Men*. The first book in that series will be published by Skyscape in the fall of 2016.

Thank you so much for reading *Dark Beyond the Stars*. To hear about special deals and new releases, sign up for our newsletter. Then join the authors and fans of the *Beyond the Stars* anthologies on our Facebook page.

And if you're looking for more short stories, check out these other anthologies edited by David Gatewood, involving robots, aliens, time travel, conspiracies, and more.

Finally, before you go, could we ask of you a very small favor?

Would you please leave a short review at the site where you purchased the book?

Reviews are make-or-break for authors. A book with no reviews is, simply put, a book with no future sales. In today's publishing world, the success (or failure) of a book is truly in the reader's hands.

Reviews don't need to be long or eloquent; a single sentence is all it takes. So please, leave a review. You'd be doing us a tremendous service.

Thank you.

Acknowledgments

What a great adventure we had in putting this anthology together! I'm looking forward to doing it again. Be on alert for the second book in the *Beyond the Stars* series of science fiction anthologies, to be released in November 2015.

I want to thank Samuel Peralta, the mastermind behind the Future Chronicles series, for inspiring me to coordinate this first collection of space opera shorts.

Thanks also to Kendall Roderick, who designed our cover, and to Hugo Award-winning artist Julie Dillon, who created the glorious art.

We had the benefit of prompt and professional work by Jason and Marina Anderson of Polgarus Studio, who formatted both the digital and print editions of this collection for us.

Julie E. Czerneda, an award-winning author in her own right, was kind enough to write an inspiring foreword that summed up precisely the feeling we were going for in this collection, and we thank her for lending her talents to our enterprise.

I particularly want to thank David Gatewood, editor extraordinaire, whose keen eye and excellent sense of story made everything he touched even better.

And of course I have to thank our wonderful authors. Each and every one of them helped shape this collection by contributing not only her words but her ideas on how to produce an anthology that is entertaining and worthy.

Finally, I want to thank the larger indie author community, which continues to supply enthusiasm and support for the exciting new ventures springing forth on the digital frontier. It's a wonderful time to be a writer.

And readers, I always love to hear from you! Feel free to email me with thoughts or feedback at:

BeyondTheStarsSeries@gmail.com.

Patrice Fitzgerald
Series Editor, *Beyond the Stars*

STORY SYNOPSES

Containment *(Susan Kaye Quinn)*
The Mining Master of Thebe is all alone… not counting the scavenger drones, foundry nanites, and magtread tractors buzzing across the tiny Jovian moon. So when a spindly tower of rocks mysteriously appears at the pole, it's enough to vex the Mining Master's machine-sourced intelligence like dust trapped in a harvester joint. Reporting it could mean reassignment to the Outer Belt… but probing the mystery further threatens to unlock something that might have been better left… *contained.*

Nos Morituri Te Salutamus *(Annie Bellet)*
The war with the Spidren is going badly; the United Fleet faces utter destruction. To snatch victory from the jaws of defeat, Commander Moira Ilvic and her hand-picked team undertake a desperate mission that might turn the tide of war in their favor. Their odds of success are low. Their odds of survival are worse. But if they don't succeed, humanity itself will be lost.

Protocol A235 *(Theresa Kay)*
Beth is a maintenance tech on the *Genesis*, the spaceship that will carry her, along with fifty thousand other passengers, to a new home in deep space. But when she comes out of cryosleep to serve her thirty-day solo shift, she finds the ship in disarray, its systems malfunctioning. Worse yet, a previously undisclosed protocol has been put into effect. Protocol A235. And now Beth finds herself facing much more responsibility than she signed up for.

Winner Takes All *(Elle Casey)*

Langlade, captain of the Kinsblade Fleet, has pulled into a station for some repairs to his ship—and to share a little down time with whatever willing female he can find to warm his bunk. But on this stop it's not just a dockside dolly tempting him to stay, it's a game of chance. There's a card game with a very interesting proposition from the girl across the table: his number three ship anted up against the gift of her innocence. And one would be hard-pressed to determine which is the more valuable pot out here in the badlands, otherwise known as Centurion 4, the farthest Dark Settlement Station in the Triangulan Galaxy.

Carindi *(Jennifer Foehner Wells)*

Stranded in a ship orbiting a dying red giant, Ei'Pio is alone and without hope—until she discovers the child, Carindi. Despite being of two different species, the two form a bond and build a life together. But that life will be a short one unless they can find a way to get their ship in motion. The star they orbit is about to go supernova.

Animal Planet *(Patrice Fitzgerald)*

Earth is hot and crowded, and Jane is ready to leave that old rock in the dust, embarking on the grand adventure she's always dreamed of, zipping across the galaxy to colonize a new planet. But when she arrives, the people are gone, and the Animals have taken over.

The Event *(Autumn Kalquist)*

Zenith has been forced to live one thousand lives. Now she must escape before she loses her own.

Dragonet *(Sara Reine)*

The inhabitants of Drakor III shouldn't have seen the invasion coming, yet when Allied forces arrive for an assault on the dragons' homeworld, the planet is teeming with life. After a desperate crash landing that leaves her Carriage destroyed, Aja Skytoucher doesn't stand a chance—unless she can find a way off the surface.

Lulu Ad Infinitum *(Ann Christy)*

Lulu is a copy of the original Lulu who once lived on Earth. Her home is a self-replicating ship, and her entire purpose is to create new worlds like Earth. But when her ship is all but destroyed by a catastrophe, she's left with only a dog for company and too much work to do. And getting her mission back on track will require a little bit more than just tanking up some new copies of her crew.

To Catch an Actor *(Blair C. Babylon)*

The only immortals now are the performers—the musicians, dancers, and actors who sell themselves to ride the near-lightspeed century ships to the many suns of the Known Worlds. If Police Detective Cordelia Hernandez can't get actor Daveen Kelly to confess to a murder a hundred years old, he'll board another ship and escape justice forever. But he doesn't realize just how far technology has advanced while he's been away.

2092 *(Rysa Walker)*

The Elisi Alliance is facing defeat in its struggle against the Lor, when Mila, an Elisi requisitions scout, uncovers evidence of a time-altering technology that could reverse the course of the war. The device is on XE7, a small planet Mila fears will be destroyed if pulled into the conflict. Can she retrieve the technology without sacrificing XE7? As a bonus for readers of *The CHRONOS Files*, this story answers the question Katherine never would: What *really* happened in 2092?